Daughter
of Skye

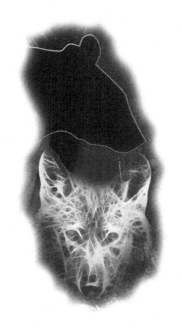

THÉRÈSE PILON

Daughter of Skye

iUniverse books may be ordered through booksellers or by contacting:

iUniverse
1663 Liberty Drive
Bloomington, IN 47403
www.iuniverse.com
1-800-Authors (1-800-288-4677)

Typography and page composition by J.K. Eckert and Company, Inc.

Cover Art by Jamie Runyan
reese-winslow.com

ISBN: 978-1-4759-3145-7 (sc)
ISBN: 978-1-4759-3146-4 (hc)
ISBN: 978-1-4759-3147-1 (e)

Library of Congress Control Number: 2012910031

Printed in the United States of America

iUniverse rev. date: 6/6/2012

This book is for my children,
Naiomi-Leah, Nickolous, Matthew, and Joshua.

To my mom, Leta Deline,

And to my husband, Dan:
Thank you for supporting me and believing in
my dreams.

Also by Thérèse Pilon

Son of Skye

Prologue

In the time of the beginning, the two-legged had dwelled peacefully with the four-legged. Each of the clans took only what they needed to survive. They had respected each other in that long ago time, and at night, when the dampness had crept along the ground, soft tendrils seeking, they, the two-legged had built their fires and had gathered about—some with drums—to sing their songs honoring the earth and all those who walked upon it.

As the moon had risen, taking her place in the velvety night, and the white mist had curled lazily about them, the Old Ones had come, their spirit-selves listening and advising as the clans of the two-legged honored them and the ancestors who had walked before.

But that was a long time ago and they had been forgotten—

1

Leah crouched in the shadows, her senses tingling, her breathing ragged. The storm had come out of nowhere, the thunder and lightning hitting so fast that she had not had time to seek shelter. She blinked against the rain that swirled about her, blinding her as the dampness crept upward while her body, numbed by the intense cold, reacted instinctively to the need to survive as she crept forward; out from beneath the copse of red pine trees into the open. Shocked at what she saw, she could only stand there, her eyes seeing what her heart denied—chaos all about her. Slowly she moved forward. Cautiously, trying to make no sound, she skirted the edge of the clearing, the knowledge layered deep within that her world, as she knew it, had changed yet again.

Gone were the towering forests, lush and emerald green with their flowing rivers set against the backdrop of mist-shrouded mountains. Gone were the caverns with their long, winding tunnels and stale musty air. Gone were the small ones, those of the earth diggers, the clans who lived beneath, they who listened in the darkened places so they could warn the clans who walked above.

All gone.

Leah covered her face and sank to her knees upon the sodden earth, while the tears mingled with the cold rain.

§ § § § §

Not sparing a backward glance for the figure huddled in the driving rain, the *Other* moved forward, his long strides taking him away.

Away from the destruction his coming had brought. Away from the young woman who had not been there but mere moments before. Somehow, she had followed him when the cavern had collapsed inward upon itself from that other place, where the Clans of the earth and sky warred with those like and unlike himself.

Looking up into the cool grey of the morning's sky where even darker clouds swirled—shadows within that churned endlessly upon themselves, the man breathed a sigh of relief. *Good.* His world had not changed in the short interval he had been gone. Sparing a backward glance toward the female who still huddled on the ground a short distance away, he dismissed her presence with the knowledge that his sentries would do what was necessary.

§ § § § §

Leah tensed as the sensations washed over her. *"Danger,"* the voices whispered as she knelt in the mud, the chill creeping upward, not from the dampness but from something else. She remained where she was, her body language not betraying what she saw within her mind as dark eyes swept the wooded area in front of her for a place to hide from the unseen ones who watched. She knew she was unprotected, here, in this place. She also knew she was no longer in Skye, that place where winged warriors guarded from distant realms—

Drawing in a deep breath, she let it out slowly, centering herself, turning inward to that other place that she and her brother, Nickolous, sometimes shared when one needed the other. Thoughts, guarded, reached out...seeking.

Leah pulled back, her mind reeling at what she sensed rather than saw. Darkness, so total, so complete...she drew in her breath sharply as the realization hit her that the connection to her brother—to that other place—was gone. She glanced around, the knowing within that she was in danger and defenseless nearly overwhelming. Carefully, she started to rise, to stand. Her attention drawn to the heavily forested area in front of her, she did not see the nearly indistinguishable form that stood just slightly within the shadows, watching her from beneath the overhanging branches of the hemlock tree. Nor, did she notice the low-lying clouds that were centered slightly above her, their shape ever-changing as the air about her became electrified, the grey, almost translucent tendrils curling down to embrace her tightly within their grasp.

Something hit her from behind, knocking her to the ground as the air above her filled with unearthly sounds. Winded from the blow, but otherwise unhurt, all Leah could do was try to draw the air back into her lungs—to breath. As the darkness closed over her, she was vaguely aware of strong arms and a man's voice. Then, there was nothing.

It was nighttime before she awakened. She opened her eyes slowly; her first awareness was of warmth, the soft glow of the fire comforting as she listened to the sounds of the night filtering through her numbed mind. Suddenly she was sitting bolt upright as the memories came flooding back, while at the same time she hit her head against something hard. Leah threw up her arm instinctively to guard herself.

The soft sound of male laughter nearby caused her to flinch as she peered into the semi-darkness; she was about to say something, then thought better of it. Leaning back, she folded her arms across her chest and waited.

"You're awake."

Leah nodded her head in reply; her senses tingling as she moved gingerly out of the lean-to while at the same time trying to center herself, to control the slight trembling that rippled through her body as she moved cautiously toward the small fire set in the clearing that beckoned with welcoming warmth. She waited for the owner of the voice to move into the flickering light.

And found herself looking up.

And up.

He had to be nearly six and a half feet tall, Leah thought to herself as she turned her head to look up into a darkly handsome face. Eyes the color of obsidian looked back. The man scrunched down so he was eye level with her; his blue-black hair was tied back in a queue, still, it fell past his waist in long dark waves. Leah suddenly found herself at a loss for words as the man studied her curiously from beneath long smoky-grey lashes. Even in the fires flickering light, his skin was dark.

Leah looked away, uncomfortable, as her mind fumbled with a memory of another time, another place. Memories, too many, crowded her, overwhelming her senses as she pushed them back. She turned her attention back to the man as something inside her stirred, awakening other instincts. She shook her head to clear it, her instinct for survival rising from deep within as she calmed herself. The knowledge that she was in a foreign place and did not know friend from foe made her stiffen apprehensively.

The man's gaze sharpened and she looked away quickly, guarding herself, her emotions, but it was too late.

"Everything is not as it seems." The voice, carried upon the unseen wind that whipped around her, rippled over her and through her as she closed her eyes against the memories and the emotions the remembering evoked.

"Are you hurt."

Leah opened her eyes, not realizing she had shut them, hoping to shut out the memories. It was not working.

"Are you all right?" This time it was a question. She spared a quick glance toward the man, his voice held a tinge of concern to it, yet it was also edged with steel. He leaned back on his haunches, studying her surreptitiously, his face shadowed by the waves of light cast by the flickering flames that licked their way upward against the dry wood. She closed her eyes, opened them. *"No."* The voice whispered in her head. *Impossible*—she shook her head to clear it, and when she looked again it was gone. But for a moment, it had been there within the black eyes of the giant who regarded her with what was now open curiosity.

Leah breathed a sigh of relief. Whoever he was, he was not her enemy. The brief glimpse into his eyes had shown her that.

"I'm okay."

"It's not often another comes through with that *'One.'*" The man had risen to his full height and was now standing, looking down at her, his gaze searching. "—and lives." The words drifted off into the awkward silence.

"Where am I? What is this place?" Leah had dared to pull her gaze away from this incredibly tall man, her attention now on her surroundings. Her breath caught in her throat as the night suddenly gave way to the dawning. It happened so fast she could hardly believe it. One moment there had been stars, a full moon and the next…

Two suns in a brilliant blue sky tinged with the lesser blue-grey hues, and below them the rose colors much like she was used to when the sun set on a brilliant day of warmth. However, there the resemblance ended, for it was not the soft kiss of the sunset upon the earth but the beginning of a new dawning, the greeting of another day. Out of the corner of her eye, she glimpsed the man in the full light of day, and stifled the gasp of disbelief that ended in a soft expulsion of air as she sucked in her breath before letting it out in a soft sigh.

§ § § § §

His name, translated by the people, was *The Hunter.* Born to the
Clans of the two-legged, his ascension by the order of his birth named
him leader. Better known as the clan of the Mukwa, or bear, hidden
from the unseen ones, he had grown into manhood. Trained by the
elders in diplomacy, guided by senior warriors who had lived for
countless turnings, the seasons had come and gone, and the warrior
had become what Leah now saw as she swung her gaze back to the
man, waiting for an answer.

Black brows drew together in a frown as The Hunter studied this
strange she creature who had suddenly been thrust through the hidden
doorway. He and others like him had guarded the gates, doing their
best to prevent ones such as that *One* from entering. Yet somehow, he
always managed to find a weakness somewhere enabling him access.
This time, however, it had been at great cost to themselves and little
cost to him. On top of it, somehow, this tiny creature had been pushed
through behind him. The only reason she had been spared was that at
the last moment he had sensed her thoughts and had caught a glimpse
of the place she had been torn from, to land unceremoniously in his
world. He was fascinated.

He looked down at her, his expression thoughtful.

"Well?" Leah held his gaze with her own despite the unnatural
chill that crept upward from her feet, wrapping around her body and
she shivered despite the morning's sun, which was illuminating the
valley set out before her.

"You are where you are supposed to be."

"And that would be?" She held her breath.

"Why, you are here, with me." The Hunter looked puzzled at
Leah's reaction. His knowledge of the otherworld places was vague to
say the least, but he had taken the small female's presence as an
acceptance of something that was to be. The reasoning as to why she
had been thrust through to him, alive, was something that would have
to be reasoned with later. He turned his head, his gaze appraising as
he moved closer.

Leah took a step back.

Surprised, The Hunter stayed his advance. The realization that she
was afraid of him or what she could not understand caused a strange
unease where before there had been none. Shrugging broad shoulders,
he remained where he was, letting her appraise him, her dark eyes
unfathomable.

Leah looked up. And up. Her gaze taking in the width and breadth
of the man, he was incredibly tall, his hair the color of dark ebony

against golden honeyed skin, eyes as black as… She blinked, then brushed at the wetness that rolled unheeded down her cheek as memories spilled out, rolling over her in waves as she saw them within her mind.

Chera. Gabriel. Jerome. Old One. The vision overwhelmed her as she remembered. Remembered her brother, remembered their mother—the shadows of winged warriors mixing with jumbled images. She breathed in deeply of the air; the scent of honeyed flowers pervaded her senses as she blinked the wetness away. From somewhere deep within she searched and found that small place, centered deep within her memories, that she and her brother, Nickolous, often went to in times of stress. Calmer now, she gazed up at the man.

"Warrior." The word was whispered. Heard.

The Hunter nodded, acknowledging the spoken word as he looked down at her, his eyes searching hers, trying to understand her distress as well as the unfamiliar sensations that were inexplicably coursing through him.

Confused by what had just happened, Leah remained where she was, unmoving, staring down at her hands that hung limply at her sides, her mind registering the fact that she had just spoken her thought aloud. *Or had she?* She stood like that for a few moments longer, and then forced her gaze upward, traveling the length of him until she was looking into his eyes.

Black eyes that were fathomless gazed back.

She shook her head as if by doing so it would clear her mind, erase the vision that danced before her, wavered—she looked once more into eyes that were no longer black but emerald green. So like—

Jerome.

The vision of that other place and those she had left behind crowded her thoughts as she pulled her gaze away from that of the warrior's. The emotions washing over her in waves as she tried to block them, but it was too late. She felt a big hand closing over hers while the other hand cupped her chin, forcing her to look up.

Into eyes that were once more the color of obsidian.

"Who are you." It was not a question. It was a demand.

§ § § § §

The day had deepened, casting long shadows against the sunlit places as Leah sat across from the one known as The Hunter. From time to time she had dared to glance into the shadows and wondered at the fact that they seemed to be always moving, shifting place; then she would move her gaze back to the man who seemed so at ease. Still—she moved closer to the fire.

She had told her story, and the warrior had listened quietly, his brows furrowed as he thought upon the words she had spoken. Behind him, he knew the watchers listened; their keen senses alert for anything untoward, their presence assurance the Dark Lord was not close. As she had spoken of the realm of the four—legged and winged—clans of earth and sky, something within him had stirred. Something primordial. His own ancestry spoke of such things, but they had been the imaginings of old women and even older men, or so he had thought.

The Hunter turned inward, his mind taking him to another place, and he saw what Leah had seen when she gazed into his eyes.

Forest Warriors. Once it had been whispered that his kind were descended from that mythical race. In dreams, he had seen such things... The Hunter shook his head to clear it. Rising, he cast more wood upon the fire. The offering of cedar, wild sage, and tobacco to appease the unseen ones was something he had always done. He straightened his back, looking out over the vast expanse of valleys rimmed in the far distances by white-tipped peaks. A no-man's land to those like him. He shifted his gaze back to the woman for a moment longer before turning away, feeling the need to be alone, to think on what he had heard this day, something he could not explain even to himself.

"Stay here." The words were tossed over his shoulder, their meaning clear. A little confused and unsure of her place, Leah decided to obey the man, but it did not mean that she had to like it.

She stood, staring into the shadows long after he had disappeared from view, her thoughts far away, and as the afternoon shadows deepened into early twilight, she began to wonder at the wisdom of having told him about the others. About Skye.

It was as she was leaning down to grab another piece of firewood that she heard it. A faint scuffling sound off to her left. She squinted in the half-light wishing Chera were here. The silver-white wolf, with her strength and wisdom, would be a welcome ally. Her breathing quickened as the noise grew louder; the knowledge that she was weaponless in a strange place did little to calm her already frayed senses as she stood there, unprepared and frightened half out of her wits as the tangled foliage gave way beneath a cumbersome weight.

What came through was not what she expected.

§ § § § § §

The Hunter picked his way warily, his senses heightened by the day's events. He had not expected the female, and her arrival at first had surprised him. It had been as he was about to loose his arrow that he had caught the scent of her, that, and the residual memories that she brought through with her.

Fascinating.

That was the thought that prevented him from the killing shot—that and what he saw draped within the misty blood memories she carried with her. He doubted even she knew the gifts she possessed.

So now what to do? Long sleek eyebrows drew together in a frown as he thought upon what he had heard this day, his warrior's training allowing him to look at what was logic and what was not. Black eyes narrowed as he pushed away the thought that most of what he had heard was *not* logical. While another part of him wished that some of the Old Ones had remained here, closer to the center of the battle. Bits of the old wisdom still lingered, but it had been too long. That *One* had taken care of that.

The Hunter ducked suddenly, sensing danger as long tendrils reached out to caress, sharp barbs barely missing his throat as he side-stepped, his hand already withdrawing the heavy obsidian knife from its sheath, the upward thrust tearing at the creature. Screams, high and shrieking, came from deep within the thing as a blue light flashed and then was gone. Back to whatever darkness had spawned it. The Hunter grimaced as he re-sheathed his knife, the heart of the stone still glowing as it slowly returned to its core.

He would never get used to that inhuman sound, he thought to himself, turning back the way he had come. The thrum of the distant drums echoed through the stillness that preceded the sudden onset of the night, the warm breeze carrying the message to him as he broke into a run, his need to reach the woman quickening as the sighing of the wind passed over him, warning him.

§ § § § § §

Snuffling and snorting, the dark form made its way slowly through the dense underbrush. It had been days since it had last fed, and it was growing weaker with each rising and setting of the sun. Nearsighted, old, and in pain, the Ancient One had caught a new scent upon the night wind, something smaller and weaker—a prey that could be easily caught.

It was this thought that made him move a bit more quickly and perhaps not as cautiously as he normally would have. As he moved through the dense underbrush, his senses, dulled by exhaustion and discomfort, failed to pick up the sounds of his pursuer.

"*No...*" Leah moved instinctively, the words shouted against the breath of the night as the lumbering form burst into the clearing, the air exploding with sound as the creature turned his attention now on another. The two combatants were circling each other warily. Both powerful, both focused. She looked up into the velvety night as something passed overhead, and then the air was filled with other things as the beast went down on all fours, its screams deafening as it backed hurriedly away from The Hunter, Leah's sharp intake of breath carrying to the warrior as he paused, his bow already restrung.

Unafraid, Leah moved forward, placing herself between the warrior and that which crouched upon the ground in front of her. Even in the dim light cast by the moon's wavering shadows, Leah had recognized him and blinked against the stinging sensation behind her eyelids as something deeper surfaced. Something within her own subconscious that threatened to pour forth.

The beast lunged sideways as if to move away, back the way it had come, but it was too weak. Leah saw the arrow that had pierced its side, and she knew the wound went deep, the shaft of the arrow buried beneath the fur and flesh. Without thought of self, she found herself moving forward, The Hunter's shouted warning lost to her senses as she knelt down. Unseen eyes followed her as she reached out to caress the brown fur gently, as words murmured softly were heard and understood. Leah felt along the rib cage, her fingers stroking, soothing, seeking the spot where the arrow protruded. The dark form trembled as she grasped the arrow firmly and pulled back quickly, the sound of stone upon hard earth all that could be heard as the broken arrow was thrown to the ground. Behind her, she heard the warrior, his tread light as he approached cautiously while beneath her touch the beast stirred, the movement subtle, the low moan falling off into the silence. With one hand, she blocked the flow of blood that seeped from the open wound while with the other she motioned the warrior back. Her hearing telling her he had stopped, she waited a moment longer before leaning down to look into brown eyes that had seen much.

Behind her The Hunter crouched, his arrow already notched, his eyes narrowed as he waited for the beast to rear up. *Where were the watchers? He would never have left her unprotected had he known—*

He drew in his breath sharply. The woman was leaning over the great beast, her long hair covering her face. He watched as she pushed it back, her attention elsewhere for the moment. His eyes narrowed. *No. He must be mistaken.* He released some of the pressure on the bow as he strained to hear the softly spoken words.

Leah turned to look at him, the soft light the moon cast illuminating her face as she moved slightly to one side. Brown eyes met black. She arched a slender brow, her gaze questioning. She, too, had sensed the others that waited just outside the fires flickering light. She had known they were there earlier, had wondered at their purpose.

The Hunter remained silent, masking his surprise at what he saw behind those eyes. *Blood memories. Whisperings of the clan grand-mothers.* He bowed his head to hide his confusion lest any of the unseen were watching. When next he looked, the woman had turned back to the wounded one, her hand stroking the brown fur softly; soothing it with gentle caresses. The dark sides rose and fell steadily as the beast raised his head, his mouth scant inches from her face, his breath warm against her skin. The Hunters fingers tightened once more upon the bow as he raised it, centering it. The warm rush of air wafting toward him embracing his senses as he pulled back on the string, muscles tensing as he prepared to release the arrow.

Leah wasn't afraid, even when the wet nose touched her face, the soft huff-huff telling her that the Old One would recover, her senses tingling as she realized that what was before her was much more than it seemed. For a moment, she thought she could hear Chera, the great silver-white wolf, telling her that what she saw with her eyes was not what she could see if she listened with her heart. She bowed her head, then reached out to brush the wetness away. Blood memories. The memories of her ancestors. Leah closed her eyes as she went to that place inside herself, seeing what was in front of her, the sudden knowing causing her to reel back in shock.

What was before her was one of the Old Ones who had once communicated with those like herself! She looked around, seeking out those who had remained hidden. Finding them gone, she turned back toward the warrior, motioning him closer.

The Hunter started forward, unsure of what he should do. The little female motioned for him to drop his weapon. Unable to argue, he found himself placing his bow, made from the wood of the yew tree, against one of the small, gnarled shrubs. It was close enough that he could reach it should the need arise, yet far enough away that the beast would not feel threatened. It was as he drew closer, his nostrils filled with the strange scent, that he felt it.

Hunger. Pain. Fear.

The Hunter took a step back, masking his shock. He and his kind had long hunted the great furred one in front of them. The clan honored them, their cunning and strength something The Hunter and those like him observed and practiced. He drew in his breath sharply at the realization that he had never really thought about the clans of the four-legged having emotions that could be felt.

Leah pushed at him gently, her gaze burning into his as she tugged him forward. Once more the warrior, he tensed as the wounded beast struggled to rise; failed; tried once more.

Leah stroked the dark fur softly, her mind going inward to that place where Chera and Gabriel were, and sensed an awakening within the creature that was struggling to his feet. She had staunched the flow of blood without knowing how she did it and now watched as the Old One rose slowly, albeit unsteadily to his feet, his gaze sweeping the clearing warily. Then, he was gone. When next she looked, the clearing was in darkness, the moon obscured by the dark clouds scudding across the inky horizon. Beside her stood The Hunter, looking down at her, his expression one of amazement—

But only for a moment.

"Come." The words were ground out from between clenched teeth as he half carried, half dragged her to where the fire had been. Mere embers glowed within a hollowed-out pit, the ash was barely warm.

"Sit."

Leah sat. Her first instinct was to argue, but then she thought better of it, which was probably a good thing given the mood of her host.

"What did you think you were doing?" The warrior's tone had a hard edge to it as he bent to the task of rebuilding the fire. The dried wood caught so fast that he pulled back as the flames reached up and out, sparking above him in the darkness, while the sudden intense heat pushed against him. There must have been, he thought, more coals beneath the ash, hidden from view. He turned away from the fire, his attention on the woman.

"Well?"

Leah had her own ideas as to why the fire had flared so suddenly against the night, the shadows pulling back, away from the warrior. She wondered at the fact that he seemed oblivious to the obvious, her instincts cautioning her to remain silent. She bowed her head, temporarily at a loss for words. As to his question: all she had done was to react instinctively. A thought, a memory? She shook her head. It was not possible. Rising slowly, she stood up, her gaze locking with that of the warrior. Black eyes gazed into hers, narrowed, widened, as a thought was passed, the words unspoken. The Hunter shook his head, his expression dark. If the woman did not wish to communicate her thoughts clearly so that he could understand—he snorted in disgust. He had had enough for one night.

Suddenly Leah found herself staring at an empty spot, the soft tendrils of the moon's pale light splayed across the path where the warrior had stood mere moments before. She shrugged her shoulders indifferently, moving back into the lean-to, the fire's warmth welcoming, the knowing somehow comforting that beyond the fires shadows The Hunter watched. Her last thought before she fell into a dreamless sleep was that some things never change.

Long into the night, The Hunter stood, unmoving, watchful. He needed time to think—to sort through what he had seen and heard this day. For as long as he could remember, he and those like him had hunted the great one. When they were cold, he had clothed them. When their bodies had struggled against the hunger the winter's wind brought, he had fed them. Strength offered. Accepted. Now—now, he had to think upon the events of the day that had just dawned and set.

The night had deepened, bringing with it the little stingers, their bite irritating, and still The Hunter remained where he was, staring into the night's shadows as he thought upon all that he had seen and heard, the morning's soft dawning bringing him no closer to an answer.

"Get up." The warrior stood above Leah, looking down at her, his gaze dark and forbidding. "I said, get up."

Leah struggled against the woven cover that she had grabbed before bedding down during the night. It was warm. Too warm. She kicked out with her feet, untangling herself and half rolled, half crawled from beneath the lean-to. Raising a small slender hand, she blocked out the bright morning light, blinking against the brightness this new dawning brought.

"Come." The Hunter was standing over her, his silhouette temporarily blocking out the sun's light. Before she could protest, Leah found herself slung unceremoniously over a broad shoulder, head down; she bounced with each step the warrior took. Away from the clearing and the unseen watchers.

"Put. Me. Down. Now." There was no response. Just the steady rhythm of the warrior as he walked, his long strides taking him away from the circle. Away from the place where the strange female had entered. He needed to think. More importantly, he needed the female where she could not confuse him, or anyone else for that matter.

So it was a little while later that Leah found herself dumped unceremoniously in a small grove surrounded by ancient oak trees or, as they were called in Skye, the Standing People.

Seething, she watched as the warrior set about making a small fire, the dry limbs that littered the forest floor within easy reach as he used his flint to strike, the spark quickly catching in the dry punk gathered from a nearby rotted log. Cupping his hands together, he blew softly on the wispy gray smoke that struggled to rise upward, then blossomed into a red flame as the punk caught, the flames slowly licking their way upward along the wood. It was not long before the fire flamed; warm tendrils reached to fan the air about them as The Hunter prepared a lean-to. Leah watched through half-closed lids as he gathered fresh boughs of cedar, their scent carrying a sweetness that permeated everything about her. Inhaling deeply, she closed her eyes, remembering...

"It's time."

Leah opened her eyes. The Hunter was standing over her, his body blocking out the warmth of the fire. As she looked up, she wondered at the need for such a large fire in the middle of the day. She was going to ask him why, but before she could, he reached for her to pull her up. She reacted instinctively. Kicking out. Rolling away. She was on her feet, her breathing rapid as she glared at the man, her dark eyes narrowing as she took in the immense size of the warrior who stood, arms crossed, looking down the length of his too-perfect nose at her. She did the only thing she could think of.

She bolted for the forest.

Behind her, the man known as The Hunter snorted in disbelief, watching as she disappeared into the dense foliage. Moments later, after banking the fire, he grabbed his bow and quiver, and without a backward glance, trotted after her.

Leah ran blindly, ducking beneath the giant ferns, their soft fronds slipping gently back into place, concealing her passage amongst them as she rolled down into a gully. The steep incline took her breath away, but she ignored it, pushing down the pain as the jagged rocks tore at her, leaving her bruised and battered. Not knowing where she was or what awaited her was better than what she had left. The Hunter would track her. She knew this. Expected it. Was prepared for it. She ducked to avoid the overhanging branches of the trees as she slipped and slid over the mossy ground, her need to escape this strange place she found herself in overwhelming. Behind her she caught the distant sounds of pursuit, knowing it was The Hunter who followed— she ran faster. Jumping and stumbling over the half- rotten logs in her hurry to escape, she did not see the shadows that skirted furtively around the sunlit patches of the forest. Nor did she see the hungry eyes set deep within the feral faces that watched as she passed amongst them, her scent heavy in their nostrils.

The Hunter followed at a leisurely pace, the tracks easy to find for one such as he. So, he thought to himself, she thought to run from him did she? He snorted softly, annoyed. She had actually kicked him—

The warrior shrugged irritably; the stinging sensation that he felt was merely an annoyance to his pride, nothing more.

Deep within the thick bracken Leah crouched, wary of her surroundings, her senses heightened by her need to escape. The wet bog she had fled through had taken her over slime-encrusted rocks, through meandering streams, and through dense underbrush. She was cold, wet, hungry, and—more than that—exhausted. It had been a while since she had heard anything except the pounding of her own heart, the sound ringing in her ears as she tried to control it. Certain that her pursuer could hear it, she crouched lower, pushing herself further back into the tall foliage The wet leaves brushing against her, chilling her. She settled back, ignoring the dampness. She would wait. Ignoring the cramped muscles, not to mention the ache in her belly, she finally gave in to the exhaustion and slept.

The Hunter drew in deeply of the scents surrounding him. He could not believe it. He could smell her, knew she was close, yet somehow she had managed to elude him. He snorted in disgust, more at his own ineptitude than anything else. He had not meant to scare her, he had only meant to protect her. It had been decided by the unseen ones, they who watched in silence, their thoughts their own. The elders who spoke without words. Somehow, they voiced unspoken thoughts, and the one known as The Hunter heard.

The day had lengthened into late afternoon, and still The Hunter stood, silent and unmoving against the backdrop of the emerald forest. The distant keening of the golden eagle the only sound to break the silence. Acknowledging the bird of prey's right to be there, he turned his attention back to the task of deep listening. Something taught to him by an Ancient who had passed this way once long ago. Once, he thought he heard her, his warrior's hearing picking up each nuance as the wind changed direction; then, there was nothing. He blew his breath out in a rush of sound as he grabbed his bow, the arrows placed for easy access in the leather quiver behind him, centered between his shoulder blades. He spared a glance back once, when he was at the top of the rise, the wind moving around him to shatter the stillness; then, there was nothing—nothing save the sound of the leaves dancing in the early twilight, their colors ever-changing as they turned in unison with the wind.

Leah did not know how long she had slept, only that she was damp and every muscle in her body ached. She tried to move forward then fell back, her legs cramped from sitting so long in one place, the pins-and-needles sensation nearly unbearable as she bent forward once more, this time to rub some feeling back into them. It took a while. She was not sure exactly what it was that made her glance up; later she would wonder why she had not sensed it—or better yet, smelled it. The pungent odor was distinct, not unlike...she was rising, turning at the same time, willing her legs to hold her steady.

§ § § § §

From his hidden place, the Ancient One watched as the young one of the two-legged clan scented the air, her posture signaling that she caught the smell of something unwanted upon the wind. He knew what it was; the rancid smell filled his nostrils even from the distance that separated them. Lowering his head, he swung it from side to side. What he suffered in nearsightedness he made up for with his ability to smell and, as the wind shifted yet again, something stirred within him. A primordial instinct to protect.

§ § § § §

Leah knew that without a weapon, she could not hope to defend herself against the shadow being; remembering all too well her brush with them when they had battled A-Sharoon, she chose the only option open to her. To run. Clearing the slime-covered bog that lay in front of her, she lowered her head as the low-hanging branches slapped her face, tearing at her clothing as she used her arms to protect herself. She was in the open now, her breathing ragged as she ducked. The nearly vaporous tendril grazed her shoulder as she turned sideways, narrowly missing the jagged rocks that protruded above ground. The greyish hard moss that clung to them laced with spores that ejected upward, caught within the wind, the fine particles swirling down the only thing to mark her passage. She did not see the dark form that loomed large and threatening in front of her, but she heard the roar of anger as she fell into the dark abyss that reached out to hold her within its embrace. Then for a time she knew no more. The day turned to night and back again. Within her dreams, she was sheltered, and a great silver-white wolf watched over her.

2

Swinging his head from side to side, the bear went down on all fours, his giant paws sweeping the hard earth away from him as he blew angrily through his nostrils, the huff-huff loud in the sudden stillness as the shadow creature stayed its downward spiral, gauging the strength of this new adversary. Behind the big Mukwa, the thing could sense the inert form of the female it had been pursuing, its ability to see as others did, not the same, for it saw in shadow, images, and color. A long vaporous tendril reached out, then just as quickly drew back. The energy the Old One emitted was powerful.

Below it, the bear reared upright, pawing the air. The low, guttural growl becoming a roar as the air filled with images that were indefinable.

Leah sat up, dazed, trying to focus, her mind registering the thought that Chera was watching over her. She shook her head. No. It was not Chera, her wolf guardian from that other place. She frowned as she looked down, then back up, as she recognized the one she had protected from The Hunter. It was he who stood guard. The air above her head hummed with sound, most of it ear shattering. As she struggled against what she could not see, the wind found her, pressing down on her as she opened her eyes and saw—saw what she had thought never to see again. Shadow creatures. Hundreds of them, and behind them were others, some she recognized, while behind them were…

Words whispered were heard. The big Mukwa slammed down on all fours, his roar carrying through the valley as he turned toward

17

Leah, while above him the creature still hesitated. It sensed the flow of power emanating from the Old One, knew that there was more. It reached out, its senses seeking. The small valley was surging with unrestrained power from a hundred different places not seen by its kind; not wishing to engage something it did not understand, it chose to retreat.

At least for now.

Behind it, the others, the watchers of earth and sky, returned to their unseen place to wonder at what they had seen this day.

"Come."

Leah looked up. The bear was towering over her, his small, close set, brown eyes peering into her own. She frowned. "But how?" She reached out, unafraid, her touch gentle as she stroked the brown, silky fur. The Old One trembled beneath her touch as the shared power flowed between them, an understanding of what had been written in the before time.

"Come," he said again. One word. It was enough. Not wishing to delay any longer in such an open place, he moved ahead of her, back toward the forest with its shaded glen and hidden caverns where one such as he found safety from those of the two-legged clans.

Leah hesitated, but only for a moment, before following. Oak trees, hundreds of years old, stood guard, their branches reaching out to intertwine as they protected those who lived beneath their boughs. Leah shuddered as the prickling sensation ran through her. She did not know it, but she was the first of her kind to enter here. The hidden valley, protected by the unseen ones had been here from the beginning. Those that dwelled within the keepers of myths, legends, and dreams. As she stood quietly, gazing up at the canopy, leaves the color of emeralds danced in the wind. And for a moment, she thought she was back in that place where wolves were guardians of the weak and warriors of the forest saw the unseen in the wind that blew, while a snow-white owl heard the whispered words carried upon the night breeze.

"None will harm you here, for it is a sacred place, forgotten by all but a few."

The words were breathed out softly against her face. Leah turned her head to look at the big Mukwa who, but a short time past, had lain at her feet grievously wounded. The fact that he could communicate was not surprising, but that one such as he had thought to attack her that night was a mystery.

He read her mind. Nearly touching he crouched, looking at her, his deep brown eyes searching hers for thoughts, emotions. He looked away and for long moments, she waited. Waited for this Old One to speak. When he did, she found herself walking where he had walked, and she listened, not with her ears, but with her heart. Within herself, she saw what this old one had seen—she saw the clans of the four-legged and the winged ones. She watched as they fell one by one beneath the weapons of those of the two-legged clans. Those ones who had grown arrogant, their being consumed with the need to conquer, their lust for power, the thing that nearly destroyed them. She wiped away the wetness as it coursed down her face, her vision taking in images so fast she felt the earth spinning, and then she saw her brother, Nickolous. He was with the others. Chera and Gabriel were flanking him on either side, behind him; Timothy and Sarah were looking at something beyond her line of vision. The Old One, her Old One was there, too, looking older but well. Beside her stood Orith, his scarred features all too familiar. While above them perched Owen, the big owl resting on Jerome's arm, the forest warrior with his immense height seeing what the others could not.

Nickolous inclined his head slightly and then was gone. Leah let out her breath slowly, calming herself. He was looking at her. She drew back, wondering if he really saw her, or was it wishful thinking...she turned at the touch upon her arm. The Old One nudged her, studying her. He would not have believed that one who belonged to the clans of the two-legged could have such power. And to hold it within themselves, burying it for turnings without count...

He looked away, at the same time acknowledging the truth of what lay deep within his own memories: that this young one possessed the knowing that many of her kind lacked. Up until the moment the arrow had pierced his side, the jagged edges of the stone cutting deep, he had considered those like her prey. Now, he had to rethink things. He must seek out the Elders, those Ancient Ones who had the knowing of the before time layered deep with their memories.

"Where am I, and what is this place? Are there more like you? How many?" Leah had suddenly found her voice.

"Here? Only a few. Other places? There are many. Some have forgotten who they are; others, like those of us who live here, try to avoid contact with those of the two-legged. You, however, are an exception. As to what place is this? It is as it was at the beginning; untouched by the darkness that shadows the outer edges of our world as we have come to know it."

Leah remained silent. There was nothing left to say. The world she had known before she had crossed realms with her brother had not been that much different, her kind had ever been at odds with what they had forgotten.

"Time grows short. The others, like you, will be searching. That one, the one we know as The Hunter, *will* find you. Even now, he seeks the trail that will bring him here, and that we cannot allow." The soft burr in the bear's voice was nearly a growl.

Leah nodded. She understood. As she followed the Mukwa back the way they had come, she wondered at the possibility that she could find a way back to the others—

Back to Skye.

"This is your journey. Yours alone to make." The Mukwa's voice echoed in the endless wind that blew around them. Leah stopped. Ahead of her, the brown form paused, his huff-huff telling her she needed to hurry up. Time was growing short, his keen senses alerting him to the fact there was another like yet unlike himself threading its way cautiously toward them.

Leah choked back the memories as a familiar face, wrinkled and wizened, eyes black and alive with the knowledge of countless turnings floated in front of her blurred vision. No. It could not be! She shook her head to clear it, the old she-rat from the clans of knowing floated into her line of vision once more.

"The Hunter seeks you even now. Through the thread of time he reaches out, his knowing buried deep within. You must awaken it." The words faded into the quickening of the morning's dawning, so softly spoken that she wondered if it was her imagination. She pushed the thought aside, knowing it was not. Moving forward, her pace quickening, she hurried to catch up to the bear who waited for her, his stance impatient. She had no idea that he had heard her exchange with the Old One and would have been surprised had she known that he was connected to the others—his knowledge of who and what she was, where she had come from, what she had left—memories awakened within, triggered by her presence. Gazing up into the clear blue sky, the elder inhaled deeply as a new memory pressed upon him. Perhaps there was more to learn after all, he thought to himself as he resumed his journey, his pace steady, his keen hearing telling him the woman followed.

They were standing at the edge of the clearing, the scene before them one of quiet beauty. Leah took a deep breath, filling her lungs with the scent of forest and stream as she reached inward to touch that place where the Old One had been. There was nothing. Sighing, she turned at the slight noise to her left, her eyes narrowed. The Mukwa was gone, melted back into the forest that shielded him. She choked back a sob, swallowed, wiped at the wetness that spilled down her cheeks, angry at the sudden emotions that rippled through her.

Loneliness. Fear. A stranger in a place she knew little about, The Hunter the only one she had seen like herself.

She frowned at the sudden thought that there had to be others.

In the darkened places, there was always light. If she had learned nothing else during her journey from there to here, it was this one thing: nothing was as it seemed. Not there. Not here. She tensed as she heard the slight movement in the underbrush. She smiled to herself. Men. Turning, she went to meet him. He was coming for her, and he did not look pleased.

The one known as The Hunter was not in a good mood. He had spent most of the day and night searching for a mere female; once he would have tracked her, run her to ground. He was not sure with whom he was more displeased. Her for running away, or himself for losing her scent. His face darkened with anger. He went to reach out, to grab her, then remembering his status as a warrior, refrained. It would seem unseemly in the eyes of the elders to behave out of anger. Instead of harsh words, he stood glaring down at her then, motioning with a shake of his head, he turned and strode away, back the way he had come, his keen hearing telling him she followed.

Leah stared straight ahead, her footsteps automatically following in those of the warrior who strode angrily ahead of her. She sensed his displeasure at her behavior but did not react to it; in fact, she did not really care. She had been tossed through time into a foreign place where everything was opposite to what she had grown used to—a stranger in a land where the clans as she knew them did not exist except in the hidden places, away from those of the two-legged. She stopped for a moment to look around her. Without looking ahead of her, she knew the warrior had stopped, his frown deepening as he watched her, his gaze narrowing as he deep listened.

Leah started forward, her step cautious, the trill of the forest creatures soothing as she followed the path the warrior had taken. He was moving ahead of her, almost as if he were in a hurry to leave the safety of the forest. Not understanding why, Leah suddenly had the urge to be away, the calm of the forest no longer lingering upon her senses. Hurrying to catch up, she did not see the watchers, but the one known as The Hunter did. Without a backward glance, he reached for her hand, pulling her along with him. He knew the darkness would come with its usual swift intensity, and he had little desire to be in this part of the forest alone, and certainly not with a small female who was fire and ice all rolled into one.

Leah found herself being dragged unceremoniously across the ground. She could hardly keep up the man was going so fast, and for the life of her she could not understand why. A part of her wanted to pull away from his tight grasp, but the still small voice within whispered, *"Do not fight what you cannot understand."*

Leah closed her eyes against the images the voices evoked. *The Old Ones. The Elders.* She sucked in her breath. Remembering. Then just as quickly opened them as she was released. Caught off balance, she pitched forward, landing on her knees, the sudden cramping in her legs preventing her from rising. Unable to move, waiting for the pins-and-needles sensations to pass, she gazed upward into the darkening dusk, the chill catching her, lingering on her already taut senses before she was unceremoniously picked up and flung none too gently on the fur-covered bed in the lean-to. Beneath her aching body, the sweet scent of cedar wafted upward.

"Sleep now." The Hunter was leaning over her, his dark eyes unfathomable. Leah was about to say something then thought better of it. Rolling over, she drew the fur robe he had thrown down with her, the sharp retort on the end of her tongue stilled as the comforting warmth enveloped her. As the night deepened and the sound of the warrior's footsteps receded, she thought she heard a distant voice calling her. *Jerome.* The forest warrior's voice resonated against her sleepy senses as she drifted off into a dreamless sleep, devoid of any images, the velvety blackness rolling over her, cushioning her in its tight embrace.

It was much later, when the night had deepened and the world as he knew it was as it always had been, that the warrior sat quietly within the circle of trees, the embers of the fire glowing red, the flames licking upward against the dry wood that he had placed crossways in the shallow pit a little while earlier. The wind sighed silently overhead, but he did not hear it; his thoughts were elsewhere, and he knew that the others watched. The silent ones. It was they who had brought him here, to this place. They who wished him to watch over the strange female. He stared into the fires depths. Wondering. From time to time, he spared a glance toward the sleeping form of the woman. She was young. He shook his head as he remembered the events of the last two days, his eyes darkening as he gazed deeply into the fire. Something was calling him. Something ancient.

He leaned closer to the fire, his attention on what he could not hear. Later, when the first rays of morning's light began to trace their way across the eastern horizon, The Hunter gave up. As hard as he deep listened, there was no reply. Leaning back against the gnarled trunk of the ancient oak tree, he took the strength it offered and closed his eyes.

3

Leah stirred, her eyelids fluttering for a moment before drifting off again. She was warm and comfortable. She had not been this warm since... Dark brown eyes flew open as everything came rushing back. Throwing off the heavy fur, she jumped up, grabbing the beam at the top of the lean-to for support as she waited for the world to right itself. She took a tentative step, then another. So far, so good. She maneuvered around the center of the fire pit, her gaze sweeping the area for *"him."*

When she turned back, he was there. He glared down at her from his immense height, his black eyes unfathomable, and for a moment, she was afraid.

But only for a moment.

"Leave me alone, you Neanderthal." Leah stepped forward as she spoke, her posture belaying her true emotions. She had she decided, had enough of this he-man stuff. She was going to deal with her new surroundings, and if that meant dealing with this warrior who thought he was all that and more, well...

She sucked in a deep breath and took another step forward, not realizing that the warrior moved forward at the same time—her nose was level with his muscled chest. Bringing her arms up, she placed her small hands against his torso and pushed.

"Keep. Away. From. Me." The words were spat out through clenched teeth. Her hands were still pushing when they were grasped in two large ones, and suddenly she found herself being held at arm's length. The Hunter remained silent, his gaze searching hers. She did not flinch, instead choosing to return his gaze in kind. She had had it. First, she was tossed from the relative safety of the cavern into a darkly gray world where nothing made sense and everything was turned backwards. The clans of the four-legged were nonexistent, or as near to it as they could be—the Mukwa was of the old clans: that much she knew, but where were the others? There were so many questions with no answers.

As to the giant who held her captive, why, she had not seen any others like him, only shadowy forms that kept out of sight, preferring to remain in the hidden places, their unseen eyes watching. Where were the others of his kind? Was he the only one? She wanted to know what she faced. She wanted to know what had happened to the others, those companions she had left behind. Her brother, Nickolous, was he well? And the others, where were they? For that matter, where was she, and why couldn't the one known as The Hunter hear her without words? She glared up at him, the tears threatening, and she swallowed, pushing them back. She would not give into emotion. Not now and certainly not here.

Put. Me. Down.

The Hunter did just that.

For long moments, Leah remained where she had fallen, her thoughts not on the jarred sensation her body was experiencing but on something else. The man had turned away, his expression guarded, and as she sat there on the cold ground looking up at his broad shoulders tapering down to a narrow waist, she thought she heard him say something. Something unintelligible.

As Leah stood up, brushing the debris from her already tattered dress, the warrior turned back toward her, his gaze now merely curious. As a senior warrior, he had never had to deal with women—and this one was really starting to irritate him. Instead of allowing her to continue to prick his masculine pride, he chose the easier route. Ignore her. Ignore her outbursts. He had not reckoned on her temper.

The sudden impact of something small and stinging struck him in the side if his neck. Placing his hand on the spot, he rubbed it gingerly, his gaze no longer curious. It was obvious that the little female was insulted, her stance reminding him every bit of that of a warrior. He bit his tongue, the words he was going to say cut off as images poured forth and he saw what she was thinking.

Him.

Now it was his turn to be confused. His frown deepened as he opened his mind to her thoughts. Her emotions. As one of the guardians of the people, he had never considered emotions. It being his belief that those of his kind put far too much importance on such things, in fact, he had very little to do with those of the opposite gender. His training had been done with the elders: those warriors who were seasoned, the wars they survived, their experience to be shared in the sacred places. A place where there were no women, and so he had never really considered them one way or another. He looked down his nose at her, his thoughts centered, acknowledging her right to her privacy, he did not press too hard, surprised when she pushed back, guarding herself so that she was shielded against his prying. Full lips turned up at the corners as he stifled a laugh.

He had never really considered females—that is, until now.

Leah stood, legs apart, her hands on her hips, glaring up at him, her eyes dark with rage. How dare he invade the privacy of her mind! She was not quite sure what had just happened, but she sensed him. He was there, inside her head, prying into her deepest thoughts. Oh, how she wished Chera was here to help her. She watched with satisfaction as The Hunters eyes widened.

Good!

The vision of the silver-white wolf with her silver eyes flashed before her, and Leah knew The Hunter saw it, too. As it faded into the silence, Leah could have sworn she heard Chera calling her. She closed her mind, weary from the strain, and when next she looked, The Hunter was gone.

"Great," she muttered into the wind. "Just great. Alone again." Except that there were others beyond the fringes of her vision. She could not see them, but she knew they were there just the same.

She had just made herself comfortable when he reappeared. Masking her surprise, she said nothing as he placed the freshly picked fruit in front of her. It was as she gazed up at him, too surprised to say anything, that she sensed something else: that he was somehow changed.

Silently, The Hunter deposited more of the fruit in front of her, his thoughts his own. He did not want to frighten her, but he was a little afraid for himself—for the things that this strange female awakened within him. He knew the Elders watched from their hidden places and he was angry that they would not explain what he himself could not understand. For millennia of thought, they had existed within their circle, observing from their hidden places where they could observe and not be seen. He had been their most apt pupil, yet now he felt like a little boy, humbled by this female's presence and the power that emanated from her.

Shivering despite the stifling heat, Leah leaned forward, her thoughts not on the food but on how to go home; she inclined her head at the warrior, her way of saying she appreciated the food and the thought, but she wasn't hungry as she pushed the food away, out of the sun. The Hunter remained where he was, saying nothing. He understood.

She could not eat right now, but perhaps later.

§ § § § § §

Unseen eyes watched from their hidden places. Words, thoughts, passed like quicksilver from one to another as they moved in shadow. Warriors. Elders. Eternal. They watched. Worlds within worlds, their realms were being destroyed, and they were helpless against it. A collective sigh arose as the eldest of the watchers leaned forward, a thin wizened hand reaching out, the air about them becoming charged as the veil that concealed them from those of the two-legged clans changed. Thinning, it became transparent as the claw-like hand burst forth, the rest of him emerging cautiously, behind him the rest followed suit until the last was drawn through.

Wordlessly they surrounded the shaded glen, the seven of them joining their powers together so that the energy flowed outward, away from them and toward the young woman who remained, head bowed, wishing.

The wind stirred at Leah's back, the warm breeze caressing her with a welcome coolness as she absently brushed her long hair back, away from her face. She turned her head to one side as the breath of something forgotten reached out to her, thoughts merging as she recognized what it was that sought her out, while memories of something familiar tugged at her senses and she saw what The Hunter did not.

The Elders. The Old Ones. Leah centered herself as she closed her eyes, opening herself to the feelings that washed over her. Through her. They were all there. Beside her. Behind her. In front of her. Within her mind they centered themselves, while she acknowledged their right to choose their center. Without hesitation, Leah accepted their gift.

Memories of a forgotten race. Leah put her hands to her head and covered her ears to stop the screaming. *"No!"* The words were shouted, the sound carrying through her numbed senses as The Hunter hovered anxiously above her, his face a mask of confusion, as he stood there, helpless in the face of something he could not comprehend. *Or could he?*

"Stay away." Leah had not looked up, but The Hunter knew that it was she who had spoken. The words drifted to him, caught by the wind, and for a moment he imagined they were spoken from afar. He shook himself as the realization dawned. It was the Elders. This was their doing, not the woman's who knelt on the earth in front of him, her tear-streaked face hidden by her long, dark hair. The wind had picked up, and the warrior shielded his face against the flying debris. He could hear them, but he could not see them, and it rankled that they had sat silent for so long and now...

Bowing his head against the wind, he started forward, leaves and sand swirled about him as he edged toward Leah. Reaching out with his mind, he pushed his thoughts toward her, probing, preparing for resistance. There was none. He was almost to her.

As Leah listened to the words that the Elders spoke, their vision became hers. She saw what they saw, and with an unspoken consent, she traveled back. Back to their time.

The time of The People. The Warriors.

Thoughts merged as she watched the earth change, and those like her with it. The clans of the two-legged began to war with those of the four, and the gift of communication was taken back; no longer able to speak the language of the earth, they now hunted one another. Always wary, always at war.

And yet...

Leah found herself at the edge of a precipice, looking down into a hidden gorge where the mists rose and curled lazily upward, the emerald green of the forest with its crystal blue waters shimmering through the haze created by the waterfall. Within the center of the forest, she saw the world as it was in the beginning: the clans of the four-legged walked with the clans of the two, while the clans of the winged ones watched from their high places. Thoughts, words, flowed together, melding, their one purpose to communicate, to join. She looked away, the learning becoming painful as she felt the pull of the elements within her as they merged so that the knowing was absorbed within her memories.

The Hunter watched helplessly as the shadows passed through Leah, her features changing as she fought to cope with the intrusion into herself of something ancient. He watched as she struggled inwardly, controlling her emotions, accepting what she could not change, embracing the Ancients.

The Grandfathers. The Seven. Their words something to think on.

She raised her head, her gaze clear. Few had walked where she had, except…dark brown eyes narrowed in a face gone white with tension as she studied him from beneath long lashes, his own gaze seeking as he squeezed her hand gently to let her know he understood.

The Ancients had known. They had waited, watching through the veil that separated their worlds, waiting for a chance to put things right.

The Hunter was on his feet, looking down at Leah, his gaze now merely curious, his immense height dwarfing hers. Straightening her back, she looked up into his eyes; they were as black as night, but deep within their stormy depths memories still lingered. Memories forgotten, held in by ignorance, but there. She closed her eyes, wishing she could find the words to explain, to make the warrior understand. She needn't have worried. She looked up; the warrior's touch was gentle as he cupped her face with one big bronzed hand, his concern evident as he listened to what she had to say, his gaze occasionally drifting toward the forest's edge as he rubbed his chin thoughtfully.

§ § § § § §

The day had deepened into the brilliant hues of early afternoon, the sun's warmth making the fire unnecessary as the warrior banked it carefully. Leah had eaten most of the fruit The Hunter had brought her earlier. Feeling better, she leaned back against the makeshift bed of the lean-to while The Hunter sat across from her, his mind obviously elsewhere as he absently snapped the small twigs he had gathered earlier into small pieces. Had she known what he was thinking, she would have been shocked, for he was not thinking of the things she had talked about. He hadn't had time to process that yet. Instead, he was thinking about her. Never one to bother with those of the opposite sex, he had never really considered them; in fact, it had been many rising and setting of the suns since he had been in contact with others like himself. He supposed that he should soon return to his clan but, then again, that thought had only crossed his mind recently.

He looked across to where she sat staring at him, her gaze unwavering as she tried to read him. He blocked her out as he felt the gentle probing. She was unlike any female he had ever known, her abilities like his, but stronger, more defined. He pulled back at the sudden thought that she was more powerful than any of the others of his clan. In fact, if he took her with him, she would have to conceal the fact she could read others and deep listen.

Inwardly he sighed. Yes, he supposed, he would have to take her with him to the Elders. Once there, he could explain her presence and ask that she be accepted so he could protect her. At least until she could center herself enough so that he could decide what to do with her.

"You wish." Leah muttered inwardly as she deep listened. Something she was not aware she was capable of doing at will 'til now. Guarding herself so The Hunter would not know she could read him so easily, she turned her attention back to her surroundings. If she pretended she was weak, frightened, unsure of her abilities—it might buy her enough time to find a way home.

The sudden change in the wind made her shiver. She hated it when that happened, because she already knew what would happen next. And she was not going to like it. She stiffened, her back straight. There it was again, the slight shift as the breeze blew against her, the prickling sensation running up her spine, the fine hairs at the back of her neck rising as her body readied itself to accept the unknown. She looked up, hoping to see something definable as it pushed against her senses, gently at first, then a bit harder.

No, she was not going to like it. Not. One. Bit...

The voice, when it came, made her almost weep, shocking her with its intensity.

Chera.

The great silver-white wolf's voice carried through the realms of the unseen, whispering words so softly that Leah had to strain to hear them.

"We wait."

Then the disembodied voice was gone, carried upon the wind back to its place of origin as Leah wiped absently at the wetness that ran unheeded down her cheeks, stifling the sob that rose in her throat. Her chest hurt, her head ached, and she wanted to run. Strong hands reached for her, pulled her up, the touch gentle. Leah looked up at The Hunter, into eyes that were fathomless, and was surprised at the empathy she saw within their shadowy depths. Yes, there was that, and, something more. She suddenly realized he was shielding himself, protecting himself, against—her?

She pulled away, in her haste nearly tripping. Just as quickly, the warrior reached out, caught her, pulled her back against him. "Let. Me. Go." The words were muffled against a chest as hard as steel. Beneath the thin covering of leather he wore as a sort of tunic, she could feel his sharp intake of breath. And then she was released, and it was his turn to stare. She wiped her face with the back of her hand, in control of her emotions once more.

"Well?" She arched a brow as she studied him. It, she decided, was time to take matters into her own hands. If Chera said they waited, it meant she had to do whatever it took to get back to the others, or them to her. The thought that they could be in danger was almost too much for her as she turned away, the need to leave this place overwhelming. She straightened her back, aware of The Hunter's scrutiny. She decided she would treat him like the Neanderthal he was, and so she did not see the smirk that crossed the warrior's face as he caught glimpses of what she was thinking. He really did not understand what a Neanderthal was, and he really didn't care. He did, however, agree that they should leave. The Old Ones were gone. Returned to their place of watching. The warrior knew they would not return anytime soon.

Yes, he decided to himself as he watched Leah prepare to leave, he would watch over the little female. He would protect her without her knowing, and perhaps they would learn to like each other.

A little bit.

Leah hurried to catch up; the warrior in front of her was striding away purposefully, his stride one to her three. Determined to give as good as she got, she picked up her pace, glad she was in shape, for if she had not been, she would have already been left behind. As it was, by the time the warrior realized she was half his height and more than half his weight, she was nearly winded. He slowed his pace immediately to allow her time to catch her breath and was pushed aside as she swept past him, her intent to keep up and ask no quarter obvious. The Hunter shook his head in amazement. So, she wanted to prove herself, did she? He choked back a snort of laughter, the sound causing Leah to turn around, her gaze appraising.

The warrior had kept a steady pace for the better part of the day, his keen hearing telling him Leah followed. He only slowed his pace once. They had been traveling for quite some time and, as the afternoon had deepened, the warm air that swirled overhead had carried a new scent to him. One entirely unexpected. He had paused long enough to glance behind him, the furtive movement of something catching at the edge of his vision, then, just as quickly it was gone. Behind him, Leah turned and looked. If she saw anything, she never showed it. The Hunter quickly resumed his pace, the knowledge night would fall soon the main reason he wished to put as much distance between themselves and that which followed behind them.

"We will stop here."

"He talks." The words were muttered beneath her breath, but were heard. Leah looked up, then just as quickly dismissed the figure before her. Was that a disapproving glare concealed behind those dark brooding eyes? She stifled the laugh as she bent to the task of gathering dry wood. She did not need to be told a fire would be necessary this night, for the air held the promise of dampness that was already wending its way through earth and wood.

The Hunter watched as the woman worked. Good. She knew what was needed without being told. He smiled in the half-light, for the night was already upon them, the sounds that accompanied it sending ripples that echoed through the forest. He knelt down, removing his flint from a leather pouch he kept at his side; he started the fire, the sparks igniting quickly, the flame flickering upward to catch the dry punk that Leah had placed in the center. He remained where he was, surreptitiously studying her from beneath half-closed lids. He was impressed. He knew of no females in his clan who were as adept as she seemed to be. Needing no guidance, she seemed to know instinctively what needed to be done.

He was impressed, but he was not about to show it. Instead, he would study her strange ways and so, in that way, perhaps better understand her.

From her hunched position, Leah watched the fire, its blue-white flames comforting, the welcome warmth reaching out to replace the dampness that had seeped upward, embracing her but mere moments before. She had read The Hunter's thoughts, the tart reply on the tip of her tongue stilled as she deep listened. A quick glance in the warrior's direction told her all she needed to know. He was not listening with his heart. "We need to talk."

The Hunter swung his gaze toward the fire's flickering shadows then back to Leah. He supposed he was not going to like what she had to say, but that she was going to do it anyway. "And what is it we need to talk about?" he said, rising.

"Oh, I don't know." Leah's tone was sarcastic as she continued. "This place. Where we are going. You. Me. The Elders. The Ancients. *The Bear.*" The last was emphasized. "The fact you have forgotten there are others."

"What *Others?*" The Hunter remained where he was, his gaze curious.

Leah was incredulous. Images. Thoughts. Memories. Everything she had, she threw at him. All her knowledge from the others, Chera,

Jerome, the Old One; learning's taught, poured forth as she showed him how it had once been between those of the two-legged and four-legged clans...

Once, when the beginning was new.

The Hunter pulled back at the force of the images that assailed him as he turned from his place by the fire and embraced what others of his kind had not. The understanding flowing through him as he absorbed it: memories awakened, quickening his breathing, increasing his heartbeat. The rush of power ebbed and flowed through him like a river. Finally spent, it returned to its center, leaving him drained of everything save the need to rekindle what he now knew lay buried within his subconscious—the decision made. He wished to walk with this small female who had been thrown through time to land in a place she did not recognize, and did not want to be.

He looked down into eyes that had seen too much, given her obvious span of turnings. His eyes widened ever so slightly as she mouthed something at him. Then, remembering she could see him in a way he was unaccustomed to, he shut the portal within himself so that she would not so easily read him in the future, or, he thought smugly to himself, at least until he was ready to control his thoughts so he would have some privacy.

Leah's face colored; she had read enough to know what he was thinking. Glad for the cover of darkness, she quit probing, something she had done unconsciously after bombarding him with visions of who he could be if he would but open himself to the possibility. As she busied herself putting out the leftover fruit she had brought with her from the warrior's earlier foray into the forest, she could not help but wonder what the next day of their journey would bring.

She spared a furtive glance toward the warrior. He did not talk a lot, and her only experience with the opposite sex had been her brother, Nickolous. She drew in her breath then let it out slowly. She could not compare the two. Her brother she knew, but the one called The Hunter? Well, he was like no one she had seen in her time, or even the darkly handsome man that had pulled her through the gate from Skye into this place that was dark and dangerous—at least to her. Oh, she had glimpsed him, that *One,* as he had hurried from the battle she knew was taking place deep within the caverns, pulling her with him whether she was willing or not. Once, as she had tried to fight the pull of the unnatural wind that held her within its tight grip, she had imagined she heard Chera calling her but had realized her mistake too late. And yes, she had recognized the darkness that lie just below the surface of the stranger—the knowing that she was caught between worlds yet again as a different wind had found them in their concealed place. Then she was falling through shadow while things dark and disembodied shrieked around her, against the elemental powers that brought them here, through the gates to yet another unknown place.

Her thoughts returned to when she had gotten lost. She had been separated from her brother after they had inadvertently found their way back to Skye. Never one to be able to gauge the direction she should have been going, she had known only that she was being followed. Weaponless, afraid, she had done the only thing she knew to do—run for her life.

Later, after she had fallen into the tunnel, she had searched for a way out. Finding none, she had followed the sound of running water, the echo as it journeyed through crevasse and fissure to spill unto rocks made smooth over countless turnings pulling her toward what she hoped was safety and home. As she had journeyed, she had caught glimpses of the others: companions who followed their hearts, teachings handed down through a millennia of thought to be passed like a flame, the embers glowing, catching as the thought was passed down to another and another…

She turned away from the warrior's intense gaze. She wanted to be alone with her thoughts.

"*Another learning.*" The words, whispered upon the unseen breeze that carried them through the endless night, swirled about her. Having found her, it retreated, back to the one who had sent it forth to seek.

The warrior stood a short distance away. Feelings, thoughts—the passage of something unknown rippled through him as he watched her. He remained where he was, unflinching against the night wind and what rode hard upon its back. He would wait for the first rays of mornings dawning, then he would begin the journey back to where it had begun. He breathed in deeply of the night air, drawing on the scents and sounds that accompanied it.

Leah supposed that she should say something. Anything. However, as she stared into the fires flickering depths words failed her. She needed to focus. On herself. On what she had heard in the shaded glen earlier. She knew Chera was searching for her.

Behind her, The Hunter coughed softly. Sighing, she drew her thoughts back to herself so they would not be seen. She supposed he wanted to give her time to gather her thoughts. Well, she had. She turned to face him, her eyes mirroring her intent and the warrior nodded his head in approval at what he saw behind their smoky depths.

"It is time to rest. Tomorrow we will travel as far as we can," he said.

"What about the darkness that follows?"

"What do you know about such things?" the warrior countered, one dark brow arched questioningly as he waited for an answer.

"What? About shadows that walk within realms? Crossing unseen bridges to wreak havoc, then just as quickly disappearing back into the nothingness that they came from?" Leah glared up at The Hunter, suddenly angry at something she could not control.

"Lots." The words were ground out from between clenched teeth as Leah bent to straighten the scented cedar boughs that had been placed there earlier. She did not want the warrior to see the tears that coursed down her cheeks unbidden.

She was angry. The warrior saw it in the way she bent to the task of straightening the makeshift bed. He heard it in the tone of her voice as she choked back the tears. More than that, he felt her anguish and was helpless in the face of sorrow he did not understand. He turned away to give her some privacy, hoping a good night's sleep would calm her. He was wise enough to keep his thoughts to himself as he gathered his sleeping robe and weapons, moving a short distance away where he could keep watch but remain unseen.

Long after the night had deepened, and the baying of wild things on the hunt had trailed off into silence, Leah lay on her bed of cedar boughs, gazing up into the starry night, her thoughts on what she had seen and heard this day. It was nearly morning before she fell into a restless sleep, and even then she was haunted by Chera's voice calling her name while The Hunter kept watch, his thoughts on the restless form that tossed and turned beneath the furs in the crude lean-to. Now and then catching glimpses of what she was seeing, he vowed to try to help her find her way home, the knowing within that they were in danger doing little to dampen his resolve to help her.

4

"Wake up." The words were breathed out softly, the speaker not wishing to draw attention to himself. Leah muttered something unintelligible then turned away, burrowing further beneath the warm robe that had been thrown over her, its warmth welcome against the cool air that blew softly through the early morning's mist. She had not really slept, and as she opened her eyes, she could feel the pressure behind them and prepared herself for the headache that was sure to follow so much lack of sleep.

"Go away." The words were mumbled against the fur-lined robe she used to cradle her head.

"Up. Now!" The warrior's tone had changed. The words cut through her numbed senses as she was pulled to her feet, the robe rolling off her as she shivered in the cool morning air.

"There's no time to lose. We were followed last night, and we need to leave. Now." The Hunter had already packed the sleeping robe into his leather bag; securing it over his shoulder with a leather strap, he grabbed his quiver of arrows and longbow and with the other hand grabbed Leah's, nearly pulling her off her feet as he headed into the forest at a steady trot.

It happened so fast that she didn't have time to think. To react. Leah suddenly found herself being half carried, half dragged through the dense underbrush, barely having time to bring her one free arm up to protect herself, to push the branches out of her way as they whipped against her face. More than once, she narrowly missed being impaled by broken branches in her path. Finally, after what seemed an eternity of stumbling, tripping, and running, they came to an abrupt halt.

They were standing at the edge of a precipice looking down into a valley so breathtaking in its beauty that Leah was in awe.

But not for long.

"Go. I'm right behind you." The Hunter knew the downward trail well, and he knew the places where they could conceal themselves from what was behind them. As he pushed her down onto the pathway, he gave her no choice but to do as she was bidden. Watching her disappear from sight before pushing off after her, he had no doubt she would be waiting for him at the end of it.

§ § § § §

Leah had been so busy admiring the wild beauty of the valley set out before her that she hadn't even seen it coming. One moment she was standing at the edge of a cliff looking down, and the next she was being pushed over the edge and dropped unto a sort of slide covered with moss—lots of moss. And water. She could feel the slime rubbing against her body as she picked up speed, and as she coursed through the water-laden tunnel, she thought of all the things she would say to the one known as The Hunter when she reached the end of it.

Oh yes, she thought to herself as the she landed unceremoniously on top of a mossy mound, winded but unhurt, yes, she would be waiting for that *One!*

She was still trying to wring the water out of her tattered dress when she heard The Hunter behind her. Obviously used to such a mode of travel, he hardly glanced her way as he removed his tunic, spreading it over a low-hanging limb of a gnarled and ancient oak tree before running his hands down the length of his body—his leather leggings clinging to him like an second skin as she watched. The water running in rivulets past his ankles to seep back into the thick moss that cushioned his feet.

Whatever she was going to say was temporarily forgotten as he turned to face her, his expression reminding her of a mischievous little boy caught in the act of doing something naughty. Leah started forward, her intent to get close enough to give him a piece of her mind without having anyone, or anything unwanted, hearing her. But before she could say anything, he placed a finger to his mouth, indicating silence. Grabbing his still-wet tunic, one dark brow arched as he motioned her to follow him through the bracken that grew thick and wild leading into the dense forest.

Leah watched him go, the giant ferns bending as he brushed against them, before falling gently back into place, leaving no evidence of his passage amongst them. Sighing, Leah followed, resigning herself to the fact that whatever she had to say would have to wait, at least for now. Determined to keep up, she moved forward, her strides nearly doubling to match his.

The Hunter knew Leah was hurrying to catch up to him. He also knew what she had been thinking, which was why he had not given her a chance to speak her thoughts aloud. Better the sound of their footsteps as they made their way deep into the forest, the song of the birds overhead distracting her from her thoughts, he mused silently to himself as he tried to block her probing. He realized with a start that even she did not realize what she was capable of...and it was growing stronger.

Leah walked slightly behind the warrior, her gaze focused on the path in front of her, littered with broken twigs and jutting rocks. And not the partially clad man who walked ahead of her. She wanted to say something, anything that would let him know how she felt. She knew he was blocking her thoughts, therefore, he knew how she felt. She sighed, the sound carrying to the warrior and he stopped midstride; turning his head to look down at her, he studied her for the briefest of moments before resuming his steady pace.

Leah stared after him for a moment before hurrying after him. "Fine. Be like that." She muttered more to herself than anyone else as she moved silently through the woods. Taking care not to tread on any small branches that had fallen unto the path, she was looking down, her concentration elsewhere, when she ran full into the warrior's back. She stepped back quickly, stunned as he turned swiftly around, grabbing her by the waist while at the same time pushing her down so that they were both concealed within the dense foliage

"Something walks within the shadowed places of the forest. There." The Hunter had one hand over her mouth, while with the other he pointed toward the darkened part of the woods.

Leah pushed his hand away from her, at the same time easing her body away from his. Balancing herself on her elbows, she edged forward just a little bit, her senses tingling as she peered out from beneath the damp ferns that hung over her head. When next she moved, it was because the warrior behind her was pulling her back, toward him.

"What are you doing?" The words were hissed as Leah twisted around so that they were face to face.

"Listen." The Hunter's face was inches from hers, his warm breath fanned her cheek as he drew her close. "Listen," he said again. "Don't you hear it? Deep listen. Now. Do you hear me?" He was nearly shaking her. She could feel the air as it fanned them in their hidden place. The smell of earth and mouldy leaves assailed her senses as she focused.

She shook her head to clear it, her vision blurring, her emotions rising as she saw what the warrior could not.

"Chera!"

The big wolf was there, partially hidden within the shadows that draped the deeper part of the forest. The limbs of the oak tree, gnarled and thick, hung low to the ground, all but concealing her. Leah was about to call out when Chera swung her gaze toward her. Silver eyes looked into brown as she bared her teeth in a snarl, her gaze sliding past Leah to the warrior. She pulled back so fast that she slammed into The Hunter. As his arms wrapped protectively around her, she dared to look once more. Only the tree with its gnarled limbs and the place where the wolf had stood remained. That, and the afternoon shadows that stretched across the limb-strewn path, reaching slowly out to cover the forest floor.

"She was there. Did you see her?" Leah had managed to turn around and was facing the warrior, her eyes wide as she looked up at him. She gripped his arm, her fingers digging into the muscles on his forearm as rising, he pulled her up with him. Not knowing why she did it, she clung to him as if he were her lifeline as she breathed in deeply, trying not to let her emotions overtake her.

"Chera." The word was released softly as she buried her face unashamedly in The Hunter's chest, the emotion washing over her in waves as she opened herself to whatever it was that was out there.

The Hunter wasn't used to such strong emotions from a woman, and he certainly hadn't expected her to take refuge within his arms, let alone cling to him as if she were his mate. The thought disturbed him that he could not see what she had, but that something was there he did not doubt as the wind blew about him, carrying the unknown with it, and he was thankful that she wanted to stay close to him.

He didn't want to admit it, but although there wasn't much to her, when she decided to hide from him, she did it well. A little too well. His warrior's pride did not compensate for failure of any kind and she had managed more than once since her arrival to infuriate him with her insolence. Yet now, holding her, she seemed so fragile and insecure. In need of his protection, he thought as he held her trembling form against him, offering her his strength as words, unspoken, nudged against her senses. Accepted.

As the day deepened and the pathway darkened, concealed by the shade that crept steadily forward, The Hunter stood quietly, his gaze focused on movement ahead of him. Beside him, Leah tensed, her senses heightened from earlier, she drew on the teachings from that other place, where the Old One was. After, when the shock of seeing the big wolf had worn off, she had tried to focus her thoughts, returning to her center, to reach out and go beyond to that place where the grandmothers dwelled. It hadn't worked. She shrugged slender shoulders. It didn't matter. She knew that Chera had seen her. Aware that the one known as The Hunter had turned his attention back to her and was studying her curiously from beneath half-closed lids, she merely nodded. Whatever had been ahead of them, embraced by the deepening shadows that heralded the late afternoon, was gone. Back to wherever it had came from.

She was ready. The warrior had given her time to collect her thoughts, allowing her to center herself. To return to her woman's place of knowing. With that in mind, she thought that she might come to like him. A little bit. And that if there were a way for Chera to cross that misty place that bridged her world and this one—she would do it.

§ § § § § §

Dampness. It crept along the earthen floor. Reaching upward, against the cold gray walls before receding back, no match for the warmth that fanned out from the center of the cavern. The fire pit was deep, evidence that the fire, which burned red-hot within its center, had done so for countless turnings. Slightly beyond the places where the flickering light cast their own ethereal shadows, out of sight from even those unseen watchers, a heavily robed figure stirred from his place of rest.

As the hood of the robe fell from him, unnaturally dark eyes looked out from a face that was almost too perfect. Dark brows rose questioningly as he turned at the sound of something or someone begging entrance.

"My Lord." The speaker moved cautiously into the cavern; careful to avoid the lighted places, it stayed within the confines of the shadows, where the fire's light could not reach.

"Yes? What is it?" The man, if man he was, moved closer, his gaze fixed on the lone sentinel.

The speaker remained where he was. Knowledge, layered deep within his being warned him to tread carefully around this *One*. Words softly spoken carried strength as he prepared himself for what was to come. "The gateway was breached when you returned." The words were spoken into the silence that now permeated the cavernous room as the sentinel tensed. Preparing himself.

The man said nothing but continued to stare into the fire's depths. Behind him, the shadows crept closer. The fire flickered as the wind, unnaturally cold, found its way through one of the many fissures that were part of the cold gray stone that made up the cavern walls. The silence deepened as the sentinel took a step back, waiting for what was sure to follow such a disclosure of failure. And was surprised when it did not.

The laugh, low and melodious, wafted though the silence as the man leaned toward the fire. Throwing something into the flames, he stood back as it flared, the flames reaching the ceiling of the cave before receding back to glow eerily in the semi-darkened cavernous room.

Inhaling sharply the sentinel shrank even further back into the darkened places, for he knew what was being called forth from the depths of the fires flame. Knew that within a heartbeat of breath that everything in his world would change yet again. It had been this way for as many turnings as he and his kind could remember—forced to serve a master who was ageless. The gatekeepers living to serve him until they ceased to be. Although, sometimes, it seemed he had once been *more*, the memories he held within him nothing more than a dream

Rising and twisting from the flames, the smoke coiled upward. The acrid smell of something unclean permeated the cavern as the air filled with unspeakable things—voices, faint and disembodied, reached out across an endless void struggling to enter a world where they could wreak havoc.

The sentinel turned away. Away from the vision of what was pouring forth into his world.

§ § § § §

They had traveled all day, not once stopping to rest as the afternoon had waned, deepening into the dusk that heralded the sudden onset of night. The moon's translucent tendrils trailed across the path casting shadows so that they had to tread more carefully. With the moon to light the way, the path still visible before them, Leah never faltered. Slightly ahead of her, the warrior paced himself so that she could keep up. He knew she would not be the first to stop, her pride not allowing a show of weakness. The Hunter grinned in the half-light as he stared straight ahead. There was much he still did not know about her, but what he did know was that he admired her courage.

Leah still could not believe it. So much to learn in so little time. *Trust no one.* Black eyes set in a wizened face floated before her, and she nearly tripped before catching herself. Ahead of her the warrior paused, the motion so subtle it was barely noticeable as Leah pushed herself forward. One dark brow rose questioningly as he stepped aside to let her pass, the question left unasked as he watched her move out of sight. Moments later he once again passed her, determined to let her walk until she was exhausted. The moon was at mid-point in the night sky when the warrior finally stopped, his motion indicating that they would rest. Leah did so gratefully, without argument, her mind numbed by the images that had pressed themselves relentlessly upon her throughout the day.

The Hunter watched from his place of concealment; the hastily prepared lean-to would serve its purpose, a place to rest for a little while before morning's dawning. He looked upward into the dark starry night as the soft rush of sound created by the tiny winged ones passed by. He knew they posed no threat and was grateful for their need to hunt the little stingers that were so worrisome to those like himself. It was a relief to see them filling the dusky night with their sound. His gaze swept the small grove. Protected by towering fir trees, their regal branches swept the ground, the sweet scent filling the air as those who walked the night went about their business. Sighing, the warrior leaned back against the tree and closed his eyes.

In her dream, Leah was back in the cavern. Her fall broken by the leaves that had gathered beneath her as she had slipped, her footsteps triggering the mechanism that had been put in place long ago to keep others out. But not her. Dazed but unhurt, she had soon realized the way out was closed, the opening gone, yet she hadn't been afraid for the cavern had been warm. The air that curled about her comforting as she felt her way along the narrow passageways, the sound of water trickling over moss and rocks guiding her. Time had passed as time does, and she had suddenly, inexplicably, found herself in a large, cavernous room. The light dancing off the walls from a fire that burned in an open pit in the center of it a welcome embrace to her exhausted senses. Dried wood had been placed nearby. Enough to do for quite some time. There was fruit, dried and fresh, as well as a small, earthen kettle. Water trickled steadily from a fissure in the rocks, collecting in a natural basin at the foot of the wall, ensuring a fresh supply of water—that and the heavy woolen cloak draped over a roughly hewn chair.

She had sunk into it gratefully, drawing the warmth to her, and had eaten and slept. The time had passed and she had felt safe, her inner knowledge telling her that she was to stay where she was. And she had. It was not until the earth had trembled beneath her feet that the first thread of fear passed through her and she felt the rush of darkness as it passed over her hidden place. Her protected place breached, she had been caught within the heart of the darkness as it sought entrance back to its own.

The moon was bright, soft tendrils reaching out to caress the hidden places, the small shadowy forms of the night creatures scurrying from path to burrow as they sought sanctuary deep within the earth. Something was coming. Something that smelled of death. Deep within the forest where the moon's fragile light could not reach, the broken branches that had fallen to earth broke beneath the weight of the unknown.

The Hunter was up and running as the screams echoed through the inky darkness that was the deepest part of the night. Leaning down, he grasped the fur robe and came up empty. He turned at the light touch upon his arm and let his breath out in relief. Leah was beside him, her breathing heavy as she tried to center herself. Whatever had awakened her was closing in on them. The air, hot and humid, clung to them both as they retreated back—back beneath the safety of the trees, the heavy scent of the towering red cedars masking their own. As the thundering sound drew closer, the warrior readied his bow while Leah knelt beside him, her heart thudding painfully as she searched the night, her inner vision seeking what could not be seen.

§ § § § §

"You seem upset."

The sentinel merely nodded his displeasure.

The man was seated at a roughly hewn table, his attention on the yellowed parchment in front of him. He did not bother to look up. He could sense the displeasure of the one who waited within the confines of the shadows and ignored it. "Things change as they must." He spoke the words to no one in particular. He knew there were others, watching, listening—gauging the sentinel's reaction.

"Speak."

"There is nothing to speak of. The gates have been compromised, and where once only the chosen were allowed to transverse the realms *in-between,* now others enter, and the veil weakens. That which you have brought forth could destroy us all." The movement was barely discernible as the sentinel moved forward, into the fire's flickering light.

The man rose to his feet, ignoring the parchment as it rolled off the table onto the earthen floor. Rarely did one of the sentinels reveal themselves fully to others. He was the master here and would not tolerate confrontation. Dark eyes set in a too-handsome face narrowed as he met the icy gaze of that of the other.

"What has been done was necessary. The female that followed me through can turn our world back. She has the memories." The man turned away, as if that were enough, his actions dismissing the watcher. "What needed to be done was done. Had you done what was expected, she would never have made it through the gate." The silence deepened as the man tensed. He could feel the others cold gaze as it pressed against his back.

"Leave. Now. There is nothing more to discuss. Return to the gate."

"There are other gates, other passageways—"

"Then see to it that they are kept closed." The man had turned around once more, his gaze level with that of the watchers. The sentinel stepped back into the comforting embrace of the darkness. Eyes the color of gray slate glowed eerily, the reflection of the fire's flickering light caught within their smoky depths as thoughts, memories, were pushed back. He made up his mind. He would not risk a challenge. Not yet.

5

The fire in the pit flared upward. Red-gold tendrils licked greedily at the dry wood as the heat spread through the cavern once more, suffusing it with warmth as the man warmed himself against it. He spared a glance toward the empty place where the sentinel had stood but mere moments before. The laughter that echoed through the many passageways to the world outside was dark, challenging. He turned aside, picking up the parchment from its place where it had fallen upon the earthen floor, unrolled it and began to read the fine script written ages beyond thought.

He was who he was.

He was the *"Other."*

§ § § § §

Leah tensed as something passed overhead. She ducked lower, heedless of the branches that brushed against her, their sweet scent masking her own as the air above her thickened. The unnatural chill gliding soundlessly above the treetops as it searched for them.

"It cannot seek lower." The Hunter was beside her, his breath warm upon her cheek. "It is of an ancient race, the night its voice, the air its breath. To touch the earth that grounds us would destroy its essence of being. It will tire soon of searching and move on. Wait." A bronzed hand covered her small one as he drew her close and was surprised when she leaned into him, accepting his nearness.

Leah closed her eyes, sensing what The Hunter could not. There was another following them, and he was close. A slender brow lifted in surprise—so it was he who had been dogging them. She shifted her gaze to the warrior.

"We need all the help we can get." She lifted her face to his so that they were nearly touching, suppressing a shiver as the wind caressed her back.

"Agreed." The warrior stiffened slightly but didn't pull back from Leah's intense gaze.

The faint shuffling drew closer as the night wind shifted course. From their concealed place, both the warrior and Leah watched as the big Mukwa lumbered into view, his huge head swinging from side to side as he peered into the moonlit night. What he lacked in nearsightedness he made up for in his ability to smell.

Pausing briefly, he looked toward them before backing up and sitting down, his expression blank. But Leah, better than anyone, knew what lie beneath that powerful body and was not fooled. Had others been watching, they would have seen naught but a mindless beast who stared vaguely at his surroundings. Seeing nothing, pausing to scratch himself restlessly as he snapped now and then at the little night stingers that harried him.

Leah inclined her head slightly as she acknowledged the Old One's presence. Knowing he would move no closer, his intent obvious. When they moved, he would. She blew out her breath slowly, watching as it caught in the chill air, swirling upward to disappear into the night. "We must leave. The Mukwa will follow, but more slowly." She was moving out from beneath the low hanging branches as she spoke, her nearness to the warrior suddenly making her uncomfortable.

Unafraid, the knowing that one of the eldest of the four-legged ones had chosen to share the path that lay before them, she hurried ahead. Behind her she heard the warrior's sharp intake of breath as he glanced at the bear, then at her disappearing back before striding after her; his snort of exasperation making her laugh as he quickly caught up. She looked up at him. Even in the scant light cast by the moon, she saw his expression and knew he wanted to shake her but thought better of it.

Leah picked up her pace to match The Hunters. He was angry, she thought to herself as she sidestepped to miss something small and furry that scampered out of her way. As they hurried through the forest, she deep listened, surprised that the ability became easier with each passing hour. She didn't have to try; she merely thought about it and it was so. However, somewhere deep within herself, she had the feeling that her surroundings had more to do with her newfound abilities than anything else. She looked around her as they passed beneath the outflung branches of ancient trees and crossed wide running streams that she was sure flowed in small eddying brooks.

"What is it you see." It wasn't a question. The warrior had sensed a change in the air and, although his senses were keen, he had to admit, the small female who walked beside him was far more astute with her feelings than he. He frowned in the semidarkness, one black brow raised in expectation. "Well?" he asked. Impatient when she did not answer, he stopped, the movement so unexpected that Leah bumped into him.

It was instinctive. Leah pulled back as if stung, and turned, the movement automatic, her intent to put as much distance as possible between herself and the warrior. Not bothering to look where she was going, she did the unthinkable. She tripped.

Then the warrior was reaching out to catch her, drawing her back toward, turning her to face him as he glared down at her. His midnight eyes seeking the unspoken answer as he deep listened.

Her answer surprised him.

"I see others, out there, in the shadows, watching. They fear what they cannot see—cannot understand. They are caught between two places. Neither here nor there." Leah drew in her breath sharply as she sensed something more. It was indefinable, but there. Fear. *They feared her.* Not understanding why, she rushed on, her voice betraying nothing of what she felt. "They have forgotten the learnings passed down by their forebears." Leah reached up to brush a branch aside as it touched her face, the slight touch electrifying as she released it to return to its place. Her breathing slowed imperceptibly as she centered herself while The Hunter remained where was, unmoving, his gaze sweeping behind him, along the winding path, back, the way they had come. Although he could not see him, he knew the Mukwa was there, hidden within the shadows, his dark fur blending with his surroundings. He looked around, his hand tightening on his bow, while with the other he found his knife. The thick obsidian blade slid from its sheath with the barest whisper of sound as he turned slowly, his warrior's sight reaching out, his grip tightening on the knife that had warmed to his touch. It thrummed silently in his hand as he saw what the woman saw: the remembrances of an ancient race. The essence of who they were trapped within the images left behind by the emotions that controlled them.

As the turnings had passed, the clans who had walked beneath had forgotten. Like the seasons that were ever-changing, nothing remained the same, and so it was for the clans of the two-legged. Knowledge, passed down from the beginning, had been lost. Forgotten by all but a few, the remembering becoming a vague dream that tugged at their senses from time to time. The Old Ones sorrowed, those Ancients who watched from behind the veil, for even they knew that with the passage of time they would become little more than vague memories. A story to tell around the fire as the people sat, surrounded by what once was, now turned to nothingness.

The Hunter looked past Leah, into the night; wondering.

"How long?"

"How long what?" Leah peered into the misty morning, still amazed at how fast the morning dawned and the moon set, the night lending itself to the light that dispersed it. No longer chilled, she welcomed the warmth as the sun spread itself across the landscape, the chill of the night all but forgotten as she turned to look up at the warrior.

The Hunter looked down at her, his gaze sweeping past to where the Old One sat, calmly cleaning himself, his small, brown eyes looking at him. Through him. He still wanted to shake her but refrained from doing so. She was looking up at him innocently, her big brown eyes full of amusement as she brushed the hair back off her face. He groaned inwardly as the wind picked it up and blew it back over her shoulders. She had, he thought, beautiful hair. It was a dark auburn as to be nearly black; the deeper threads of red were muted within the waves that trailed down her back, curling gently at the ends. It suited her. With that thought in mind, he pushed back the urge to grab her and all but hissed the words through clenched teeth. "How long is that *creature* going to follow us?"

He had agreed they needed all the help they could get, but this was not what he had envisioned. The answer not what he wanted to hear.

"Until the end."

They continued on, walking in silence for some time, neither one speaking, the Old One lumbering steadily behind them. Occasionally, Leah felt brave enough to look up, but the warrior's face showed nothing of what she knew he felt. His world was changing as he moved through it—not a subtle change, but the kind that struck one with disbelief that all they had known, all they had been taught, wasn't exactly what it appeared to be. She sighed inwardly.

She knew just how he felt.

Behind them, the Old One growled, the sound low and throaty. Only Leah knew what it really meant. She kept going, ignoring the puzzled look the warrior shot her from beneath dark brows, while behind them the Old One snorted again, his head swinging from side to side. Leah suppressed a grin as the sound of laughter echoed in the stillness behind them.

§ § § § § §

"Chera—?" The sound was muted, the silver-white wolf guarded as she scented the wind. There was nothing. Just the wind that circled her restlessly. Not a natural wind, but a telling wind. She shook her head to clear it, beside her, Gabriel, her mate, watched her, his concern evident.

"What is it?" Nonetheless, he knew the answer even as the wind caressed his back, the prickling sensation running the length of his spine.

Leah.

Words unspoken were heard. They echoed hollowly in the silence as both wolves stared at each other. It had been but a few short turnings since Lord Nhon had been sent to earth and the world as it had once been was turned back to what they remembered.

"She isn't here but somewhere we cannot reach," Gabriel murmured softly, more to himself than anyone else, at the same time reaching out, probing the unseen places. His knowledge, layered deep, went beyond what they were now. It went back beyond remembrance, back to their primordial time of remembering when what they saw *was*.

Chera growled softly, the sound resonating from deep within her chest and spiraling outward as she saw what Gabriel saw. It hadn't been a dream. Leah had called to her from out of the darkness, and she had answered, her instinct to protect this young one of the two-legged bridging the worlds of the *between*. The veil that separated their world was thinning; something dark had merged with the two. Her silver eyes narrowed as she stared thoughtfully into the distance. They needed to find the others.

Nickolous, Orith, Owen, and the Old One. They were with Jerome, the forest warrior who could look beneath and above, descended from an old race, he could see into the darkest of hearts.

Then there was the Old One. An ancient she-rat, she was of the *knowing* clans. One of those who could see the unseen and interpret its meaning along with Orith, the snowy white owl—scarred from battle, but still able to read the ancient runes etched deep within the rocks that sheltered them all. Together since the battle for the sacred flame, the two had become inseparable.

Finally, yet importantly, there was Owen, brother to Orith. The eyes of the night, he could go where the others could not and ferret out the unwanted.

They were all with Nickolous. The young warrior who had walked between two worlds, a half-son of Skye. Son of Aleta, a daughter of Skye, he had chosen to walk within their world, the other place he had been born naught but a fading memory as he learned how to channel his extraordinary abilities.

"Come." One word, spoken succinctly.

Gabriel watched as his mate loped off, her svelte form disappearing into the welcoming forest. He paused a moment longer—visions of the night hunt and the pull of the moon upon their instincts guiding them to where they belonged crowded his memories.

Sighing deeply, he pushed them back before following in her wake. They would have to wait.

§ § § § §

The Hunter knew that something was different. Had known for a while, the first inkling being when the little female had been pushed through after that *'One.'*

He should have left her to the cloud creature, he mused silently to himself, and just as quickly regretted the thought, knowing it would not have mattered, that somehow she would have survived such an attack. She was strong, this one—not so much physically but spiritually. He frowned as he stepped over a fallen log, the little dwellers that lived beneath its shade squeaking in protest as they fled for safety, away from him and any others who followed.

Aware that Leah had stopped, he paused, his gaze impatient as he waited for her to catch up. She ignored him, her attention on one of the small ones who had narrowly escaped being stepped on. Too young to flee, it had stayed where its mother had dropped it in her terror and haste to get the others to safety. Teeth bared, hissing, it wobbled on tiny legs, nonetheless, its stance challenging her.

Watching, the warrior suppressed a laugh as she knelt down, then masked his surprise as she murmured something he could not hear— the words alone for the little one who stood, glaring up at her balefully. The Hunter moved closer, his eyes shuttered. He could feel the change in the air as the small earth digger, no longer hissing, placed its head to one side as if listening. Impossible! He shook his head in disbelief. Reaching out to pull Leah forward, the growled warning at his back was enough to stop him as he turned slowly. Looked up. Small brown eyes glared at him from a few feet away. Cursing himself for not having paid attention to where the bear was, he simply did what was practical.

Remained exactly where he was.

Leah knew the warrior was staring at her in astonishment, but she did not care. Leaning closer to the little one, she concentrated, envisioning the others of its kind, they who lived beneath—the little ones, the earth diggers, the heartbeat of the earth. They must, she thought, be similar. She was right.

The small one wavered, its fear replaced by awe. It belonged to the smallest of the four-legged clans, taught since birth to avoid those of the two-legged. Those clans having lost the memories long turnings past; they were considered to be little more than savages at best. Now, as it looked up at Leah and heard her thoughts, it did not know what to think. When she put her hand out, it hesitated, as if weighing its options before carefully stepping unto her palm. Moving slowly, she went to the edge of the path and, kneeling down, released it to its mother, who was staring up at her with wide black eyes.

"Thank you." The words were hers alone to hear as she stood for a moment longer, watching as the little family of earth diggers moved deeper into the shadows. When she turned around, she found herself staring up into The Hunters eyes, his expression one of astonishment.

"You see with eyes that see nothing." She glared up at him, exasperated that he could not see what she did. She was tired and hungry and had just about had it. All around her the forest spoke. Was she the only one listening? She wanted to put her hands over her ears and run, but the lumbering form of the bear stopped her.

"Patience." The voice whispered, and she paused, not quite sure who had just spoken. Shrugging her shoulders indifferently, she moved away, back onto the path, away from the warrior and the Mukwa, both of whom watched her for some moments before following her.

In the silence that followed their departure, the little ones waited. After a while the bravest of them, an elder who had lived longer than most, poked his nose out from beneath the bushes where he had been watching and moved slowly into the open where he could be seen by the others. Slowly, cautiously, the others appeared, carefully edging their way to where the Old One stood; alert for anything untoward, they waited for the eldest of them to speak.

"She saw us in our hiding places and knew us for what we once were," the elder spoke loudly enough that all could hear, his voice surprisingly strong for one so old. "Well?" He waited for others to speak. To say the words that would trigger the remembering in them all. From somewhere deep within the midst of the crowd, a small voice was heard. The elder motioned for those in front to let the speaker pass through. To be seen. He was surprised that it was one of the younglings, barely out of her first youth. He nodded, beckoning her closer. It did not matter her age, for wisdom had many faces, and age was not always one of them.

"You may speak." The elder leaned forward, his gaze searching, waiting to hear the words, to see what had been learned.

"Once we were more than what we are now, our purpose to protect the sacred places. We have forgotten who we were..." The voice trailed off into the poignant silence as the elder studied her intently.

"And now?"

"Why, we must remember. We must return to the earth and be who we are." The youngling was looking around, clearly puzzled by the question. A small brow furrowed in a tiny face as she fell silent. After all, did they not already know these things?

The elder remained where he was, unmoving, as the thread of thought was passed to another and another, the remembering shared. Memories awakened to who and what they were: they were the little ones, the earth diggers; the smallest of the four-footed clans, their purpose was to live beneath—the watchers within the unseen places.

The elder was the first to move, back toward his burrow, the others of his clan following slowly behind. He looked to his center knowing that many others followed the path to the tunnels deep within the earth.

§ § § § §

Chera had traveled far into the night, her loping pace matched by that of her mate, Gabriel. As they moved swiftly through the darkness, their thoughts met, merged, the need to speak unnecessary, while ahead of them, the lesser of the night clans sought refuge, their eyes peering fearfully out from beneath their hidden places as they wondered at the sudden passage of such hunters amongst them.

From his perch atop the jack pine tree, the large snowy white owl surveyed the distant horizon, his keen eyesight carrying him beyond what others saw. Long wings stretched, his body taut as he caught the sudden movement out of the corner of one golden eye, his head swivelling as he focused in the morning's dusky dawning.

No, it could not be. His mind stretched, reaching out to intercept as the intruders loped easily into view. Were recognized. *No...* The words were in his mind, then unheeded, they spilled forth to be heard by the others who watched.

Something was wrong. Something had happened, else why would Gabriel and Chera be in the forested wood, their haste obvious to one who knew them so well. As the great owl took flight, the branch that he had perched upon trembled. The vibrations carrying to those who dwelled beneath, the little ones picking up the thread of thought, the soft thrumming carrying swiftly through rock and earth to the others.

Chera never broke stride, not even when Owen dipped low, the tips of his wings caressing her back as he acknowledged her need to find the watchers. Soaring high, he winged his way southward, away from the heavily trodden paths that those of the forest clans used, toward the sacred place where the forest warriors kept council.

6

Warmed by the fire, the one known as the *Other* stood at its edge, gazing into the heart of the flame, his thoughts on another realm and a sister who was as cold as winter's breath. He had become complacent over these many turnings, he mused silently, his dark eyes narrowed angrily as he threw another piece of wood on the fire. Never before had there been a reason to watch where he walked; the few who challenged him had not lived long enough to do it again. His judgment was swift and final. It had never occurred to him that, when he had bridged the worlds *between,* any would have followed his path. He squared his shoulders. He should have finished the intruder off himself instead of relying on others...

§ § § § § §

The sentinel was nearly to the gate when the first tremor hit, taking him by surprise. Slate-grey eyes darkened in a dusky face, and where the irises should have been, there was nothing—only a smoky mist, swirling, ever-changing, back to its cold grey center. He was not human, neither was he one of those brought forth in the beginning by the one he now called master.

He belonged to the earth.

Once he and others like him had been guardians of the sacred places; their presence neither felt nor seen, they had moved freely across the earth, grounded by the rich black soil and what lay beneath. Then that *"One"* had entered their world, and all that they had been, all that they were, had changed. Now they served a dark master.

57

One who sifted through time, his abilities to change their world a constant threat—it had been left to them to guard the hidden places. There would be none to challenge him.

In that way, they were allowed to exist. Not as what they had been, but who they had become.

The sentinel stiffened as he caught the scent wending its way through the forest. His chest tightened, memories crowding one another to be recognized as the earth beneath his feet awakened, and for a moment he was incapable of all thought save one:

The little ones. The earth diggers. Mole and shrew, they who once had lived within the darkened spaces.

The earth beneath the sentinel's feet resonated, the ripples moving upward, spreading through him as the emotions washed over him. Moving quickly, he who had once been *more* positioned himself in the center of the gateway. Once there, he closed his mind against all save the subtle movement of the earth beneath him as the little ones returned to what they once were, and as the twilight that heralded the night embraced him, he dared to once again dream.

§ § § § §

"Well?" Leah had climbed ahead of the warrior and was standing on a grassy knoll, waiting for him to catch up. Ignoring the look he leveled at her, she looked past him; back the way they had come. She knew what The Hunter wanted from her, but she wasn't sure she was ready to try to explain it. Not just yet. Besides, he owed her an explanation. She knew there were others like him; she had heard them that day when he had rescued her from the cloud creature. As to why she had seen none since? She arched a dark brow, her stance broking no argument as she crossed her arms. She wasn't moving one step farther until she got some answers.

The Hunter knew what the little female wanted. She was directing all her energies at him, and as fast as he threw up the barriers to ward them off, they dissolved. He was about to move around her, unwilling to explain the ways of his kind to her just yet, when the warm breeze pushed against him. The leaves of the poplar trees overhead resonated with a haunting melody as he stopped, listening.

The power of the Women, the Grandmothers.

He bowed his head, acknowledging the whispers.

"Where are the others?"

"They wait for us at the hidden place."

"Why did they have to travel ahead? Why couldn't they make the journey with us, help us, guide us? They were there that day in the clearing—I heard them. There were others, like you. They were there." Leah's voice trailed off as she looked at him, gauging him as she waited for him to speak.

He looked down into dark brown eyes and glimpsed a little of what lay behind their depths. It was the *knowing,* and his warriors' heart told him to tell her the truth. There were others, but they never stayed long in the same place. They were the hunted. The Dark Lord and his cloud beings ever seeking them. It had been The Hunter's choice to stay behind while the others had returned to their villages to wait while he had sheltered her and protected her until she was able to speak. In that way, he would see for himself if she posed a threat, the decision his to make about her fate. Instead of a weak weeping female who would endanger them all, he had been taken aback to discover she had courage, an inner strength, and knowledge that most others would have envied in one so young.

"My people, those who are left, wait beyond those mountains." The Hunter spoke softly as he pointed toward the distant horizon. "It is there we will find the answers you seek. It is not my place to teach you the way of the people. It is the women. Those old ones who have lived turnings beyond count that will listen and decide."

"Decide what? Decide that I shouldn't be here? That I'm an intruder who should never have been allowed to survive?" Leah's eyes had narrowed as she studied the warrior, her voice rising as the bear reared up just behind the warrior, his soft huff-huff warning the warrior he was there.

"You have forgotten who you are. The forest moves around you, yet you do not see it. The clans of the four-legged. The winged ones. The little ones, the earth diggers. *They* move around you. Above you. Beneath you. You are so blind." Leah threw the words at him, her anger rising. She felt the change in the air as the Old One wavered behind the warrior, his senses picking up the subtle nuances as the wind changed direction. Frustrated, she turned from the warrior's gaze.

"Fine." She flung the words over her shoulder. She turned away, her shoulders squared. She needed to think. She fixed her gaze on the distant horizon, her focus on the white frothy mist that curled its way upward, long tendrils reaching out to spread across the tops of the treetops. It was so ethereal that it reminded her of the land beneath Skye, and for a brief moment she was there, with the others. Still, the

voice that carried to her through the coolness of the late day nonetheless startled her. A quick look behind her at the warrior told her that he, too, had heard. She made up her mind. Regardless of where the others were going, she was heading toward the misty places, and if The Hunter wished to follow her, he could.

"Stubborn woman." The warrior muttered the words under his breath, not caring if she heard. He was tempted to let her go on alone, let her see what lies ahead, but even as he thought it, he dismissed it, knowing he could not do it. Sighing, he shouldered his bow and followed her. She didn't realize it, but the trail she followed would lead her home.

His home.

From his vantage point, the Old One watched as the woman moved away; the direction she took was one he knew. This had been his forest long before the seeds of change had taken root and spread like a festering sore. The others like him had vanished, their path their own, while he and he alone had stayed to watch and wait. He batted at the biting flies as they worried him, irritating his skin so that he sought out the coolness of the shaded places and where he could, roll in the boggy places to ease the itching.

He was the *Old One*. Once, long ago, in the time before remembering, he had sat at the sacred fire of the two-legged, and his kind had been honored.

But that was long ago.

A short while later, after he had eaten his fill of the wild berries that were so abundant in the forest and found a log filled with the small larvae of the fly, he continued his journey. The memories pushed back once more as he followed the path to where he knew the two rivers would meet. It would be there that the little female—she who could speak to him in the old way—would find the answers to her unasked questions. And so it was that he followed a bit slower, the warrior ahead of him her protector for now.

§ § § § § §

Jerome placed his wooden gourd upon the ground, rising from his seated position as he did so. Something, he was not sure what, had happened—he was being called. He could feel the pull of the forest as the little ones, the earth diggers, beat out a steady tattoo against the earth. So it was that even before Owen flew into their midst, the wolves not far behind, he was prepared.

"Leah," the Old One whispered softly, the words trailing off into the silence. She stood beside Jerome, her staff held before her as she summoned the others to them. "She calls to us. She calls to *you.*" She pointed her staff at Chera as the silver-white form loped into view. Orith stood beside her, his familiar cloaked form comforting to the weary travelers who had journeyed fast and far this day.

"Where's Nickolous?"

"He is not here, he is in the high places with Lord Moshat," the warrior of the forest answered as Chera wavered unsteadily before him. Exhausted from the hurried journey, she needed to rest. Jerome nodded at the Old One. Motioning with her staff, the elder led Gabriel and Chera to a secluded spot beneath the willows, and it was there, the shade cool and comforting, the moss thick and soft beneath them, that they told Jerome and the others what had brought them here.

Jerome listened to the words being spoken, his heart heavy. After the battle between the clans and the *Fallen,* they all had assumed Leah had found her way to a safety. Her journey her own to make, there had been no indication otherwise, but now—he reached out, his mind seeking the hidden places. Places where he alone could walk. Tendrils of knowing stretched out as he went to the farthest reaches of the four corners, and the answer, when it came, shocked him.

"She is no longer here. She is not in Skye." Jerome shook his head in disbelief as he looked down at the companions.

"Where is she?" Chera asked as she looked up at the forest warrior, her instincts warring within her as she tried to see what he had seen and failed. Beside her, Gabriel had risen from his resting position and was standing over her protectively. He, better than anyone, understood her concern. After all, he had been bound just as tightly to Nickolous, the bond they had forged on their journey together just as strong as that of Chera and Leah.

Jerome met her gaze evenly. He wished he could get a message to Nickolous, but he was in another place right now and would be hard to reach. After the battle for the Living Flame, after A-Sharoon had returned to her forest and the *Fallen* had been defeated, all the companions had separated for a time. The warriors of Skye had left, and Nickolous had returned with them. He had grown swiftly to manhood, and this was his time to journey *between* and so learn. His path was now a warrior's path.

"She is in another place, a place we cannot reach. Unless..." The Old One leaned forward, her face inches from Chera's. The big wolf stared into small black eyes that had seen much, the inner knowing something her kind carried with them from the moment of their birth. "You must find the way. It is you that she calls out to, you who holds the bond to her. We, at least some of us, can follow, but it is you who must lead the way." The old she-rat drew back from the wolf as if the knowing was too much. But it wasn't that. She had reached out and saw where Leah was. Saw the darkness and what encompassed it. Saw that *One,* the *Other,* and knew that Leah was in danger. She turned at the gentle touch on her shoulder; the forest warrior nodded, understanding, as he whistled, the sound high pitched and fluting. From deep within the forest, an answering trill sounded.

"My warriors will seek out those who guard the hidden places, we will wait and see what they say," he spoke softly, his concern now for Chera. She was worried, and it went without saying that she wanted to leave—to find a way between realms so that she could help Leah. Straightening to his full height, Jerome stroked his chin thoughtfully as he looked down at her, thinking about what needed to be done. "Don't worry, we will find her."

Chera nodded assent.

§ § § § §

"You need to rest." The Hunter had been walking slightly behind the woman for some time, keeping his distance and his thoughts to himself as he studied her surreptitiously. There was something feral in the way she moved, her body language warning him to keep his distance. And he had, before deciding to catch up to her. He had hoped she would calm down if he gave her enough time to be alone with her thoughts. Behind him, he knew the Mukwa followed at a distance and was not at all sure if he would have preferred its company to the woman's. She stopped so abruptly that she startled him, her dark brown eyes looking up into his black ones.

"You need to look, to see into your place of knowing. The forest speaks, yet you do not hear it. The little ones, the earth diggers, they wait patiently for you to listen. To hear them. You do not..." She motioned him to silence as he tried to speak, her voice rising to be heard above the blowing wind, the far off cry of the eagle as it flew from its aerie echoing throughout the forest. She wasn't finished with him, and he knew it. Her brows drew together as she glared up at him. "You do not feel the earth move beneath your feet as they beat out the message to those clans who walk above, warning of the darkness to come. You are so blind. You have lost the knowing that is born within us all." Leah paused, her gaze sweeping the area in front of them as she drank in the wild beauty of their surroundings. "Nor, does it appear that you wish to awaken it," she drawled sarcastically, waiting for the warrior to answer.

The Hunter remained silent, staring down at the young woman who stood gazing up at him with such defiance in her posture, her gaze speaking volumes. As much as he did not want to admit it, she was right. He could not remember a time when he had felt any of those things of which she spoke. Although, sometimes in his dreams, he walked the unknown places, his footsteps marked clearly as he looked behind him. And yes, the animals spoke to him, but then again it was just a dream—or was it? Something had pricked his subconscious as he had listened to her words—something was pulling at him.

"It wasn't a dream." Leah reached out to touch him. Her gaze had softened as she watched the myriad expressions that shadowed themselves within his features, even though he tried to mask them. She knew now that he had seen the things she talked about, had felt them, but did not understand them. He had pushed them away like the rest of his kind. She understood that now.

"Patience. He will remember." Leah didn't bother to look around as she acknowledged the words, accepted them. *"Fine."* The words were muttered to no one in particular. The Hunter remained silent, his expression thoughtful as she turned away from him. Her intent was to follow the worn path through the forest as long as she could; the afternoon was deepening, and she knew how fast the night fell. As far as she was concerned, the sooner they made it to wherever the others were, the better. Perhaps there she would find the answers to her questions, that—and food.

Good food.

The warrior watched the woman go. The words he was about to throw at her dying on his lips as he thought better of it. Moments later he followed, careful to keep her in sight but allowing enough distance to give them both time to cool off. Although, had he admitted it, the distance he kept between them was more for his own benefit. *Women.* No wonder he had chosen to live by himself these many turnings. His home the forest, his bed, the ground upon which he lay, and the sky with its starry night the only comfort he needed. He snorted in disgust.

If Leah heard him, she gave no indication.

§§§§§

The sentinel closed the gate. The ancient ruins with their crumbling etchings lay protected beneath the shadows of the gigantic oak that had guarded the secret pass turnings beyond remembrance. But he remembered. He had been within the forest that surrounded him since the beginning. He and his kind. He frowned in the half-light, his unnatural grey eyes were nearly translucent as he caught glimpses of what he once was before that *One* changed his world.

And the clans forgot who they were.

Guardians of the earth.

7

The Guardian had moved easily over the forest floor, without effort or thought, the clans of the four-legged at ease in his presence. He was, after all, their protector. Without face or form, he Was. Born into the beginning of existence as the earth drew her first breath, he belonged to them all. Those of the two-legged sensing his presence around them as the faint prickle of the unknown racing up their spine. It was these ones that would look around as if searching, the feel of unseen eyes watching. Sometimes, however, there would be exceptions. Sometimes, there would be one born with the knowing, and it would be one of these who would "see" him for what he was—something ancient. He would pass them in the dark of night and would stop, wondering that they could see what had passed over them and would wait as they silently acknowledged his right to be there, and he, theirs.

Then the Other had entered their world and used his dark magic to change his kind. Caught unaware, they had not had time to protect themselves, and within the space of a breath, they had been changed to what they were now. Their chains forged by the very earth that had borne them at the beginning..

The sentinel shook his head to clear it.

"Enough." The words were not his own. He had been careless with his thoughts, for the *Other* had seen.

§ § § § §

Chera turned her head, listening, her nostrils distended as she scented the air. The swirling white mist had settled over them, curling slowly about them. She shivered despite her resolve to show no discomfort lest there were watchers amongst them. They hadn't bothered with a fire this night, for they had been too busy, and the coals that remained were little more than dying embers. Orith, feeling the cold more than most, had left to find Jerome. The warrior was somewhere in the forest, and the elder, sensing this, moved ahead, knowing he would meet Jerome somewhere in between. His bones ached more lately, and the Old One was fretting over what she could not see. He looked up as the silhouette passed overhead, the shadow caressing the moonlit path in front of him as the shrill cry of the hunter seeking its prey echoed softly against the night.

Owen. Orith inclined his head slightly. It had been a long time. Too long since he had felt the song of the night against his back, the wind curling against him as he soared beneath the moon's wavering light. Shadows, cast against the trees; the rustling of the leaves as the dew glistened on their tips casting the reflection back. The elder sighed, remembering. He had healed slowly, his wounds had been deep, the resulting scar tissue disfiguring. A constant reminder of why he would never again fly. Orith bowed his head, accepting what he could not change, so deep in thought that he was startled at the sudden appearance of the forest warrior as he stepped out from the forest's depths, unto the path in front of him.

Jerome suppressed a chuckle as he bent to the task of gathering the dry wood that littered the path in front of him. It was forbidden to use the living wood within the forest, but with the dead fall that lay scattered about in such abundance, it wasn't long before the comforting warmth of the fire rose upward to curl gently about Orith and the Old One. The aches and pains of the day dissipating in the face of such strength.

Leaning down, Jerome laid more wood carefully across the top of the fire pit before removing the leather bag tied to his side. Placing it carefully upon the ground, he gently shook out its contents as the Old One leaned forward, her gaze on what now lay exposed to their view. "Jerome," she whispered, hardly daring to believe what she saw. Turning inward to her place of knowing, she said no more as she stood beside Orith, both of them looking down at what Jerome had brought.

"The scrying stone of the Ancients..." The Old One's voice trailed off into the silence as Orith moved closer to the stone. Nearly transparent, it was one of the most ancient of relics, lost at the dawning of their world, or so it had been believed. He glanced up at Jerome; the

warrior remained where he was, shaking his head as he put a finger to his mouth indicating silence. What must be spoken of could not be. Not yet.

Understanding, the elders leaned back, gathering the warmth to them. Content in the knowledge that, when the fire died down to red embers, they would place the stone in its center.

§ § § § § §

Remaining where he was, concealed within the shade of the mighty oak, the man watched as the sentinel positioned himself in the "between." He had been caught off guard. The sentinel was one of his best. Always, he had been obedient to the letter, and so the man had never thought to question his loyalty. Until now—something that was about to be remedied. A thought passed between the man and the watcher beside him. A vaporous cloud creature without form or thought. It just was. It obeyed without conscience and was a formidable ally, or enemy, depending on which side it was on. As the man turned away, he motioned silently, his meaning clear.

The sentinel watched as the *Other* moved out of sight. He knew that beneath the dense canopy of trees there was another. One of the unseen. He knew because it was he who had opened the gateway to the in-between to allow ones like it passage—creatures spawned from the dark time when the worlds were forming. Caught within the center of the worlds within worlds, they had become vaporous beings with no solid substance, their innate drive to destroy all within their path a thing that fed their very existence.

Grey eyes glinted with a pre-eternal light then dimmed as the sentinel closed his mind against further intrusion. He would not be so careless again with his thoughts, for he knew what now moved beneath the ground upon which he stood.

§ § § § § §

"We're close to the village." They were standing on top of a hill, looking down into a lush valley of rolling hills and running streams. From her vantage point, Leah could see the not too distant forest, its thick canopy of trees more than likely concealing an entire community, and although they had eaten generously of the fruit and wild leeks that they had found along the way, she was hoping that once they reached the village, there would be something more. Looking down at her, the warrior grinned. He knew how she felt.

"They will be expecting us." The Hunter spoke the words softly as they moved quietly through the forest. Leah nodded but didn't look up; instead, she picked up her pace.

"Are they watching us?" She was moving ahead of him now, her pulse quickening.

"The runners should have seen us some time ago," the warrior replied as his hand slid slowly downward to rest against the leather sheath fastened securely at his hip. The sound of the drums and the smoke from the fire should have been heard and seen some time ago. That they were not—saying nothing, looking straight ahead, he carefully unsheathed his knife, the black stone cold upon the palm of his hand; he waited until the obsidian warmed to his touch. Then, and only then, did he acknowledge what crouched within the shadows.

Leah tensed, the hair on the back of her neck prickling as she caught a faint movement off to her left. Whatever it was, it sensed them, because it moved farther back, the branches of the trees bending slightly to allow it passage.

"There. Between the trees." Leah was crouched down. She motioned the warrior to lower his weapon as she focused her attention on one spot. Her eyes narrowed thoughtfully. It moved again, farther back into the shadows. Something tugged at her memories as thoughts passed between one like yet unlike themselves. Knowledge, layered deep within the center of the being. One memory. One thought. Together. Leah barely had time to get out of the way as the rush of wind blew over her, the form within its center taking flight. The sharp *screeee* echoed loudly as she turned sideways, her elbow catching the warrior in the side as she tried to catch a glimpse of the watcher. Beside her, The Hunter quickly resheathed his knife, realizing it would have no effect on one of these—those of the winged clans having the ability of flight. Leah's reaction was instinctive. It happened so fast she barely had time to react, but she did manage to knock the bow out of his hand as she slammed her whole body into his side. As they went down together in a tangled heap, she had the further satisfaction of bringing her head up to slam him in the nose.

"Idiot!" She hissed the words as she scrambled hastily away from him. "What do you think you are doing? You, who have walked this land since your beginning, would harm a *watcher?*" Then she was standing over him, glaring down at him. He was still sitting on the ground, holding his nose and looking up at her in disbelief. She had hit him. She had actually whacked him. A good one, too. Leah backed away, wary, unsure of the warrior's reaction, aware that they were no longer alone, the soft huff-huff telling her the Mukwa had returned. Outwardly, she was still upset; inwardly, she was shaking, aware that she had just taken on someone twice her size...and got the best of him.

"Unfair tactics," a small voice whispered. Was it hers? Leah grimaced. Yeah, right, she thought to herself as she dusted the dirt off her clothing. "All's fair when it comes to stupidity," she muttered to no one in particular, her gaze now locked with that of the warrior. "You shouldn't have done that, you know." She arched a brow as she absently brushed her hair off her face, at the same time tucking a long strand behind one ear as she stood, looking down at him, prepared for the storm that was sure to follow.

The Hunter was stunned. He had been bested in battle by a woman. And a small one at that. He couldn't believe it. It hadn't even been a battle, he thought ruefully to himself—it had been more of a skirmish. Rising from his sprawled position on the ground, he touched his nose gingerly; it wasn't broken, but his face hurt. He was looking down at her, big brown eyes set in a face that was white with apprehension. Beyond her the Old One sat, his small honey-colored eyes watching him with unnerving intensity.

The Hunter pulled back, startled at what he saw within their velvety depths. *It was a knowing.* Shaking off the feeling that the bear was speaking to him, he shook his head in disbelief. Those were nothing more than legends, taught to the small ones at their mothers' knees.

It was the people's way of soothing the young ones to sleep. To dream. The warrior turned his head, listening. There it was again.

The bear sat back, putting all of his massive weight on his haunches, his expression watchful as he studied the warrior. Unnerved, the one known as The Hunter turned away, the sound of laughter, soft and mocking, echoing in the wind. He bowed his head, confused, not wanting to acknowledge the truth of it.

It was not his.

8

Time before time.
Time of legends.
Time of shadows…
Once, the Mukwa and others like him had walked within the misty places of the *"Between,"* their warrior spirit communing with that of the two-legged.

Within the mists of swirling shadows fed by the sacred fire, they had sought each other out in the old way: the way of the spirits. Dreams within dreams as the Elders held counsel while the pull of the moon ebbed and flowed through them, the mists that rose within the bogs and rivers rising up to embrace the night and those who walked within it. The warrior spirit of bear. The warrior spirit of man. Together, they had almost become as One.

Almost.

9

Orith threw more wood on the fire, pulling back as the flames shot up, the dry wood catching so fast he barely avoided being singed. The night had brought with it a dampness that chilled them to the bone, and so the old she-rat had stayed close, the warmth seeping into her aged body as she watched the flames, watched what flickered within their white-hot depths.

"Here." Orith sat beside her, his thick woolen cloak pulled tightly about him. It had been a gift from Nickolous—ages ago, it seemed, for it was tattered now from wear, but still serviceable. He bowed his head, remembering their journey together. The ending. Ahhh, he glanced to where the Old One sat, watching the flames of the fire entwining around the log as it burned white-hot. The center slowly falling inward upon itself. Orith blinked. It was gone, but he had seen. The Old One had seen. They both looked at the crumbling coals, then at each other. The scrying stone of the Ancients had spoken.

It was time to call the others back.

"Chera." The words echoed softly through the dusky night.

Jerome was returning from his short foray into the forest when he heard the first whispers carried upon the wind that blew so restlessly about.

Orith. Old One. Their thoughts reached out and found him in his sacred place. Beside him, Chera tensed, the silver-white wolf trembling as she looked up at him, her silver eyes reflecting the moon's light. The warrior of the forest pulled back, startled, for deep within

73

their pewter depths he had glimpsed something. His heart racing, he pushed his thoughts back so the wolf would not see—

"We need to go. *Now.*" Chera was already racing ahead of him, toward the distant fire and those who kept it.

§ § § § §

From beneath earth and rock they came, pushing themselves forward, farther into the moonlit places. What they lacked in nearsightedness, they made up for in their ability to sense what was above, below, and ahead. They were the little ones. The earth diggers. Shrew and mole, they now lived in the *beneath*. They were the voices within the darkened places; by choice, they sought out those ones who practiced the dark arts, their voices rising to warn others.

The man turned from his place at the fire, the faint sounds of something within the earth reaching him as he deep listened. Turning his head slightly, he nodded, the motion barely perceptible, nonetheless acknowledged by the vaguely visible vaporous watcher in the shadows. Confident in the creature's abilities to seek out the unwanted, he turned his attention back to the scrolls with their ancient writings, unaware that beneath his feet, deep within earth and rock, the little watcher waited. Waited for the silence that would tell him that he was safe from that "*One.*" Waited for the cold draft of air to pass him, the breeze wending its way through rock and crevice from the outside world to the furthest depths below, seeking out those things that did not wish to be discovered.

§ § § § §

"What is it? What do they say?" Chera was standing in front of the Old One, her gaze searching. She knew that behind her the warrior of the forest and Gabriel followed. She snorted impatiently, the need to know where Leah was something that was unexplainable, even to herself.

Orith stayed where he was, his gaze never leaving the fire. Beside him, the old she-rat leaned heavily upon her ornately carved staff, her dark leathery face unreadable. Chera sighed, the sound carrying to Jerome as he moved into the open, his guard up. Something was not right. His senses tingled as he grasped the huge war club looped at his side; beside him Gabriel tensed as the fire leapt upward to curl lazily about the dry wood, which had been placed there moments before their arrival.

"Watch." One word, spoken softly. The Old One stroked her staff with a gnarled paw, while with the other she withdrew a pouch from somewhere deep within the folds of her robe.

Jerome moved closer, his fingers stroking his war club, readying himself for the unknown as Gabriel edged toward his mate. Something was riding hard upon the night breeze, and his instincts were warning him to be cautious. As it was, the flash, when it came, was blinding, the night filled with unspeakable things as the Old One threw the contents of the pouch into the fire that burned blue-white, the flames leaping skyward as Jerome ducked. The brush of something unpleasant grazed against his skin. Beside him, Gabriel growled a warning, but it was too late—Chera was gone.

Gabriel leapt after her fading form, only to meet empty air. He hit the ground hard. Rolling, he was up almost immediately, his howl of outrage and confusion echoing in the night.

"Chera!" The caress of the wind and the silence it left in its wake the only answer. That, and the sound of the flames as they lapped hungrily against the pine that snapped beneath the red-hot flame.

"Where is she? Where is Chera?" Gabriel stood inches from the Old One as he eyed her staff apprehensively. He had seen the powers that lie contained within the heart of the wood. Carved from the wood of the cherry tree, its many burls thrummed with pulsating power.

It had been handed down from elder to elder, and the Old One was well versed in its use. It had been a gift from Lord Moshat, the elder of Skye's way of thanking her; at the same time, it was a replacement for the one she had lost during the battle with the *Fallen.* Since then, it had grown stronger, the tiny burls within the wood growing each time it lent its power. He wasn't sure, but he thought that the staff had something to do with her disappearance.

He was right.

§ § § § §

Leah spun around, the brush of the little bat as it flew by startling her. Something touched her face. Something cold and damp. She put her hand up, and it came away wet.

"What. Is. That." She brushed at the wetness again. Night had fallen and, like usual, impossibly quickly. She had barely enough time to adjust to it before the fine, white mist descended, seemingly out of nowhere, its damp tendrils reaching out, enveloping everything in its path. The warrior, used to such a phenomenon, wasn't too concerned.

He had seen this kind of thing before, but he wasn't prepared for what happened next.

Leah saw the blur of something flying past; in the ensuing chaos, she was aware that the bear still sat a short distance away, his unconcern evident. Then the warrior was beside her, unsheathing his knife, the black obsidian glinting in the pale light of the crescent moon above them. Her dark eyes widened as something hit the ground near her, rolling a few feet before stopping. A throaty growl coming from deep within a chest that flashed silver-white.

The Hunter stared at the apparition, his mind focusing on what stood within the center of the mist that wrapped itself tightly around him, and everything else...except...he spared a quick glance to where the bear was. Small brown eyes stared back as he remained where he was, nonplussed by what was happening around him. The warrior shook his head to clear it. Before he had a chance to swing the deadly blade, he was knocked down by a rush of wind and fur. As he lay sprawled on the ground, held down by the weight of something large and heavy, he found himself looking into silver eyes, flecked at their centers with gold. He drew in his breath sharply as he struggled to rise, to push whatever it was off him, the scent of the unknown clinging to the thing that held him down. He tried to roll over. His knife was pinned beneath him; he could feel the edge of the blade as it dug into his side. Inwardly he cursed himself for being so careless. He should have known better.

A warning growl. The breath warming his cheek as he stilled beneath the weight as whatever it was shifted enough so that he was pinned flat. Large paws lay heavy against his chest as he looked into the eyes of a predator and saw death.

His.

§ § § § §

The Old One leaned forward, her breath catching in her chest. The staff she held still thrummed softly beneath her touch, the wood slowly returning to its normal color. She stared into the fires depths, the blue-white flame had died down, merely flickering now and then as the remaining wood turned to hot ash. She was waiting for the storm to pass—waiting for Gabriel to calm himself so that he could prepare. But the silver-grey wolf was in no mood to guess this night. He wanted answers, and he wanted them now.

"Calm down, my friend," Jerome spoke quietly. He had positioned himself between the elder and Gabriel as they had spoken, for he knew that the events leading up to this moment had confused them all. He had an idea where Chera was, and he sighed inwardly.

His world had been quiet of late, and he was loath to change it, yet he knew what lie within the heart of the big wolf who stood in front of him, his gaze unwavering as he sought answers. He also knew how much Gabriel cared for his mate. Sighing, he gave it over and waited for the Old One to speak.

"Where is she?"

"She is where she needs to be."

Gabriel snorted derisively, the sound unusually loud in the stillness that surrounded them; beside him, Jerome tensed, ready to intervene if necessary. The Old One stared at him from her place beside Orith, her brow wrinkled thoughtfully as she continued to caress her staff. The low hum it emitted caused the forest warrior to take a cautious step back, wary, lest he be next. Gabriel, ignoring the soft sighing, edged closer. The wind still held the scent of his mate as it blew about him, and he had no intention of letting the trail go cold.

§ § § § § §

Leah stared at the bear, then at what held the warrior at bay. He had lost his weapon in the scuffle and was lying there, pinned beneath fur and fang. It took a moment longer for her mind to register what her eyes could not.

"Chera." The words were no more than a sigh, carried upon the breeze that wrapped itself tightly around her. "Chera?" Leah moved closer. The movement, almost indiscernible caused her to pull back a step, the recognition slowly dawning as silver eyes looked into her own. "Chera!" She met the wolf halfway, rolling with her as the warrior struggled to his feet. He shook his head in disbelief at the thought that within the past day he had been bested by a small female and now a wolf.

He did not have to look beside him to know that the bear was close by, watching.

"Where are the others?" Leah asked as she stood up, brushing the leaves and twigs from her clothing as she did so. She could hardly believe it. Chera had heard her calling and somehow found her. She wiped at the moisture that slid unheeded down her cheeks. "The Old One, Orith…" her voice trailed off as she waited for Chera to speak. In her excitement, she almost missed the look the wolf shot her, the silver eyes with their strange swirling depths speaking what her heart could not.

"They are where they need to be, young one." Chera lowered her head, not wanting Leah to see her pain at being separated from her mate, then, remembering herself, she turned her attention toward the other one—the one of the two-legged clan who stood at a distance, watching her, his gaze narrowed, wary. She scented the night wind, catching the heavy musky scent that rode upon it. Silvery eyes narrowed then widened as she recognized the bulky form of the Mukwa near the man. Lowering her head, she searched her memories from the before time.

Ahhh, there it was. She let out her breath slowly, the steam rising in the cool night air. Thoughts passed. Heard. The bear lumbered slowly forward, his bulky form swaying slightly as he stopped in front of the wolf. Leah watched with bated breath as both Chera and the Old One stood their ground, their gazes locked. Unable to read their thoughts, she remained where she was while the one known as The Hunter stepped back into the shadows, his grip firm on his knife, the black stone comforting as it warmed against the heat of his hand.

Chera knew who stood before her, for like the old she-rat, he, too, was of an ancient race. A knowing race. One of the Old Ones. So called because their count of turnings lived went beyond what others remembered. There from the beginning, they had watched from within the mist-shrouded places—that ethereal place between wakefulness and sleep.

It was here, between the darkness and the dawn, when the sacred fire of the people flickered in the stillness that was the night, that Old Ones such as these had once sat—their presence acknowledged—accepted.

"Old One." Chera dipped her head slightly, the gesture one of respect. Once, long ago, her kind and those like the one before her had sought counsel each with the other. Centered deep within her primordial memories, she saw the way it had been. She saw the bond that had held the clans together. All of them. From the smallest to the largest, the clans had acted as one.

That was before they had forgotten who and what they were.

Worlds within worlds. Each of them unique. Some of them old. Some of them new. Some of them just beginning…Chera saw them all within a hearts beat of her indrawn breath. She saw her world where the clans had struggled to overcome a darkness that threatened to turn their world back upon itself. The struggle between the light and the dark something they all had shared, no matter the realm they lived in.

"Chera—?"

Chera turned toward the speaker, her bond temporally broken with that of the Old One; at the same time she saw the warrior, crouched in shadow, and knew what it was he held within the palm of his hand. She cocked her head to one side as she studied him, her silver eyes glowing eerily in the shadows cast by the moonlit night. She knew that beneath his shuttered lids, his black eyes studied her surreptitiously. She turned away, not caring, for she did not fear ones such as he. Her vision saw beyond what he was, therefore she did not notice him.

She took a step forward, her silver-white head tilted slightly to one side as she studied the young woman standing before her, seeing past her dishevelled state. It wasn't that which caught and held her attention. It was something else she saw layered beneath Leah's tense expression, for like her brother, Nickolous, her maturity had somehow accelerated.

Gone was the young girl she had watched run so carelessly through the forest, to fall down an ancient tunnel built before the time of remembering. In her place stood a grown woman and within her—

—Memories of the grandmothers lingered! Now Chera understood. Turning, her gaze seeking that which was unseen, she caught the movement of the watcher, her eyes seeing in the darkness what the warrior and Leah could not. The soft huff-huff telling her that the Old One saw what she saw. She turned her attention back to Leah. Words, unspoken, passing between them as she relaxed, thankful that this one thing at least had not changed.

§ § § § § §

Gabriel paced the length and width of the cavern, his blue eyes scanning the shadows for the unknown. He was waiting, had been for hours, for the Old One to give him an answer. Pausing at the entrance to the cavern, he scented the wind and that which lingered upon it. Chera's scent was fading! Agitated, he turned back toward the fire that burned in the middle of the cavernous room, his low growl of inquiry drifting through the silence, not surprised when there was no answer.

The Old One had retreated to her kind's place of knowing. It was an ancient place nestled safely between realms. Shrouded in mist and imagery, caught between waking and sleeping, those not gifted with understanding awoke remembering little at best of where they had been. Even then, she felt the big wolf reaching out, seeking counsel.

Withdrawing to her center, she shut out the emotions that whispered to her and focused on something else that was there.

In her sacred place of shadow, merging with the light, it reached out, tentatively seeking.

Gabriel pulled back at the feathery touch that sent chills racing up his spine—the prickle of something unknown tracing a soft shadow across his vision before disappearing, vanishing into the smoke that curled idly upward from the fire in the center of the cavern.

The sudden dampness curled around him, caressing him, flowing past him as he stepped reluctantly toward the light cast by the flames, the warmth strangely comforting. Not bothering to look behind him, he waited for the forest warrior to join him, the slight rustling as Jerome pushed his giant frame further into the cavern a telltale thing. Even though the big warrior preferred the open places, at such times as these, he made allowances.

"It won't be long now." Jerome was crouched down, bent nearly double, his immense height preventing him from standing. Beside him, the big wolf paused long enough to glance behind him, his acknowledgement accepted. At this, the forest warrior fell silent, for he knew the other's heart. As long as he had known Gabriel, the silver-grey wolf had never left his mate's side for more than a short time.

He looked to where the Old One was, her eyes closed, a warning against unwanted intrusion. Knowledge, layered deep, told him where she had ventured, and it was for this reason that he had left the fresh air of the forest to crouch uncomfortably in a dark cavern. In this state, she was vulnerable, unprotected, her return journey dangerous. For her. For them.

He gazed into the darkness, searching out the hidden places.

§ § § § § §

The Hunter let his breath out slowly. The moon hung low, just above the treetops, her soft white light brushing here and there haphazardly against the leaf-strewn path, pointing the way to where the woman and wolf stood, their attention focused on each other.

Watching them, the warrior wondered at the events that had brought him here, to this day, this place. He gripped the knife tightly, the black obsidian, formed from the hot breath of a volcano long since silenced back into sleep, bit deeply into his palm. He tensed. The Mukwa was standing close. Too close. The slight rustling sound as he settled back, his massive frame outlined by the backdrop of soft light cast by the moon's trailing tendrils was enough to remind him not to be rash. Whatever was happening between the woman and the wolf was not to be interfered with. At least not yet.

Black eyes narrowed in a darkly handsome face as the warrior slowly relaxed his grip on the knife. Silently replacing it in its leather sheath, he swung the longbow in front of him; his quiver of arrows beside him, he hunkered down to wait.

"Young one, what has happened here? This one?" Chera motioned toward the warrior who remained where he was, watching her warily.

His eyes were the eyes of a hunter, she thought as she caught his scent. It rolled off him in waves. Hunter. Predator. It mattered little to her—she who had lived turnings beyond count. She who had walked in the night beside unseen entities that guarded the earth and air with a fierceness that would have made the warrior before her cringe. Because he could not see...she looked closer at the warrior, her silver eyes narrowing. At the same time she felt Leah's hand upon her fur, thoughts passed between them, and the words she was going to speak aloud were passed one to the other.

"He does not have the memories."

"They are there. He has but to awaken them."

Chera looked up at Leah, her expression doubtful. She lowered her head to accept Leah's touch as Leah strained to hear the words she muttered beneath her breath.

"This is a place of savages."

Beside the warrior, the Mukwa snorted derisively, the sound carrying to the woman and the wolf, both realizing too late that their thoughts should have been guarded. The warrior's eyes narrowed, Chera's low growl meaningless to his ears—but not to the Old One, who reared up, his stance clearly defensive.

The movement, unexpected, caused The Hunter to pivot, black eyes widened as something faint but intelligible caught at the edge of his consciousness, the words—if words they were—drifting into the night as he settled back once more to wait.

The Old One snorted again, this time louder. Chera raised her head, tilted it slightly to one side, her silver eyes glinting strangely in the half-light as she apprised the warrior who met her unspoken scrutiny with that of his own.

She was nearly there. Leah let her breath out, relieved that the warrior had controlled himself. Placing herself in between them, she nodded curtly to the wolf before swinging her gaze up to boldly meet that of the warrior's. One dark brow arched thoughtfully as she studied him for a few moments before relaxing. He did have the *knowing.*

§ § § § § §

Orith watched as the old she-rat journeyed back to them. She was getting too old for this, he thought to himself as he stirred the hot coals, the dry wood catching quickly as he placed the pieces cross-wise over the logs. Beyond the fire's warmth, he knew that the forest warrior waited with Gabriel, the big wolf impatient for news of his mate. Finally, after what seemed like an eternity to the watchers, the Old One opened her eyes.

"Gabriel."

Jerome watched in silence as the big wolf moved quickly to the Old One's side, his head lowered, the words spoken for him alone to hear. Seeing that Orith was making his way toward the outside, he followed, neither of them looking back as the leather covering fell into place behind them. Jerome breathed in deeply of the night air, a quick look at the eastern sky telling him the morning's dawning was still a little ways off.

It would be later, when the dawning washed away the last remnants of the night, that they would heed the call of the Old One to return. The howl of the silver-grey wolf dropping off into the eerie silence as the worn leather covering was pulled back to reveal the Old One, her leathery face streaked with tears, her body trembling with fatigue, that they would acknowledge silently to themselves that their world had changed yet again.

10

The man glanced up, irritated that he had been interrupted, his attention momentarily distracted from what lay in front of him. Although he was well versed in the language of the Ancients, he had to admit, albeit grudgingly, that some of it was beyond even his comprehension. Thus the reason he searched and re- searched the documents, trying to access their hidden meanings. He was so focused on his studies that he failed to notice the first tremor beneath his feet. The second one, a bit stronger, caused him to look up, the unfamiliar emotion of unease taking him by surprise as the table and the parchment shook, the ground beneath his feet heaving just enough to throw the fragile documents in disarray.

He drew himself up quickly, at the same time gathering the scrolls to him, gently placing them back in the wooden cedar box that protected them against the small ones. The little eaters of dust and debris. Kneeling, he placed his hands full upon the cold earth, his eyes narrowing to mere slits as he drew the sounds that thrummed upward into himself so that he could see…

A few moments later, he was moving swiftly toward the outside and the sentinel who guarded the western gate.

§ § § § § §

The lone watcher saw the *Other* racing toward him. Knowing that the next few moments were going to be unpleasant, he steeled himself for what was to come. He no longer cared about the consequences his actions had wrought. Better to suffer this *One's* wrath than to exist in the unnatural state he had been forced to maintain these countless turnings. Closing his eyes, he prepared himself.

He wasn't disappointed.

§ § § § §

"What was that?" Leah asked no one in particular as she steadied herself, while at the same time peering upward into the starry night. The rolling thunder in the distance the only reply as the warrior, his bow already strung, sought out the unseen danger. Beside him, the wolf crouched, her ears back, her muzzle high as she tested the wind. Nothing. She turned to look at the Old One; he too, looked a bit bewildered.

"Wait." Chera tilted her head to one side, her hearing picking up something. It tugged at her senses. "Don't you hear them?" She looked from Leah to the Old One, her impatience showing as she shifted her weight from foot to foot. After a moment, the Mukwa nodded, his close-set eyes narrowing as he went down on all fours, the soft under pads of his feet picking up the vibrations deep below earth and rock.

The sound was muffled but there, beating out a rhythmic tattoo against rock and earth, rising upward through narrow passageways to reach the outside world.

The Old One remained where he was, centering himself. Not wishing the link to be broken, he listened long after the thrumming had stopped, now and then glancing at Chera, his gaze hopeful.

The silver-white head nodded. "They have returned to earth. All of them. It is the first of many changes. Come." She spoke to no one in particular, but everyone understood her meaning. Even the warrior.

There was danger here. Something was coming. Something dark and deadly.

The Hunter watched silently as the wolf moved ahead of them, away from the main path they had been following, her lithe form disappearing into the darkened places, the giant bracken moving quickly back into place to conceal her passage. A moment later with barely a backward glance Leah followed, leaving the Mukwa and the warrior to stare after them.

Shrugging his shoulders indifferently, the warrior shouldered his bow, the quiver of arrows within easy reach strapped securely at the center of his back before taking off at a trot. Feeling as if his place in his world had been usurped by a tiny woman and a great silver white-wolf with silver eyes, the centers the color of polished pewter rimmed with flecks of gold—

For once he was grateful for the company of the bear, who trailed behind them at a more leisurely pace.

At least he and the Old One belonged here, the warrior thought sulkily. Then another thought occurred to him. This one not entirely pleasant: if these two had bridged his world, others might.

§ § § § § §

Orith felt the sudden shift in the wind, the temperature dropping quickly as he called the forest warrior to him. The sky above them was overcast; a dark sickly gray that swirled unnaturally as the rain spattered them, a warning of something worse yet to come.

They had sent the Old One back to the cavern earlier amidst her protests, and now they waited for the darkness to pass. Far below them the valley, lush and green, stretched as far as the eye could see, the vast expanse of it breathtaking. It had grown and flourished since the defeat of the *Fallen.* The sound of small rocks tumbling down the grassy incline behind him told him Jerome was close. Moments later, they were standing side by side, the snowy owl dwarfed by the warrior's immense height.

Jerome could see everything; his warriors were spread out, the guardians alert for anything untoward. The sacred flame was back where it belonged while the Ancients—the circle elders—once again slept. Even A-Sharoon, the Daughter of Darkness, had remained unusually quiet of late.

The warrior sighed as he looked into the distance. Of one thing he was certain: whatever was happening was not her doing. After the *flames'* brief embrace during the battle, she had seemed somehow changed…he let his breath out slowly, and beside him Orith glanced up, his concern there, mirrored deep within his amber eyes. "What is it—what do you see?"

Jerome didn't answer at once and, when he did, it wasn't what Orith expected to hear. "Something rides the wind, something from the places *between.*" Jerome shifted his gaze, centering it on the scarred owl. As he did most days, Orith's woolen cloak with its heavy hood was pulled forward far enough that most of his features were concealed.

Never one to be in direct light, he stayed mostly to the shadows, instead preferring the cover of night. In this way he avoided the stares that his appearance brought when others saw him for the first time.

"A-Sharoon?" Orith was looking up at his friend, his expression incredulous.

"Not A-Sharoon."

"Who then?" Even as he asked Orith knew he wasn't going to like the answer.

"The *Other.*"

§ § § § § §

"The warrior has the memories. Deep within they may be, nonetheless they are there."

Chera looked up at Leah, her expression one of curiosity. She was wondering at the changes she sensed in her young charge. The last time she had seen her she was a young girl, untried, frightened, now she seemed—more. She kept walking, waiting for her to speak the words that would assure her she was the same—that nothing had changed.

"The Elders have said so."

"When?" Chera tensed, but her voice remained calm as she centered herself, her thoughts reaching outward, her mind's eye seeking what was hidden. She needed Gabriel. Here. Now. She flipped sideways, the sudden movement knocking Leah down. As she slammed into the hard earth, she silently berated herself for having been so careless. The cold rush of air that accompanied the shriek telling her that the warrior's arrow had found its mark little comfort to her pride.

The warrior had smelled the thing before he had seen it. A loathsome thing, its elongated face and dull yellow eyes gleamed menacingly as it hurtled toward him, bearing little resemblance to anything he was familiar with. Not sure where it had come from and, more importantly, if there were more, he ignored the warning growl as the wolf with the strange silver eyes sprang forward, her howl of outrage carrying through the inky night.

Quickly stringing another arrow, he went down on one knee, at the same time pulling the bow taut, readying himself for another creature like the first. *"Steady."* The words drifted in his mind, the speaker unfamiliar. The bow strained beneath his weight as the warrior waited for another to dart forward.

Something struck Leah in the side of the face, her hand coming away wet as she wiped at it. Around her the night exploded with sound as the Old One and Chera joined the battle, their cries echoing throughout the forest as they fought side by side with the warrior, neither giving quarter nor asking for it. The attackers were small feral creatures, with dull lifeless eyes, narrowed in elongated faces.

They moved swiftly, darting in and out between blows, long fangs snapping at their prey as they tried to wound. But the warrior was faster. The Old One and Chera casting them aside as quickly as they appeared, and then just as suddenly they were gone. Back to whoever or wherever it was that had called them forth.

"What. Are. Those. Things?" Leah swayed, her gait unsteady as the warrior grabbed her, at the same time drawing her close while he searched the darkness for others. It was some time before his hold on her relaxed. and when it did, she leaned into him, grateful for his warmth. She was so cold. Her teeth chattered as she fought the nausea that threatened. Swallowed it. She was drifting, falling into the emptiness of a dark void where long dark tendrils reached out to embrace her. The last thing she heard was the warrior's uttered oath as she slipped into darkness, her last lucid thought that at least they hadn't been changelings.

"She's been hurt. We must get her to the village of the people." The Hunter spoke to no one. Everyone. He looked from the Old One to Chera, his thoughts reaching out, opening to them both, but drawn to the grizzled Mukwa. A part of him acknowledging what he knew, hoping that the Old One might see what was in his heart and speak. He knew that somewhere ahead of them his people waited, and he turned back to the bear, his gaze hopeful.

It was not to be. Not yet.

"Come." Silver eyes stared into black. Unsure whether he had imagined it, one dark brow arched questioningly. For a moment the moon's reflection caught and held within the silver eyes, the effect startling him. The pull of the night wind tugging at him as she took off, her lithe form moving quickly through the dense underbrush, the warrior silently following in her wake. Behind him the Old One snorted, coming down on all fours as he raked the earth in front of him with a gigantic paw.

The warrior had asked for help and had been answered, the answer not what he wanted. The big Mukwa snorted again. It was not time yet, and so he followed the wolf and the warrior, but more slowly, his snort of disbelief lost in the night as he scented the wind, keeping his thoughts to himself.

The Hunter still had much to learn—trouble was, he did not believe enough in his own instincts to acknowledge that he had heard.

§ § § § § §

It was like a fist hitting him in the center of his chest, except that when he looked down where his chest should have been, there was nothing. Nothing except the forest in front of him and behind him. He felt himself falling, but he never hit the ground. Instead, he changed form, writhing as he floated above the *"thing"* that had held him captive for so long—never his body, but something that the one known as the *Other* had forced him to wear, so that he and others like him could serve a Dark Lord they all despised.

He glanced down once more. The earth was moving around him, over him, and he accepted the shelter offered. From somewhere behind him, he felt the soft sighing as the form that had imprisoned him for so long released him, the movement so subtle that it went unnoticed while the towering form stood over it. Again and again, the cold flames caressed the already used up vessel that for so long had held him prisoner. Turning, the restless entity flew over the Dark Lord. Back to the earth. Back to the forest. More importantly, back to his freedom and what he had once been.

The man stiffened, his senses tingling. *No!* He flung his arms up, the binding spell cast, but it was too late. The sentinel had escaped.

Gone back to what he was.

The man cursed as he kicked the empty vessel at his feet. In his rage at being betrayed, he had forgotten what had been embedded deeply within the runes that he himself had written.

Even more importantly, he had to make sure that none of the remaining sentries betrayed him as this one had.

He knew what the sentinel had done. Trouble was, he didn't know who had bridged the world within worlds, the power emitted from their passage telling him little other than that they would be formidable adversaries. His face darkened as his hands clenched and unclenched. He regretted now that he had left his realm, and for what? To traverse a forbidden path to aid a sister he had barely known...

More words spewed from bloodless lips as he used an ancient spell to strengthen the already closed gate, ensuring that none would enter. Beneath all his reasoning, a seed of thought had been planted. Perhaps when he had left that far off place of warriors, his return trip hurried because of it, he had been the one to inadvertently leave the gate open to allow others access.

Black eyes narrowed as he cast a thoughtful look at what could no longer be seen.

One more thing he didn't like. Not. One. Bit.

From his high place the one now returned to the earth watched. Once more an unseen entity, he was once again free to soar through air and earth. A protector to the clans above and below. The return to himself was filled with bittersweet memories. Too late he had realized what the one known as the *Other* had done. The joining of his spirit-self to a body that chained him, confined him to a prison that held him fast—he hadn't even seen it coming. By the time he had realized what was happening, it had been too late; the incantation had already been cast.

The entity sighed, remembering the long endless night he had endured. Too long had he walked in the darkness created by one who did not belong to his world. Caught within the winds caress after such an endless time of waiting, he soared high. Away from air and earth to gather his powers back unto himself. His mind reached out. There was nothing. Nothing save the emptiness of the wind as it found him. Reaching out, seeking, meeting, melding, so that they were once again one.

The sentinel sighed. He had forgotten, it had been so long.

Time passed. The moon rose. The pull of the earth drawing him back to himself. To his center. He leaned forward, the breath of the night the mirror within.

The others. Those ones who guarded the entry points to and from his world to other worlds—realms within realms—and all of them in peril. The sentinel who had never thought to go beyond himself, to communicate with others unlike himself, now moved earthward to seek out those of the clans who by their own birthright could be chosen and made to see the unseen.

§ § § § §

The Other. The words were whispered, as if speaking them out loud would call that which was unwanted back.

Jerome had waited in the silence with Orith. Waited as the shadows had deepened. Waited as the dusk had fallen, her velvet mantle enveloping them, covering them in the blackness that was the night.

If Orith was cold, he never showed it. The snowy owl simply drew his woolen cloak more tightly about him, his ability to see deep into the night the one thing that had remained unchanged.

And still Jerome waited. Waited for the moment when the moon and stars were perfectly aligned. Waited for the mist, which curled its way lazily across the ground, seeking, coiling upward, long tendrils reaching out to grasp...

Jerome braced himself for what was coming. He sighed wearily.

It had been a short time of peace.

§ § § § §

Leah opened her eyes. Closed them. The night with its shadows surrounded her, the faint light cast by the moon tracing a pattern across the forests floor. It was still the darkest part of the night. She laid there a while longer, her senses slowly returning as she became aware of the dull throbbing at her temples. Unsure of where she was or how she had gotten there, she waited to hear something familiar. Reaching out, she sought out Chera. Her gentle probing received an immediate response.

Yes. She was here.

Another gentle probe. The Old One responded. She felt safer now.

She closed her eyes; her senses still reeling, she lay there, quietly waiting until her emotions stilled. This time when she slept, it was more peaceful, the dreams that had pushed against her giving her a brief respite.

When next she opened her eyes, it was morning. She was in a sheltered grove, protected by red cedars that towered above her, their trunks thickened and gnarled with age. They were ancient, some knew them simply as the Standing People.

She did not have to turn her head to know that the warrior was close by, his dark gaze full of concern. Somewhere, out of her line of vision, she heard others.

"Chera?" Leah called softly as she struggled to sit up. Carefully easing herself back against the tree trunk, she waited until her breathing slowed. Her head still hurt, but she refrained from touching it.

Something brushed against her, and she nearly wept with relief as silver eyes flecked with gold looked into hers.

"Oh, Chera..."

The Hunter rose from his place beside the Elder, for the sound of the woman weeping caused a strange unease within him. Something he was not used to. The unexpected touch on his arm startled him as black eyes looked up into his.

"Sit down."

She was the oldest in the tribe, her years beyond count, she had endured where others had given up. She was one of the eldest of the clan mothers. It was she who listened. It was she who would decide.

"Warrior, she must grieve." The voice was soft but edged with steel.

The Hunter looked at the elder in surprise. The woman was strong. She communicated with the spirits. *What,* he wondered out loud, did she have to grieve?

"The loss of her friends. Her world as she knew it. Many, many, things." The woman pointed a long bony finger at him, her eyes narrowed, she signed that he should sit down, to be at her level. At her age, it was hard to look up. Besides, he still needed to learn that he did not know everything.

She leaned forward into the smoke that whorled restlessly up from the sacred fire. For too long had her people faded into themselves, their memories lost to the dark wind that had risen from the North. Her mind turned back. She was a young woman, naive, trusting, and like the others of her clan, eager—

Too eager.

One day, many turnings past, she had watched as the dark one had entered their world. Young and full of promise, he had brought new hope to a people who were struggling with their way of life. They had listened, had accepted what the stranger said, had allowed him to convene with the leaders, the meetings held in the hidden places. They had trusted him—had shown him their sacred relics.

She bowed her head, remembering when the storms had come. Sweeping like wildfire across their land, leaving in their wake terrifying things that had hunted her people and destroyed their villages. Nights. Days. All spent in hiding. The terror of being discovered. Memories washed over the elder as she went back to that place and saw again the death and destruction that had nearly decimated a once strong people. *Her* people. She sighed.

The warrior was still watching her, his thoughts his own. She knew what he was waiting for. She turned away from him, her attention brought back to the fire and the flowing flames within its center.

"Wait for her grief to ease, warrior. She must throw off that which binds her to that other place, and so, in this way, she will release one way of life to embrace another. Within herself, a power grows that must be nurtured. Her gift of speaking to the clans of the forest was once our gift as well…"

The voice trailed off, and she leaned forward to place more dry wood crosswise on the fire. Leaning back, she looked toward the place where the wolf and young woman rested. Her gaze swept back around her. Them. They were alone. The few remaining villagers had given the strange visitors a wide berth. The elder also knew that the giant one, the Mukwa, was close by. To know that he had returned was enough—she had endured years of age and aching joints in hopes to see this day. She released her breath in a soft sigh, the sound carrying in the morning's stillness.

Knowledge was a hard thing to bear when the truth could not be told.

§ § § § § §

The sentries stayed where they were, heads bowed, unmoving. The master had returned to the cavern in a rage and, so far, anything that could be thrown had been.

Dismissing them with a curt nod, he had gathered to him what was necessary and fed the fire so that the flames leapt high, soft tendrils of ice fire reaching out to explore the ceiling before receding back. Awakened from eternal sleep, deep within the heart that burned blood red, something moved, drawing the man closer.

Peering into the flames' center, he turned his head as if listening to something that none save himself could hear. Nodding, he drew back slightly as the greyish-white plume wafted up, the acrid smell burning his nostrils as he removed a powdery substance from a small leather packet at his side. Throwing it into the fire, he watched as the flames swept upward and out, arcing toward him as he took another cautious step back.

He feared little, yet even he understood that there was a fine line between arrogance and respect.

"They wait at the gates," he whispered as the smoke from the fire thickened, a form slowly taking shape within the center that glowed red-hot. Soulless eyes looked out from a face that was terrible to look upon. The ruined spectre moved closer as the silence deepened. Where there should have been a mouth, there was nothing but a slit. No feet, just ruined stumps that it hobbled on, its gait slow and deliberate.

The man motioned silently toward the long tunnel that led to the cavern's opening. Not bothering to look up, he remained where he was. The rush of cold air left in the creatures wake enveloping him as he bent once more to the task of carefully unrolling the parchment in front of him. He needed more time to decipher the scrolls—which was why he had summoned the creature, for he would watch the remaining gates, thus ensuring that there would be no further interference.

They must remember the present. Not the past. The quill pen splintered in his hand. Cursing softly, the one known only as the *Other* merely tossed the feathery remnants onto the earthen floor before calmly reaching for another. He knew where the creature was going. Knew that it would shadow the others' minds so that any lingering memories they had of what they had once been would be nothing more than a distant memory.

11

"It is time."

Leah ignored him. She had waited in the stifling heat as the warrior and the old woman had talked, her patience thinning as the day deepened. The shadows of mid morning were tracing their intricate patterns across the ground in front of her. She remained where she was, looking straight ahead, saying nothing, her mind on the silver-white wolf who crouched not far from her in the cooling shade.

"Come." The touch on her arm was warm. Reassuring. This time she looked up, her eyes taking in the shadows that were etched in the warrior's face.

Funny, she thought to herself as she allowed him to help her rise, that she had not noticed them before.

She looked up at him again, noticing for the first time how exhausted he looked. Not realizing she did it, she took the hand he offered and walked with him into the clearing where the elder waited for her. For them both.

Memories. So many memories. The elder put hand to her head as if that would stop them. It didn't. She watched through half-closed lids as the warrior walked back toward her, the young woman following, her stride nearly matching that of The Hunter, but not quite.

She was small, the elder thought. Long, dark hair with tints of copper in their burnished strands trailed down her back, nearly to her waist. The color of her hair matched her eyes, which were framed by long lashes set in a small oval face that looked back at her, the gaze open and appraising.

The elder didn't react. Didn't pull back. Yes, she thought decidedly, this one was special. She just didn't know it yet.

She looked at the warrior, caught the sideways glance her gave the young woman, saw what lie beneath the look. She settled back against the many robes that had been placed there for her comfort and waited until the warrior and the young woman had reached her. Watched as they both waited patiently for her to speak. Looking from one to the other she chuckled, the sound low and melodious.

Sometimes the unseen ones had a sense of humor even in the midst of chaos.

Leah listened to the elder, her head bowed as she tried to shut out the images that coursed through her mind with the telling. Something dark and dangerous crossed her vision, but when she tried to focus, it was gone. Beside her the warrior stiffened as if he also sensed it, but then she realized that only she was seeing what the elder saw with the retelling of her remembering from her distant past.

She was beginning to understand. She remembered now what had happened. Knew what had brought her here.

Although she had been deep within the caverns depths, sheltered within the living rock, she had known that her brother, Nickolous, had fought a fierce battle with the aid of the forest clans. What she had not realized was that, this time, A-Sharoon was not the enemy.

There had been another. Darker. More dangerous. The Daughter of Darkness had…she frowned as she tried to sort the memories, make sense of them.

A-Sharoon had a brother!

Leah closed her eyes, shutting out everything except the images. Beyond her vision, she sensed Chera, the big wolf centering her thoughts so that Leah saw through her eyes—saw the battle for the sacred flame—saw the one known as the *Fallen*—saw his destruction and imprisonment.

She was now at a place where even Chera could not go, the wolf's presence a comfort to her as she deep listened, her abilities to see the past awakening as she went back even further.

There had been two born to the shadows on that night so long ago.

Like, yet unlike. One cold as winter's breath. The other, warmth and darkness. Combined? *Deadly.* The unspoken word hung suspended in the air between the two women.

Leah opened her eyes, the warrior watching her intently, his concern evident. She knew he had been gently probing to see if he could see what she saw, but she had shut out all save the wolf and Mukwa.

She turned her head as if listening to something that only she could hear, her eyes sweeping upward, centering on the warrior's face. He knew even before she spoke the words that he wasn't going to like what she had to say.

"We must prepare. I know who it is you battle. Once, turnings ago, my brother and I fought his sister with the help of the four-legged and winged clans. As dark as she was, I fear, he is darker. Somehow, during the last battle for our world he journeyed *between.* When he returned, here, I somehow was pulled back with him. I don't belong here, but then neither does he."

Leah looked up to see the warrior watching her. Behind his black eyes, she saw something more. He looked away, into the forest as if he had seen something. Something within himself? Leah wasn't sure. She swung her gaze back, meeting that of the elders.'

The Ancient One said nothing. She didn't have to. If there was anything that could have convinced her that she had lived this long to see hope, this was it.

"What can we do?" The warrior's voice, close, startled her.

"Do?" Leah focused her gaze on the stand of cedars, she knew that, behind their concealing depths, Chera and the Mukwa watched. She turned back to the warrior. *"Do?"* She repeated, the words sounding strange even to her own ears. She heard her voice, but it wasn't hers. It belonged to another. Words, not her own, poured forth. The sharing of thoughts with another a thing that was hard to do.

"The clans of the forest begin to awaken. You," she pointed a long, tapered finger at the warrior, "must remember. The clans of the two-legged have forgotten who they were. They have forgotten when they walked with the others. All of them. Clans of earth and sky. You have the memories. *Remember.*" Leah turned her face away from the warrior and the elder, her emotions obvious. She reached out with her mind, hoping others had somehow heard her pleas for help—

—Caught a brief glimpse of silver-grey fur, and blue eyes, which glinted strangely clouding her vision. She could almost see him as he came through the mist. Almost touch him.

Almost.

"Leah!" Someone grabbed her, twisting her around. She felt herself being pulled roughly to her feet. Then she was being shaken. Not roughly, but enough that she was jolted awake. Had she been sleeping? She looked dazedly from The Hunter to the elder. The warrior was looking down at her and he wasn't trying to mask his emotions; he was trying to understand what it was she wanted, this strange little female who had been thrown into his world. He looked from Leah to the elder, his silence begging help to understand.

The elder, like most of her predecessors, remained silent. She had seen what Leah had seen, had walked the path, unseen, with her. She had watched the wolf and bear in their hidden place, had glimpsed another—unusual blue eyes that saw both worlds as they had been at the beginning. She nodded to the warrior, her voiceless approval of the one he had rescued carried in the slight nod of her head. The one known as The Hunter reached out with his senses to seek understanding and reeled back as if he had been struck.

It was there. Carried in the air that surrounded him. The low rumble that reverberated through the air, throaty and deep was…

Questioning?

Black eyes narrowed as he brushed the sweat absently from his brow. It beaded up again. He was suddenly aware of every nuance around him. The birds. The trees. The warm wind that wrapped itself around him. Everything. Everywhere. The warrior turned around, his gaze sweeping the clearing before falling upon the place where the wolf and bear waited. The leaves trembled with the passage of the silvery-white form of the wolf. Silver eyes flecked with gold looked at him. Through him. Behind her the bear came, his gait slower, more methodical.

The forest around him melted away.

He was in a high place. There were no clans. Nothing. Nothing save the wind that blew restlessly about. seeking that which was not there. Above him, the sky was dotted with thick grey clouds that roiled and frothed. The Hunter's hand moved to his knife sheath. It was gone. He was looking down into a lush valley. It was primitive. Unspoiled. Untouched. The warrior drew in deeply of the air. It was cool, filled with moisture. A thousand beginnings. A thousand endings.

The Hunter shook himself, trying to brush away the prickling sensation that ran up his spine, the fine hairs on the back of his neck standing up. He was being watched. Pivoting swiftly around, he caught himself. He was at the edge of a precipice, behind him there was nothing save empty space. Drawing in a deep breath, he let it out, the wind catching it, drawing it away from him. Beneath his feet the earth moved with its own heartbeat. His awareness heightened, he became aware of other things. The breeze, which wrapped itself around him whispered softly, carrying with it memories of endless wanderings as it moved over the earth.

The warrior shook off the feeling that he had always known these things. That there was more. Much more. Layered deep within memories. Blood memories of the grandfathers. The seven. He closed his eyes. Opened them to find himself deep within the heart of the valley, surrounded by trees. Tall and stately, they bent beneath the winds gentle caress.

Another thought. The warrior blinked in the bright light, at the same time shadowing his eyes with a bronzed hand he looked up. Where there had been a stand of mighty oak trees, there were now warriors. the like of which he had never seen. A familiarity tugged at his consciousness as something caught at the edge of his peripheral vision. The movement was barely discernible, but it was there.

Forest Warriors. Protectors of the deepest heart—

He had thought them nothing more than a myth. Stories told to the little ones to ease them into soothing sleep. The Hunter didn't flinch, not even when one of the warriors brushed him in passing, the touch something he would always remember. The shock electrifying. *He was in an ancient place of knowing.* He drew in deeply of the scents surrounding him, his lungs expanding in the pure air filled with sound. With life.

The ancient warriors circled him, and he blinked against the sun's bright glare as he looked up into eyes the color of the very forest that surrounded him. He saw himself, mirrored within their swirling depths, within the seeing he knew there was more.

He was at the beginning. Before the time of forgetting. Before those of his kind had buried their memories in a distant place deep within themselves. He didn't flinch. Not even when the forest warriors spoke, their voices heard as they looked at this stranger who had entered their midst uninvited. Instead, the warrior was welcomed, acknowledged. Who he was—what he had been—all these things were remembered.

And more. Much more.

The warrior was jolted back to the present. Startled, he looked around. At Leah. The elder. And beyond them to where Chera stood with the Old One. The big Mukwa swung his head from side to side, one giant forepaw sweeping the earth in front of him; the dust rising into the air, to hang suspended in the light that danced between the leaves of the trees.

"The journey *'between'* was a good one?" The elder had risen with some difficulty and was watching the warrior; gauging his reaction to her words. The Hunter said nothing. He couldn't. This was his journey and his alone to make. What he had seen—what he had heard—these things were his to think on and decide. He merely nodded to the elder, his respect for her would not allow him to be rude. She smiled, the corner of her mouth twitching slightly.

It was good.

§ § § § § §

The Old One had watched as the warrior dream walked the *in-between* with the forest warriors. They were one of the oldest of the knowing clans, an ancient race. Part of the living earth, they protected all who lived beneath their watch. Born at the time of the beginning of learning, they and they alone saw the true heart of the clans. That they had allowed him to walk among them meant there was still hope. The big Mukwa snorted, the sound unusually loud in the silence that surrounded them. The villagers had long since vanished into the forest, afraid of what they could not understand.

Small black eyes blinked in the bright light as he shifted his gaze to that of the wolf. Silver eyes stared back. Reflections of what lie within pooling in their depths. The Old One understood. Like, yet unlike. It mattered not...

Once, when the worlds were new, and the clans were young, her kind and his had sought each other out. It had been a time of learning. Of healing. The sacred fires had burned bright, the clans of the two-legged seeking out those of the four, as well of those of the winged ones. Guardians of the skies. Together, they had learned. What one of them took, they shared with another, and another. In this way, they all had been teachers and the earth that gave them life had prospered for they had been *One.*

The Old One closed his eyes as the remembering became almost too much to bear. He had not thought on these things in a very long time; he shook his head from side to side, as if by doing so he would shake away the memories.

It *had* been the dreaming time. But that was long ago.

He spared a look at the wolf, his eyes filled with pain It was true that wisdom wore many faces and his world, as he knew it, was changing—something brushed against him—something that reeked of darkness and death. He turned, his gaze sweeping the clearing for what was not there, the challenge thrown out, answered. The *whoomph* as he brought his forefeet down upon the earth resonating as he started forward, but Chera was there ahead of him. The high-pitched shriek as she flung herself at the thing echoing throughout the nearly deserted village as her jaws closed around its neck.

It happened so fast that the warrior had barely enough time to unsheathe his knife, the black stone vibrating softly within his grasp as he shoved Leah unceremoniously to the ground. He brought the knife up, the elongated head of the thing facing him, dripping saliva as it skewered itself on his blade. Mere inches from his face, it glared balefully at the warrior as it struggled to remove itself from the dark obsidian that held it captive.

The warrior plunged the blade deeper, twisting it, but the thing merely slithered off, its movements resembling that of a serpent. The Hunter's eyes widened as he watched it scurry into the shadows, its narrowed eyes staring at him from beneath an overhanging branch as it turned to glare at him. To change.

Leah rolled out of the way, her heart thudding in fear. She knew what *that* was. Memories pushed their way upward as she fought down the nausea that threatened to choke her. Changelings! Here? Her skin prickled as she sprang to her feet, uncertain of what to do. She heard Chera's howl of outrage as one of them pinned her to the ground, the big wolf twisting, turning, protecting her soft underside from the deadly curved claws of the thing's hind feet as it struck out, its intent to kill. As it rolled off her, it began to change, growing bigger, stronger with each moment that passed. Leah knew that in this state it was most vulnerable; she shifted her gaze to the warrior. He looked from the wolf to her, then back to the changeling where it crouched in the bushes. Rocking back and forth it snarled viciously, its jaws working as it spewed red-flecked foam from a mouth that would not stay closed.

The Hunter saw his chance and took it. The strangled cry of outrage as he snapped its neck was cut short, the dull thud as he flung it from him resonating through earth and stone. Then the air was filled with unspeakable things as the white frothing mist came out of nowhere, curling about them, embracing them, so that it was hard to tell friend from foe.

The Old One hurled the struggling form from him, his snort of disgust lost in the heat of battle as yet another changeling appeared out of nowhere. He shook his head to clear it, the red haze clouding his vision, the dull thud of the thing as it fell lifeless to the ground a warning to the others. A warning, that was ignored.

Leah stood mesmerized by the creature's eyes. It had come out of the mist unseen. Bigger than the others, it had moved warily toward her, the deep sounds emanating from its throat threatening as it placed one clawed foot slowly in front of the other. She sidled back, careful not to trip, her movements slow and calculated. Out if the corner of her eye she saw the elder rising slowly to her feet, her eyes following the beast as it drew closer. Her lips moved silently as the mist found her, curling about her it wove its way up and over her, momentarily concealing her.

The Hunter threw the thing from him in disgust, cursing himself because he should have known danger was close. He squared his shoulders, reached for another arrow. It mattered not where they had come from, he would send them back; he loosed the arrow, the *thunk* as it hit the thing satisfying. It was as the warrior reached for yet another arrow that he sensed rather than saw another of them; it crouched in the shadows, nearly out of the range of his vision. It was watching him, its eerie yellow eyes following his movements with intelligence. The warrior roared a challenge, the war cry carrying through the heavy white mist that encircled him, the damp tendrils seeking.

Leah watched in horrified fascination as the thing moved closer, flecks of foam flying as it shook its head from side to side. Its features shifting, changing. Long, yellow fangs growing as it snarled at her. It slashed at her with long curved claws that promised death. She moved swiftly, tucking and rolling as the elder shouted something at her, her stance challenging the beast as it half jumped, half flew—the thick leathery wings that sprouted from its back not yet completely formed as it opened its mouth. The sound it emitted deafening.

The elder was not afraid. Even of things she did not know. She was too old. Had seen too much. As the thing towered above her, she saw her death mirrored within its soulless eyes and embraced it.

Screams. Shrieks of rage that tore through the mist even as it dissolved, taking with it the rest of the dark beings. The warrior blinked in the bright light, shielding his eyes with a large bronzed hand. He knew the Old One and wolf were close. He could hear them. Hear their heartbeat as they willed themselves to be calm—heard the woman, her footsteps falling softly upon the damp earth as she slowly made her way toward him, felt the touch upon his arm, the wetness as she brushed at the tears that ran unheeded down her cheeks. He felt everything.

"No!" The shout carried upon the wind echoed in the clearing as Leah stopped, one slender hand pointing to where the elder lay, still and quiet. The red that seeped into the ground beneath her inert form

a telling thing. The warrior went deathly still, his hands balling into fists, the knuckles white, bloodless. For a moment he ceased to be, the anger was so great. Then, going to the elder, he bent down, his hand searching for a pulse where there was none.

Gently closing her sightless eyes, he cradled her against him, his grief obvious to the others as they stood back, shocked that one of them had fallen.

"She must be taken to the sacred place before the sun sets. Whatever they were, they're gone now; back to whatever darkness that spawned them." The warrior was standing, holding his fragile burden with little effort. He turned to Leah, his black eyes searching her face for understanding. She nodded assent as Chera pushed against her, the wolf's thoughts reaching out to her, soothing her.

"Those things smelled of A-Sharoon." Chera was staring straight ahead, watching the path the warrior and the Mukwa had taken. The day had deepened into late afternoon and, even though the wolf had disposed of the changelings remains, the stench still lingered. A vivid reminder of their immortality.

"I don't think she had anything to do with this. At least not this time." Leah was leaning down, placing more wood on the fire as she spoke. She knew how fast the night fell and was preparing for it.

Watching her, Chera could not help but wonder at the changes she saw. Like her brother, Nickolous, she had grown. Gone was the frightened young girl. In its place stood a young woman, the knowledge of who and what she was something that would serve her well in the days to come, for their world as they knew it was no more. Thrust into the unknown, they could not sit idly by when all about them chaos reigned. Sighing, she gave it over.

It was not A-Sharoon they faced, but something worse. Much worse. Memories pressed upon her as she remembered what Jerome had said about the *Other.* There had been two: one cold as winters frost—the other? Darkness and warmth. Combined? Chera snorted despite the look Leah shot her, silver eyes widened as the wolf realized why *they* had been able to journey so easily between worlds.

The dark one, the one known as the *Other* had once been part of their world. Now, they were part of his.

12

There it was again.

The wind wrapped around the forest warrior, but nothing else moved. Not even the leaves on the nearby trees. The warrior reached out, his thoughts centered deep within. Below him, the little ones, the earth diggers, moved closer to the surface. They were part of the whole, and they knew that more was needed.

The Old One, the old she-rat, had patiently explained to both Jerome and Orith why they could not make the same journey as Chera and Gabriel. At least not in the same manner. They must, she explained, journey instead to the sacred place. Once there they would know what to do. The one known as the *Other* must not be allowed back, must never traverse their realm again. He must be bound to his own realm. His own time.

He had been gone too long from theirs—the balance had been tipped. They had to trust that this was the task set for them, that those who watched, the Elders, the Old Ones, knew.

It no longer mattered that the one known as the *Other* had begun his existence in their world. He had left, had become part of another—had caught it at the beginning of its existence.

Was now part of it.

The forest warrior reached out with his mind, searching for something that was not there. Beside him, Orith watched, his cherrywood staff with its many small burls was glowing, the soft white light that flowed from its tip pointing the way.

All things revolved in a circle. All things returned to their center. Now, they must look to themselves for the answers.

§ § § § § §

"They come."

Leah had just finished replenishing the fire. The embers beneath the thin layer of white ash glowed red-hot as she turned them over, the wood catching quickly as the flames curled around the tinder dry wood.

Although she would never have admitted it, she was glad to see the warrior, the Mukwa, following slightly behind. She saw the pain etched in The Hunter's face and grieved with him even as she tried to speak the words that would give him comfort, but none would come.

The warrior reached out; cupping her chin in one large hand, he slowly raised her face so that she was looking into his. She did not flinch. Did not pull way as she gazed up into black eyes, the words she tried to speak trailing off into the silence. And so she said nothing, for she sensed that no words could take away the grief that the warrior felt. The thoughts and feelings his alone to think on.

"There are more of them, out there, watching, waiting." The warrior's breath was warm against her cheek as he leaned down, his dark eyes guarded as Leah looked into their swirling depths. She nodded mutely. Aware that the Old One and Chera watched, she moved back, the warrior's hands sliding down her arms as she did so, confused by emotions she could not understand, her heart beating wildly as she looked at the warrior as if for the first time.

Something stirred in the pit of her stomach as she felt the warmth spreading throughout her body. Suddenly discomfited, Leah looked away, her gaze momentarily locking with that of the big wolf's, before bowing her head, even more confused by emotions she could not explain, even to herself.

But Chera knew. She had known from the first time she had watched them together.

The warrior and the young girl.

"Time passes, some things change while others do not," the Old One drawled softly as the wolf passed him. She stopped, her head raised, her silvery eyes appraising him. Sparing a glance back to where the warrior stood, his attention riveted on Leah, Chera nodded, acknowledging the truth in the words that were spoken.

It made no difference where they had started from. They were all the same. Thrown into a new beginning, like their forbears, they had struggled against insurmountable odds. Their abilities challenged to survive in a world where they were considered less than those who walked the same path as they. The clans of the two-legged instead choosing to walk a separate path, their walk now different from the rest of the forest clans.

Chera shrugged silver-white shoulders. It did not matter. She was here to protect Leah. Where she went after that, well, that would have to wait until she got there. She turned aside, her senses tingling. Leah was beside her, her touch gentle, her hand running the length of her back as if she sensed what the wolf felt. It was time.

The warrior watched, bewildered and a little awed at the interaction between the wolf and woman. Instead of pulling away, the beast seemed to welcome it. He shook his head, confused. He still did not understand how she did it. Perhaps it was a gift that was hers and hers alone. His people believed that the spirits sometimes favored those who were special. The Hunter's eyes narrowed as he looked at the woman.

The whole of her. She was small. Smaller than most of the women belonging to his clan. Long, dark, auburn hair hung to her waist in waves as she absently brushed at it, pushing it back from her face, tucking the wayward strands behind her ear. She did it so often she was probably not even aware of it—it was something that made her even more appealing. The warrior tensed as he realized that he thought of her as *more*. More than something weaker and frailer.

The men of his clan had long been taught to protect the women, for without them there would be no continuation. The people would cease to be. It was as simple as that. He turned away and nearly ran into the bear, who was staring at him, appraising him. The warrior took a step back, caught himself. *Too late*—the Mukwa had seen the shadow of confusion that crossed the warrior's brow.

"Careful." The word drifted to him on the wind that blew around him. The warrior shaded his eyes against the bright light that sifted through the trees, unsure if it was his imagination or if he had heard the word.

"Well, whatever they were, they're gone now." Leah spoke quietly. She had come up behind him, her steps so light that she had nearly caught him unaware. The warrior looked down at her, his gaze shuttered. Like him, she searched the shadows as she spoke. Whoever—whatever—had been out there before, watching—was gone. As the night breeze drifted throughout the nearly deserted village, she edged closer to the warrior. The need to be next to him was something that she could not explain, even to herself.

Looking down at her, the warrior wondered at her sudden frailness, for it wasn't like her. Perhaps, he thought, it was the day's events. The elder's sudden passing had been unexpected, true, but this was the way it had been for his people as long as he could remember. You were born. You lived. And when it was time, you died. Whatever those things were today, he would know their smell and be ready when next they met, for he had no intentions of traveling the blue road yet.

Reaching out, he took her hand, the slight touch meant to be reassuring. She was cold, he could feel her trembling beneath his touch. Removing his heavy fur cape, he draped it about her shoulders so that she was buried within its many folds.

Leah accepted the robe gratefully, drawing the warmth from the garment to her, the warrior's scent permeating her senses as she sank into it. The scent of earth and cedar calming her as she wondered at these new feelings.

"Come," he spoke the word softly, gently guiding her toward the fire that burned in the center of the village.

Leah absorbed the warmth gratefully. She was cold. Unnaturally cold. She fought the urge to throw up as she drew her arms close to her body, grateful for the warrior's support, for without it she would have collapsed. Aware that he was looking at her strangely, she ignored it, her concentration focused on the fire and the warmth as she reached out, her mind seeking, into the darkness to reassure Chera that she was okay. Not waiting for an answer, she gratefully accepted the fruit placed in front of her, while behind her she heard the soft pad-pad of feet as the wolf came into view, followed by the Mukwa. Placing themselves just out of reach of the fire's flickering light, they hunkered down, waiting.

"You must eat." The warrior had placed more food in front of Leah. Although he hadn't said anything, he knew that she was hungry. Deep within he was upset at himself, for he wished he had more to offer, other than the fruit. He saw the dark circles beneath her eyes and wished he could hunt for her. She needed meat, the warrior knew she was weakening and didn't know what to do; there was little food to be had in the village. What the villagers hadn't taken, predators had. The fruit would soon be gone, and he needed to know she would be safe.

The elder had said to keep her close, not to leave her alone.

He placed more wood on the fire, his thoughts reaching out as he wondered if the wolf or the bear would hunt for her, the low growl so close, caused him to stiffen, his hand automatically reaching for his knife. Silver eyes gazed into his as Chera brushed past him, then she was gone, plunging deep into the forest and the night that engulfed her.

The warrior pulled back in disbelief. Had she really heard him, or at the very least perceived his thoughts? Sparing a glance toward the place where the bear had been, he caught the slight movement as the branches fell back into place. That and nothing more. Unsheathing his knife carefully, he placed it within easy reach as he leaned back, bracing himself against the massive trunk of a red cedar. His longbow and quiver of arrows within easy reach. He knew something was out there, watching them.

What he did not know was that, somewhere deep within the forest, a wind blew toward them, an unseen warrior riding hard upon its back.

The Hunter opened his eyes, sweat beaded his brow. He was close to the fire, too close. He wiped absently at the sweat that ran down his face, sparing a look toward Leah, grateful that she was sleeping peacefully. Reaching for his knife, he noted with satisfaction it was where he had placed it, as were his bow and arrows. The night had deepened but the little ones, the creatures who ruled the night were out, their song filling the air with sound, a good sign that nothing was amiss.

Their silence would let him know if danger lurked close by. Rising, he banked the fire before retrieving his weapons.

The first defense was a well thought defense. Sighing, he retreated to an ancient oak tree, there to watch and wait. Even though the night carried with it no signs of danger, it wouldn't do to get careless. In his world, being careless could get you killed, and he had every intention on living a long time yet.

§ § § § § §

Leah was running. Hard. Something, someone, was chasing her, had been since she had been separated from her brother, Nickolous. She watched, helpless, as the frothy white mist curled about her legs, snaking its way around her, over her, passing upward as it disappeared into the trees.

She ran faster. Whatever it was, it was now behind her. With each labored beat of her heart, she could sense it. Knew it was closing in on her, could almost feel its heated breath as it gained on her. Casting a backward glance over her shoulder, she saw nothing, but she knew something unseen watched: moving when she moved, stalking her.

Later she would realize that it was the fear that had taken her. The fear of the unknown. It had heightened her senses with each labored breath she took as she ran blindly, the brambles from the thorn trees tearing at her hands, her face. That's when she missed it. The slight swell of the leaf-strewn mound and the deeper indentation in the earth.

She had tripped, falling into a cavern that smelled of earth, mold, and mildew. At first she had lain where she had fallen, winded but unhurt. The opening above her head had already closed, the howl of the wolf as she scrambled to her feet reaching her at the last moment. Its echo fading as she tore frantically at the moss and stone that barred her way, back to the outside world. Too late she realized it was Chera who had been trailing her as she had stood there in the darkness, calming herself, drawing deeply of the scents around her.

Somewhere ahead of her there was water. She could hear it as it trickled over the rocks, falling into a small pool that had been worn smooth from countless turnings. The fresh air that wended its way through the many crevasses telling her that somewhere there was an exit. As she grew more accustomed to the darkness and her surroundings, she became aware of something else: the little ones, the earth diggers.

They watched her from their hidden places; waited until she was no longer frightened, then revealed themselves. After a short time, when she knew her way was well and truly barred from above, she had looked to her center. Finding the answer she sought, she reached into the darkness, seeking out the oldest amongst the watchers, then had silently followed them as they led her to a wide cavern.

There within the center, a sacred fire burned. Here, there was warmth and food. Content for now to watch and wait, she had sat beside the fire, gratefully accepting the gift of warmth offered and the fresh greens and fruit that had swept away her fatigue.

How long she had waited there, she wasn't sure, she had slept, ate, slept again. Time had passed, and she had been content to wait, she had not bothered to look for the way out, her inner instincts telling her that Chera and the others would come for her.

She had been unprepared for it when it came. The unexpected rush of wind that had ripped through the cavern, the thunder followed by the lightning. Then there had been nothing but the darkness. It had pressed down upon her, smothering her, and she had known no more for a time.

Until she had awakened. Here. In this place. With a strange man known as The Hunter and a bear, one of the old ones from the forgotten time: each hating the other for the monster they thought each of them had become.

Or at least that's what they had come to believe, because they had forgotten the unwritten laws cast down for them to honor from the beginning.

Leah tossed restlessly in her sleep. Something was there, at the edge of her consciousness, reaching out, pulling at her, the need to communicate almost desperate, keeping her where she was, holding her prisoner. She fought back, trying to strike out as she struggled in her sleep, unaware that the warrior was beside her, his black eyes full of concern as he tried to awaken her.

The warrior reached out, his touch steadying her as she lay trembling beneath the robe he had given her. Helpless, he could only watch as sweat beaded her brow and upper lip. He was tempted to reach out and brush it away but refrained from doing so. It was a dangerous thing to awaken one from such a deep sleep.

Instead, he leaned over her, his breath fanning her cheek with warmth, he gathered her to him and held her gently. And when she cried out once again in her sleep, he simply held her more tightly in the hopes she wouldn't be too angry when she awakened in his arms.

Looking into the fire's flaming depths, he sought out the elders. Those old ones who watched from their place in the unseen realms, asking for help to understand this small female who was so strong, yet at the same time as fragile as the blossom of the rose.

He marveled at himself for caring as he disengaged himself carefully so as not to awaken her. Beyond the fire's warm glow, he smelled blood and knew the wolf had returned with food.

Chera snorted derisively as she watched the warrior. The hunt had been successful, and she had dropped the limp form at the edge of the shadows cast by the fire's wavering light.

She still didn't trust him or his motives. Beside her, the bear huffed softly, the sound carrying on the warm breeze.

From his place near the fire, the warrior glanced up. He had released his charge long enough to prepare the food Chera had brought. The rabbit was already turning on the spit, the aroma reaching out, tantalizing—it had been too long since he had hunted wild game. He had been existing on the dried meat and berries these many days past, not by choice but by necessity. He peered into the darkness, relaxed.

The woman moved restlessly within his arms as he pulled her back, against his chest. Chera, seeing this, shook her head in disgust.

"She's not a cub." The bear had moved closer, yet still maintained a respectful distance from the wolf. He could sense her underlying anger toward the warrior and understood it.

"Maybe so, but she is still a youngling," Chera retorted, her silver eyes gleaming in the pale moonlight.

"Ahhh." The bear nodded mutely. He understood. The wolf looked upon the female as she would her own pup. Interesting.

He turned his head aside. It wouldn't do to let the wolf see his thoughts. She wouldn't like it, and he had no wish to argue. They were from different times, he and she. She was at the beginning of her world; well, he was somewhere in the middle of his.

He stretched, yawning. Some things were best left unsaid. He knew the warrior cared for the woman—so did the wolf. Remaining silent, he moved a short distance away. He would take first watch, for he had no fear of the night and that which walked within it. Stretching to his full height, he scented the wind. The night carried no threats. At least not yet.

Chera cast a sideways look at the bear. She would not let him know she could see what he saw. Not yet. Her purpose was to protect this small Daughter of Skye. It was why she had been allowed to pass through the portal unharmed by one of the guardians. One who still remembered

She closed her eyes against the images that suddenly assailed her senses. Gabriel's face floated before her, the vision almost painful, the blue eyes searching, Chera stiffened as the realization hit. It wasn't wishful thinking. Gabriel had passed through another gateway. Was searching for her. For them.

She swung her gaze around as she came up on all fours, the fur along her spine and neck ruffling. They might not be able to communicate on this plane of existence as they had in their own, but in the name of all her ancestors who had lived and died before her, from this time forth, they would try!

§ § § § §

Leah reached out, her mind seeking. Gabriel was calling to Chera. To her. Crystalline blue eyes flashed as he looked about. Her eyelids fluttered as she fought to awaken, so deep was she in the between realms, she felt as if she were being smothered as she returned to that place—

She had broken free of the cavern, the rock and rubble crumbling away as the wind tore at her, and had stumbled after the man.

A-Sharoon's brother! It was he who had caused the rip in time. *He should have stayed where he was.* She turned restlessly, mumbling in her sleep. If he had only stayed where he had belonged, she would be in Skye, safe, with the others.

But he hadn't.

Oh, just great, she thought to herself as she struggled against something that held her fast. A dream within a dream. Where had she heard that? Was that her? Talking to herself? She mumbled something.

Against. A. Warm. Chest?

The resounding *thunk* as her head snapped back caused her to look up into black eyes set in a bronze face. She tried to scramble back but got tangled in the fur cloak that was still wrapped tightly about her. Then she was struggling out of it, kicking it away from her as she tried to remember how she had gotten wrapped up in it in the first place. Her eyes locked on that of the warrior. He remained where he was, silently watching her, rubbing his chin gingerly.

Leah closed her eyes, momentarily embarrassed. She had whacked him with her head! She stifled a laugh. Then Chera was there beside her, nuzzling her, checking her to make sure she had come to no harm.

"Gabriel." Chera growled the word softly.

"I know. He's here. He made it through." Leah said, exhausted by the rapid exchange of unspoken thoughts between the two of them. She leaned into the silver-white wolf, hugging her, glad that they had returned to themselves. She looked up, past the wolf, at the warrior, opening her mind to him.

The Hunter pulled back, startled, the roar of the Old One deafening as the smaller of the forest clans scattered in alarm.

13

The yellowed parchment began to crumble as soon as the man picked it up; cursing softly, he passed his staff over it; the blue-white light acted like a magnet, drawing the tattered pieces together on the table in front of him. Light from a dozen candles illuminated the words that had been hidden from prying eyes for turnings beyond thought as he leaned closer to study them.

Behind him, in the farthest corner of the cavern, the shadow being watched as the master of the night read the ancient script, trying to decipher their meaning.

The candles burned low, the wax dripping slowly down the crude stone holder to pool onto the wooden table. And still the being waited. Waited in the shadows as the light that crept through the crevasses from the outside world waned and the darkened places loosed their hidden sentinels into the night to hunt.

"You're still here." It wasn't a question, merely an acknowledgment of fact. The man had risen from his place at the table. He stretched leisurely, for he feared little, and there had been barely any resistance of late. The fact that the young woman had survived his guards—more than once—had ceased to surprise him.

He shrugged broad shoulders. It didn't matter, she would be dealt with at a later date.

Drawing himself up to his full height, eyes, full black searched through the darkness that lingered just beyond the protective rim of the fire. Sometimes visitors appeared unannounced, and he was in no mood to deal with some power hungry entity whose real intent was to usurp him—to claim his power and rule in his stead.

Laughter, dark and deep, echoed in the cavern as he lit another candle. More fools they! He smirked at the shadow being; watching with satisfaction as it shrank further back, into the darkness.

He had ruled this world he walked upon nearly since its first breath of thought. Had watched as the four-footed and winged ones had struggled to find their own way. Had manipulated the gates so that he could travel *between* and so allow what was in other worlds of mist and imagery entrance.

It mattered not that each time he left one world to journey to another, the return brought with it more change. Creatures that were bound by their own laws were thrown into an alternate time, leaving a void in their own world. And so it would continue.

The one known as the *Other* looked around the dimly lit cavern. The creature was gone, probably back to its own realm, but he knew that it would return after a time. After it had sated its hunger.

There was little enough to sustain it in this one of late, he mused thoughtfully to himself as he bent over the yellowed parchments on the table, his staff within easy reach beside him. Time was growing short. The moons in the sky were changing while the currents that determined the direction of the tides were shifting.

He stopped long enough to stroke his chin thoughtfully, his dark eyes peering into the hidden places, for, like the elders of old, he had been gifted, but it was a dark gift. A gift that most would not have been willing to pay the price for. He frowned, his dark brows beetling together as he pushed at the shadows—pushed them away so that he could see what was concealed behind them.

After a time he leaned back, his expression thoughtful, watching the fire until it had burned down to embers—something he normally wouldn't have allowed unless there was a reason. He sensed the shadow creature, knew it had returned, was watching him. He beckoned it closer, coaxing it from the shadows, willing it to do his bidding.

It would be much later that he would return to the cold ashes of the fire. Kneeling down, he began to dig, pushing the blackened coals and bits of unburned wood aside until he found what it was that he sought. Carefully removing the stones that were layered on top of one another, he took something from a small stone case, the silver glint unmistakable even in the darkness that gathered, thick and foreboding, about him.

Quickly gathering more wood, he pushed the cold ash back on top of the layers of thin rock and sand, before lighting the fire. Then stood watching as the flames flared upward, the dry pine crackling in the silence as the sparks flew against the shadows that retreated, back to crevasse and tunnel.

Beneath his feet, the little one, the watcher, waited. Waited until the man had returned to his place near the fire. Then and only then did he retreat, back to his burrow, while the man, born of the darkness, bent over the scrolls that opened before him. At first, the pages seemed empty, the writings so faint they were barely legible, sighing, the man removed something from his pocket, the clink as it rolled on the roughly hewn oak table a telling thing. A clue to what it was.

Lighting another candle, he placed it next to the first. The wax dripping from it as he tilted it slightly to one side, cursing softly as the hot liquid pooled on the table, spattering on his hand as he shook it off, onto the yellowed parchment spread in front of him. It didn't matter. The fact that the ancient script was proving difficult to translate only meant that he would have to find another way to unlock its secrets. He leaned forward, focusing his thoughts, channeling them.

A vision of a young woman with long, dark, auburn hair, big brown eyes peering up at him in fright as she was pulled through the gateway after him—

The one known as the *Other* jumped up, startled, as recognition dawned. He knew her face! Drawing his woolen cloak tightly about his shoulders, he hurried outside, into the forest, his staff gripped tightly in his hand. The dull thrumming sound it made inaudible to mere mortal's ears.

Yes, he thought to himself, as he chose his way carefully through the dense underbrush, the thorns and thistles tearing at his robes as he pushed his way through them. Yes, he would seek her out, the woman known as Leah, and when he found her…

§ § § § §

The bear fell back, puzzled. Shaking his head from side to side, he snorted, the sound loud even to his own ears.

The Hunter turned, his attention focused on the bear, before swinging it back to Leah.

She was standing alone at the edge of the wood, her gaze turned toward the dark shadows that shaded the inner depths of the forest, her expression wistful.

The Mukwa was beside him, silent and watchful, his small brown eyes registering nothing of what he sensed. The Hunter's eyes narrowed angrily.

What was she doing exposing herself to unseen watchers?

The Hunter drew himself up to his full height, his black eyes glittered dangerously as he started toward Leah, then, thinking better of it, paused. Whatever had startled the woman and the wolf was gone. The shadows cast by the moon's wan light traced indefinable patterns along the leaf-strewn floor, the musty odor that wafted upward the only indication that something had passed this way recently.

The Hunter turned his head to one side, deep listening. Yes, something had come through upon the endless wind—something unseen.

He took a step toward the forest, its thick canopy of trees a shield for those who sought sanctuary within. For a moment he thought he saw something. A shadow perhaps? Then there was nothing save the faint prickling of the unknown as it moved up his spine.

Sparing a quick glance at Leah, he noticed for the first time how pale she looked, the dark circles that rimmed her eyes making her appear even more fragile. He knew she wouldn't show her discomfort, at least not to him. Aware that the wolf watched him, her unusual silver eyes with their swirling depths missing little, he spoke softly.

"Come." He spoke the word gently, turning her back toward the fire and the meat roasting upon the spit. If he could do nothing else this night, he would at least make sure she ate. For a moment, he thought she would argue with him, but she merely looked up at him, her expression guarded, then walked past him, toward the fire and the food.

Leah felt guilty as she ate the succulent meat; she knew the warrior must be just as hungry as she was. They had eaten nothing but dried berries mixed sparingly with bits of dried meat, a few greens, and some fruit for the last few days; already her clothes were looser, not to mention torn and filthy.

She sighed, the sound carrying to the wolf who watched her from the edge of the shadows. Thoughts, feelings, passed between them while the warrior remained where he was, gazing into the darkness, looking for shadows that were not there.

§ § § § §

From his place within the center of the night, the *unseen* watched from the shadows as the big warrior hunkered down. His weapons within easy reach. Once, glancing his way, the warrior had half risen, his dark gaze probing the darkness. The entity that had been forced to serve as a sentinel rode higher, the night wind swirling about The

Hunter as he glanced upward, the sudden chill causing him to draw his fur-lined cape more snugly about his broad shoulders.

A short distance away, the silver-white wolf stood, her senses tingling. The watcher relaxed. This one he knew. It had been he who had allowed her passage through the gate he had once guarded against unwanted intrusion for the *Other*.

Drifting closer, he caressed her back. The night wind aiding him as she tensed, alert, her strange silver eyes catching the slight movement that most, not born to the forest would ever see.

Tilting her head to one side, Chera acknowledged the Ancient One. Acknowledged the guardian of the forest and his right to be there. The soft huff-huff nearby telling her the Mukwa also sensed what rode upon the night wind. Above them. Around them. The sound of sodden leaves being displaced by tiny feet distracted her, but only momentarily as the source was recognized. The little ones, the earth diggers. The heartbeat of the earth.

The silent breeze caused the fire to flare brightly, the sparks rising, carrying high into the inky blackness that was held at bay only by the flames that surged upward and out. Leah pulled back, the sudden surge of heat searing her arms as she rose quickly to her feet.

"Something calls to us. Something ancient." Chera was standing once more at the edge of the shadows, her silvery eyes catching the fire's light, reflecting it back like a mirror against the darkness that was the night. The otherworldly glow not altogether lost on the warrior who watched from a distance. His knife already unsheathed, the blade warming against his palm.

She looked down then up. Beneath her feet the movements had stilled. The big wolf took a step back, masking her surprise. They were there—dozens of them. Chera's eyes narrowed as the eldest of the earth diggers approached. Wizened, bent nearly double from living turnings beyond count, the Ancient One stopped in front of her, the soft humming of the staff he carried speaking for him as he held it out in front of him.

Chera took another step back, startled at the force of the blue-white light that emanated from something so small, her nostrils scenting the night for anything untoward. She had to be sure. She reached out to Leah, her thoughts heard.

The fine hairs at the back of Leah's neck prickled as something brushed past her. Sparing a backward glance at The Hunter, she moved forward, toward Chera and the Old One. She drew in her

breath, held it, then released it. Whatever apprehension she felt dis-
solving as the night wrapped itself gently around her.

Then there was nothing. Nothing save the warrior, who now
moved slowly toward her, a bear, a wolf, and the little ones.

The smallest of the four-legged clans.

They had come to warn her, and as she listened, she felt the
strength of the man who had moved from the shadows to stand beside
her, his breath warm upon her cheek as he stood close, offering her
his strength as he looked down at her.

She knew him. Knew he watched and listened. His mind, at least
partially accepting the gift he had been given. The fire snapped as the
flames caught, taking hold. The dry tinder beneath the wood placed
there moments before throwing the sparks upward into the night that
wasn't the night, and the *Unseen,* born upon the breath of it spoke—
hoping the words would be heard.

§§§§§

Jerome whistled, the sound high pitched and piercing. He didn't
bother to wait for an answer for he knew his warriors were close by.

He had been following the trail upward for hours, the snowy white
owl trudging steadily ahead of him, the staff he carried pointing the
way. The strange humming sound it made trailing off periodically
into silence, then becoming deafening as they once more traversed the
winding path that led upward into the high places.

Jerome sighed resignedly as he watched his friend pick his way
carefully along the rocky trail. Every so often, he would pause, his
head tilted to one side, listening. The forest warrior shook his head in
amusement. Of one thing he was certain, it did not seem to bother
Orith. He had come prepared, his heavy woolen cape wrapped tightly
about him, his cherrywood staff with its small burls resonating as he
picked his way carefully toward the hidden gateway.

Orith bent down to examine the rock; reaching out, he brushed at
the surface gently, the dry lichen crumbling beneath his touch as he
held his staff against the markings that had been etched so deeply
long ago.

This was once a sacred place—a place where the Old Ones had
gathered. Orith drew himself upright, the staff trailing down the side
of the rock as he turned to face Jerome. The forest warrior raised a
brow questioningly as he knelt down, his gaze going to the place
where Orith pointed. The faint humming the staff emitted telling him

they had found what they were seeking—the gateway that the Old One had sent them to protect.

Jerome reached out, placing a weather worn hand on a large grey rock, he bent slightly forward, listening. He could feel it. There. Buried beneath the rocks that had sealed the entrance turnings ago. He turned toward Orith, who met his questioning gaze with that of his own.

The Old One had been right. There had been another gateway. One that the dwellers of darkness had missed these many turnings. At any rate, *none would trespass here,* the big warrior thought to himself as he rose slowly to his feet, alerting his warriors as he did so that they were in a sacred place and that any intruders would be well met. Looking up, he shaded his eyes against the bright light as he whistled, the sound echoing through the hazy heat of the late afternoon. None would gain entrance from either side.

Jerome settled down, his back to the stone wall, his war club at his side. The leather thong looped loosely around his wrist. The shrill call of his warriors echoed in the valley below them as he watched Orith through half closed lids. The snowy white owl eagerly reading what had been written upon the rocks at the beginning.

"What is it that has been written turnings ago beyond thought?" Jerome was curious. It wasn't like Orith to not to share his thoughts. The afternoon had waned and the day had deepened, the shadows cast by the sun as it moved steadily across the sky telling the forest warrior that dusk but a few hours off. He leaned forward, the hair at the back of his neck prickling. The air that curled about him had changed.

There was a feel of the unknown lingering here, midst the rock and shrubbery.

He spared a glance around, noticing for the first time that the trees looked different; for that matter, so did everything else. Squinting up at the blue sky, he watched as the clouds skirted across the distant horizon, the silver beneath reflecting the sun's light. Jerome froze as recognition dawned, at nearly the same time Orith looked up, his amber eyes blinking in surprise.

Once of Skye. Returned to Skye.

Jerome shook his head to clear it, the moisture that ran down his craggy face dripping off his chin irritating him. As fast as he mopped his brow, it returned. Beside him Orith coughed, a gesture meant to get his attention. Jerome ignored him. His attention riveted on the cloud creature that Nickolous had helped but a few turnings past.

It moved lower, the air that surrounded him was humid. *Unnaturally so*...he thought to himself as he grew more aware of every nuance that surrounded them. He looked at Orith in surprise, the great snowy white owl returning his gaze in kind as they both felt the earth trembling beneath their feet. The sound of thunder deafening as the earth beneath them, and the sky above, changed yet again.

Jerome rose shakily to his feet, his war club lay some distance away, just out of his reach. Still dazed and a bit disoriented, he looked around for Orith and was relieved when he spotted him on a ledge that jutted slightly out of the rock face a few feet above him.

Orith was looking down at him, his expression unreadable. Beneath him, the tremors had ceased, but he could still feel the slight thrumming deep within the earth as everything returned slowly to its center. It was only as the aging elder made his way slowly down through the fallen rock and debris that now littered the path that Jerome realized what had happened. A quick glance at Orith confirmed it.

They were at the hidden gate all right, but somehow they had sifted through, to the other side.

Jerome glanced up at a sky that wasn't theirs. The Old One had said they could not follow, and yet...

The Old One had never said they could not follow the path the wolves had taken. She had said—not the same way. The still small voice whispered as Jerome remained where he was, looking at Orith, who seemed just as perplexed as he. Jerome fell silent, his intuition telling him that they were not alone. He reached down and ever so slowly retrieved his war club, his hand running the length of it.

Letting his breath out slowly, he masked his relief that at least he wasn't weaponless in a strange land. Beside him, Orith leaned heavily upon his staff. The warrior's eyes widened slightly as he gazed at the cherrywood staff with its many burls. Even from where he stood, he could feel the heat emanating from it. The power reaching out. Testing. The burls glowing softly even as they began to grow bigger.

Jerome tore his gaze away from the throbbing burls and focused on Orith, words unspoken but heard passing between them. Edging closer to the center of the living rock that was the gateway to the realms within realms, the warrior settled back, watchful as Orith placed the staff carefully beneath his robes.

There was a storm coming. The wind was rising, coming from the northeast. Even so, the coolness that swirled about them was a temporary respite from the stifling heat.

§ § § § § §

The Hunter moved away from the fire and the shadows it cast, his focus on the young woman who walked with the four- legged ones as if they were her equal. He caught the look she shot him, her face upturned in the light as she peered at him from beneath long lashes.

The one known as The Hunter looked away, suddenly uncomfortable beneath her close scrutiny, his gaze swept the area in front of them, his skin prickling as the unknown raced up the length of his spine. He spared a glance once more to where Leah stood with her companions. The fact they did not seem to be aware of anything was little comfort as he struggled to understand what it was that he was supposed to know. He turned his head slightly to one side, listening.

There was something out there. Something…

Eyes darkened as a brow arched questioningly. Voices. Whispers in the dark. The Hunter closed his eyes. Opened them. Leah was there, her hand warm on his forearm, her breath soft upon his face as she stood on tiptoe, her wide brown eyes searching his as she waited.

Waited for him to acknowledge what he already knew existed even as it embraced him, the soft sigh of the wind as it curled about him answering him.

It was everywhere. Above him. Beneath him. Below him. It surged upward, racing through layers of earth and stone. Thousands of turnings old, it had been there since the beginning.

The Hunter staggered back as Leah moved with him, her grip upon his arm firm as she saw what he saw, felt what he felt, while the air about them thickened so that it was hard to breath. In the distance thunder rumbled while the sky lit up with bolts of lightning that zigzagged against the distant horizon.

From his high place within the wind the *Unseen* watched, his presence felt by all who walked within his forest. It had been a long time—too long. As he moved swiftly away, carried by the wind to where the others waited, chained within their pitiful mortal bodies, hope surged through him.

The Hunter had heard.

14

The *Other* retraced his steps through the forest, cursing softly beneath his breath as he found the return path. The night was unusually warm, and he had removed his heavy woolen cloak, the need to hurry something that he wasn't used to.

He had thought about sending one of the watchers out in his stead, then just as quickly dismissed it. *Some things,* he guessed, you had to do yourself, and as much as he regretted allowing the woman to pass through with him, he knew it wouldn't have changed anything—knew that he would still be faced with dissention and rebellion for it was everywhere. It surrounded him like a festering sore, and it was growing.

He drew in deeply of the night and that which was in it, seeking out any nuance that would lead him to the one he sought. But the wind kept its secrets, and the earth remained silent. Finally, exasperated, the one known as the *Other* withdrew a stone from deep within the folds of his robe. Warming it in the palm of his hand, he blew softly on it, the swirling depths within the smoky quartz becoming transparent as the stone awakened from its eternal sleep.

The man looked closer, his mind opening to the voice of the stone. His by birthright, it served him and no other. As the dark head lowered, the whispered words reached out into the endless void that was the night, carried upon the unnatural wind that swirled through the forest, seeking what was needed.

§ § § § § §

The Hunter pushed Leah down as the wolf leapt past, her growled warning lost in the rush of wind that blew around them. Frustrated, Chera paced back and forth, angry that she could not fight what she could not see. She knew something was out there, could feel it. And as she peered into the shadows, she sensed something else riding the night. This one closer.

Gabriel.

The night breeze that wended its way through the forest carried the scent to them. The distant howling drawing closer as the warrior restrung his bow, tensing, readying himself for battle.

"*No.*" Small hands pulled at the warrior, his attention temporarily diverted as he stared in surprise at the small female as she tried to pull his arm down. The understanding dawning slowly as he deep listened.

Whoever, whatever, was out there was not an enemy. At least not hers, nor the wolves. He lowered the bow, but kept the arrow nocked. Beside him, Leah relaxed as she waited expectantly, her thoughts joined with that of Chera's.

As it turned out, they did not have long to wait.

§ § § § § §

Gabriel wasn't sure where he was, but he knew it wasn't Skye. After Chera had disappeared, he had sought to follow her, his instincts guiding him as he had passed through the gate, the lone sentinel that guarded it allowing him passage unhindered as he had centered himself.

He hadn't had time to ask any questions. The gateway had closed, and the sentinel had vanished, and all was as if it had never been. But it hadn't mattered, for Gabriel had caught the faint odor of something—he turned inward—reaching up and out as he focused on Chera. Unspoken thoughts raced ahead as he scented the night wind that rode fast and hard toward him, enveloping him within its embrace as he shuddered beneath its soft caress.

It wasn't an ordinary wind. He stood still, his primordial instincts shattering his forgotten memories. Blue eyes widened as the moon, white and luminescent, crested just above the tree tops, its reflection caught and held within the still shallows of the small river that flowed below him. He turned his head, listening intently to the sound of the water as it wended its way slowly around the bend sheltered by the massive oak trees.

Crouching down, he peered intently into the shadows while the wind stilled. It had been a long time.

Too long.

The sentinel pulled back, the one known as Gabriel had heard. It was enough.

Gabriel stared up into the night. The stars shone brightly against the backdrop of black velvet, while the light from the moon traced her fragile beams across the forests floor. The silver-grey wolf scented the night wind, for that is what it now was. The ancient entity was gone, but he *had* been there, Gabriel was certain of it. The feelings that it had evoked still lingered deep within his breast.

He took a tentative step forward, the path before him clear. Chera had been here; her imprint left for others to follow. Gabriel tensed as he sensed something else—Leah! The images, unexpected, assailed him. His mate walked with others also, their smell foreign to his nostrils. He searched the path before him for more signs. Something. Anything. There. In the sodden leaves that littered the ground, an imprint of a small foot. The fur along the silver-grey back rose as the familiar prickling of recognition raced up Gabriel's spine.

Something, someone, followed in the steps of the others. Something dark and dangerous, not unlike—

Blue eyes darkened as the moon's light reflected eerily within their center. The low warning growl abruptly silenced as the swirling white mist frothed across the damp ground toward him. He pulled back, wary, his instincts warning him to tread carefully. The strong musky scent stung his nostrils as a memory of a sacred place and a young man turned warrior, his sacred staff held before him, swirled before him, wraithlike.

He shook his head to clear it. The answer given. He knew this one. The *Other.*

Moments later, the big wolf took off at a fast trot, the need to find Chera and Leah the need that drove him forward as he moved deeper into the forest. The shadows that reached out to envelope him guiding him to his destination.

§ § § § §

"How far?"

"A long way. Too far for us to make it under cover of darkness." The Hunter stood looking down at the woman, his warrior's instinct warring with his emotions. He knew that there were others ahead of him at the waiting place, but it was another day's journey from where they were now. Perhaps a bit more.

If he were to travel by himself—he shrugged, knowing it was a useless thought. He couldn't leave the woman by herself; even with the wolf and Mukwa to protect her, it would go against all he had been taught. Beside him the wolf growled, the sound low and throaty and The Hunter paused, his thoughts centered in that other place. Black eyes widened as he stepped back in surprise, Chera was peering up at him, her expression questioning as Leah reached down, her hand caressing the silver-white fur.

The Hunter watched as the wolf turned her head, her strange silver eyes with their swirling golden depths looking through him, to another place that even he could not see.

The shiver that rolled slowly up his spine spread out to the tips of his fingers as he drew Leah to him, his one thought to protect her from whatever was out there—unknown—unseen. Then the night with its dark mystery surged with primitive power as the translucent mist roiled upward from the ground enveloping the warrior and the woman within its damp embrace.

Chera turned away—away from the warrior who held her young charge tightly to him. *Too tightly.* She snorted derisively while at the same time she suppressed the urge to growl. Instead, she focused on the night and what was riding upon the wind toward them. Chera stood at the edge of the forest, poised, ready for battle if need be, her senses so acute that she felt the shift in the wind before the Mukwa did.

Something, someone, was approaching. The Old One rose up slowly, scenting the night wind and that which was carried upon it. Massive shoulders bunched as he went down on all fours, his body taut as he swept the earth back and forth in front of him, his nails digging into the hard ground, the soft huff-huff as he blew the air forcefully out through his nose carrying to the warrior and the woman who stood a short distance away.

They too sensed the change in the night and even though The Hunter gripped the handle of his obsidian knife tightly, the Old One knew it would be useless against what was coming.

§ § § § §

The *Other* moved slowly, his instinct for preservation enabling him to be patient. There was, he knew, a time for everything; although his powers were beyond what most of the clans could comprehend, there were, to be sure, exceptions. He waited in the shadows, his night vision taking in the height and girth of the Mukwa.

True, he was old, but his age carried wisdom, and he was not to be underestimated—neither was his strength. Then there was the wolf. The one called Chera—a memory of a moonlit night in another realm—shadow beings—the one known as the *Fallen*—he didn't bother to wonder how she had gotten here. It wasn't important. She was a creature of the forest. He dismissed her as a threat; his eyes resting on the warrior who held the woman to him as if to protect her.

The watcher stifled a snort of disbelief. Dark eyes set in a darkly handsome face narrowed as he began to change form, the incantation cast to became one with the night. It would serve no purpose to be discovered yet. The warrior was strong for one of his kind. The *Other* could sense the underlying power that was within The Hunter—knew that its holder had not yet awakened to the gifts given. His attention focused on the young woman who peered into the darkness, her senses heightened by what she could not see.

Yes.

The *Other* leaned forward, the slight trembling of the leaves in the trees that surrounded him giving little indication as to his presence as he used the darkness to look at her. He pulled back, careful to maintain the spell lest she see him through the veil that separated them one from the other. At the same time wondering why he had not known what she was capable of that day, when he had pulled her through, after the battle between the clans and the *Fallen*.

He had merely thought her a nuisance. Something his shadow beings would easily dispose of. Dark brows furrowed as he moved further, back into the shaded spaces, his gaze once again appraising the female.

The one known as Leah was not unlike her brother, Nickolous. He who had wielded the staff given him by the warriors of Skye.

The far-off trilling that heralded the days dawning pulled the *Other* away from his thoughts. Never a lover of the light, he was not, however, as averse to it as A-Sharoon had been. He peered into the pre-dawn. Something was moving toward him, he tensed, surprised. Dark eyes focused on the frothing writhing mist that snaked its way toward him but it wasn't that which had caught his attention. No. It was something more. He started forward, then caught himself. Now, was not the time to be seen. He moved back into the shadows, waiting.

It would be a decision that he would later regret.

§ § § § § §

The big wolf leaned into the wind, her ability to *"see"* things that others could not heightened as she caught the faint movement off to the side, cloaked within the shadowed places. She started forward. Stopped. Whatever it was, it was not there now. The feeling that they were being watched still tugged at her, and she was glad he was there. The Old One, his small brown eyes seeing what she could not.

Her gaze swept over Leah while at the same time she drew in deeply of the scents that swept around her. The fur along her silver-white back bristling as she felt the rush of something evil as it swept silently by, and knew that something dark beyond remembrance had been close enough to touch them but for some reason had not.

But why? Why hadn't whatever it was that was watching, waiting, shown itself?

The thought remained unspoken as she turned toward the warrior, her thoughts reaching out to touch his. He was tense. They all were. The question went unasked as the Old One once again raised upright, his immense height allowing him to see what The Hunter could not.

The sudden howling echoed through the mist that was slowly dispersing beneath the rising sun's warmth. Then, the unasked was answered as Gabriel leapt through the remnants of the last of the white stuff that receded back, into itself. Into the emerald of the forest that had nurtured it. Something to guide. To cloak. To protect.

"Gabriel." Leah breathed the word out softly as the apparition took on form. The great wolf lowered his head in acknowledgment, his gaze swinging toward Chera, who remained where she was, silent, watchful.

She stood like that a moment longer, looking past her mate, her gaze following the last of the frothing mist. Then, there was only the silence, which deepened as the three companions from that other place joined thoughts. Words, unspoken, flowing as easily as the spoken while the warrior watched, his expression masked.

Once, he thought he could hear thoughts flowing like quicksilver between the two wolves and the small female, before dismissing it, his attention on the movement, barely discernible, deep within the darkened wood. He blinked. Whatever it was, it was gone now.

"It is good to see you, little one." Gabriel greeted Leah with his usual stoicism. Never one to openly show emotion, it was a rare thing when he did. Leah, however, had no such qualms as she engulfed him in a hug. Stepping back, she gazed at him, her emotions threatening to spill over as she wiped at the tears that ran unheeded down her face. Beside her, Chera said nothing. She didn't have to.

As Leah moved back, the Old One moved closer, out from the edge of the forest's concealing shadows, into the soft light that heralded the new days dawning. Head down, he stared warily at the newcomer, his thoughts reaching out to probe gently.

Gabriel centered himself, his thoughts guarded. The Old One (for he instinctively knew that this was an Elder of the forest, his life span and turnings outweighing his own beyond count) brought his head up, his gaze even with that of the silver-gray wolf's. Memories poured forth, entwining with Gabriel's, sharing, learning, interrupted—

"There is danger here. We must leave. Now." Leah looked up into black eyes as the warrior moved closer, his hand on his knife, the feel of the stone as it warmed beneath his touch, giving him little comfort as the cold rush of air swept around him.

The air that swirled about them was poignant, charged with unbridled power that reeked of ancient things. Leah looked from one to the other of the companions, her mind made up. Something dark had passed over them, of that there was no doubt. She shivered, despite the warmth of the morning's sun, her senses tingling.

The *Other*...

The warrior gathered his weapons. Not bothering to look back at the wolves or the Old One, he moved swiftly forward, his keen hearing telling him that Leah followed, the others close behind. It was almost too much. The knowing. But what was worse was not understanding quite what it was he was feeling; or more to the point, how to use it. At times he could almost see the thoughts that swirled about him, they reached out, entwining, merging into a cascade of colors each more brilliant than the last.

He was untaught in the ancient knowledge, and he knew it—knew that his kind had lost the vision to see the unseen. He drew in deeply of the morning air, his gaze following the path that his people had so recently taken; away from that which they could not understand and wondered at the changes that just a few short turnings had wrought.

Memories of the elder, her wisdom and quiet strength, her patience—the warrior closed his eyes briefly against the pain the memory evoked, then opened them. Leah was beside him, her large brown eyes mirroring his concern, her hand warm against his skin.

"We need to talk." The warrior nodded. His warrior's instinct telling him that he wasn't going to like what was coming next.

He was right.

§ § § § §

Cloaked deep within the spell he had cast earlier, the *Other* watched from his place of concealment. He knew now how the wolves had gotten through the gateway, and he marveled at his own negligence that had unwittingly allowed it. He had been so busy attending to other matters elsewhere that he hadn't seen the dissention within his own house. A mistake he intended not to repeat.

He was one who could command an army of darkness without fear or thought of self, yet here he was hesitating. His cold gaze swept over the young woman. Her youth was but an illusion to conceal what lie deep within. *Yes.* He focused his attention solely on her, probing her inner senses before pulling back in surprise. One black brow arched thoughtfully as he stared at her, for she had, quite simply, pushed back.

She knew he was there and was guarding herself. She was the *One.*

The one known as the *Other* reconsidered his next move and thought better of it. Not one to fight a battle unless he was sure of the outcome, he decided to return to his cavern, hidden deep within the side of the mountain. Once there, he would plan his next move. A smile curved his darkly handsome face as another thought crossed his mind. The possibilities merging into one cognizant thought as he deep listened one last time, the sounds of the forest receding behind him as he moved swiftly away, toward his cavern with its protective ruins and preternatural beings that waited for his return.

§ § § § §

The warrior was turning, his fingers tightening on the already strung bow as something brushed against him. Something unseen. The sound of primeval laughter rippled through the air, dissipating into an uncomfortable silence.

"He returns to his lair to draw more dark ones to him." Leah's voice broke through the stillness.

The Hunter looked down at her, his gaze narrowing as the silver-grey wolf with the strange blue eyes trotted to her side, the fur raised along the length of his spine. Chera was already there ahead of him. Her silver eyes with their smouldering swirling depths looking around them, her muzzle held high as she scented the air, drawing the scents of the forest to her as the warrior slowly lowered his bow.

Leah felt the caress of the cool air, fed by the nearness of the running streams as it brushed by her, startling her, while the fine hairs rose at the back of her neck.

Once, the shadowed places had frightened her. Not now. Not anymore. She leaned into the gently swirling breeze, grateful for the brief respite. It reminded her of the shaded mossy places where she had once walked beneath an indigo sky, the gentle breeze welcoming in the heat of the day. She pushed the vision away.

Standing close to the warrior, she looked up into eyes the color of obsidian. She needed him to understand what it was they faced—needed him to see what this Son of Darkness was capable of.

So many questions and none to ask. There were no answers, and yet she frowned, trying to remember what it was she had forgotten. There was something—she wasn't sure what—there—just behind her memories, layered deep within her consciousness.

No matter. She pushed the thought away, squaring too taut shoulders, the tension easing somewhat as she centered herself within her woman's place of knowing. How she wished the others were here. But they weren't.

She straightened to her full height, her focus still on the warrior who remained silent, looking down at her, his gaze unwavering. She reached out with her thoughts as the words, unspoken were heard.

The one known as The Hunter recoiled as if struck, then caught himself. The darkness that crossed his inner vision quickly displaced as he saw what the woman saw. But it was more than that. Beside her, the wolves watched, their stance protective, and for the first time he saw them as something other than feral beasts, without thought or purpose.

From the beginning their kind have protected. The warrior glanced uneasily about, unsure if it was his imagination or not. The wind grew bolder as it blew about them, the small whirling circles of dust rising as the warrior leaned forward into the wind and, without thought of self, embraced part of who he was.

"Finally, he begins to see," Chera growled, the sound low and throaty. She was close to the warrior. So close that she was nearly touching him. Her thoughts reached out. Testing. Something was coming. Something dark. She had sensed it more than once. If the *Other* were anything like A-Sharoon, then they would need all their wits about them.

She looked deep into the warriors' being. Seeking his memories, probing. Her silver eyes widened.

She turned back to her mate, her thoughts carrying to him. To the others. She turned her thoughts outward so that the others could see what she had seen.

Maybe there was hope for this two-legged one after all.

Behind her, the Old One snorted loudly. Chera paused, drawing her personal thoughts back to herself—

Then again, maybe not.

15

The sound of breaking glass as it shattered against the rock walls echoed throughout the many unused caverns that crisscrossed one another deep below the earth, while the faint smell of something putrid wafted through the cavernous room where the *Other* paced, his face dark with rage. How could he have been so complacent? One moment of neglect. One moment! The rage was so great he had to fight to control it—to unleash such a power would serve no purpose.

The darkly handsome head lowered as he stared thoughtfully at the yellowed parchment spread out in front of him, the etchings on its surface nearly indiscernible.

The passage of time had not been kind to it; the dampness of the below places even more so. The markings were faded, the fragile paper cracked and curling at the edges and in some places totally obliterated.

His frustration evident, the *Other* rose slowly from his place at the table. It was here, in this place of utter solitude, that he had labored turnings beyond count. The hidden knowledge just within reach, if he could but see with eyes of knowing.

But he couldn't. Hands the color of burnished copper reached up to prize a piece of rose quartz that was wedged tightly within one of the many crevices out. Holding it up to the fire's light, he turned it so that the light reflected through it, for there were those who believed in the power of the stone.

The very stone that now warmed and thrummed beneath his touch.

He should have recognized the woman for what she was, even before he allowed her passage beyond the gateway. If he hadn't been so eager to return from Skye—the unspoken thought remained as the silence deepened, the stone cutting deeply into his hand as he leaned forward, his gaze following the wisps of smoke that roiled up from the center of the fire's hearth.

His grip upon the stone tightened as the red liquid dripped slowly from between his fingers, the shattering sound of the stone as it slid from nerveless fingers, unto the flat rocks at his feet startling the sentries who guarded the cavern's entrance.

It was some moments before he moved away from the shattered remnants of the stone. Away from the shadows that moved slowly toward him from their place of concealment deep within the depths of the darkened places, where they had stayed, unseen, waiting for their master to call.

§ § § § § §

The world as the sentinel knew it had shifted yet again. Ever-changing, the power within the power waited—waited for those who would come forth to help. Even so, it was a hard thing. Waiting.

Once transformed back to what he had been, there were none to see, or feel, for to most his passage amongst them was no more than the faint touch of the breeze as it brushed against their cheek. He had done what he could to awaken their senses and now he waited—waited for the awakening.

The wind shifted, and he with it. Beneath him, he watched as one, like yet unlike himself, begged entrance to the cavern where once he had walked in a body not in his own form, but forced upon him so that he could do the Dark Lord's bidding. He brushed against the watcher then quickly withdrew, disappointed. He had hoped that on some level the one who had once been like himself would know he was there. That he was offering him hope, for none of them had served the *Other* willingly.

He shifted yet again, his intent to return to the forest warrior and the one called Orith, pausing at the last moment, for he had caught something—a flicker of remembrance in the watcher's eyes—eyes that saw nothing. Eyes that saw everything. He looked around as if seeking and for a moment longer waited, hoping. But the sentinel, he who was once one of the unseen, quickly resumed his posture, his only duty to serve the dark one.

The *Other.*

The leaves on the poplar trees danced in the sudden wind that brushed against them, the sound carrying in the silence that spread swiftly across the forest floor. A warning to the clans to prepare.

§ § § § §

Jerome moved cautiously, his warrior's heart missing little as he searched the ground in front of him for a sign. Anything that would tell him the others had passed this way. There was nothing. Standing there, his war club thronged loosely at his side he reached out, spreading his feet wide so that he melded with his surroundings, his ability to sift through earth and rock to seek out the smallest of the guardians—the little ones. Earth diggers who no longer lived in the light, they had long ago taken it upon themselves to guard the sacred places below.

The unexpected silence startled him. He crouched down, using his broad hands to dig through the soil. He pressed himself against the dampness, listening. There was nothing.

The warrior of the forest pushed himself up, balancing himself he leaned back, crossing his arms across his chest as he did so. Something was wrong. Where there should have been movement beneath him there was nothing. The stillness made him wary, and he drew his war club to his side, preparing himself.

Orith was so busy trying to interpret the ancient script that he nearly missed it. The first small fluttering of apprehension deepening as he brought his head up, his cape falling back over his shoulders as his staff warmed beneath his touch, the burls within the wood glowing as the snowy owl straightened slowly.

He stood where he was, unmoving. The knowing that there would be nothing there even if he turned did not make it any easier to remain calm as he reached deep within to his place of knowing, searching for an answer.

Jerome centered himself. The forest warrior could sense the entity within the air that surrounded him and, although unsure as to the guardian's intent, he nonetheless acknowledged it. Gifted with the knowledge passed down by the Ancients, the big warrior opened himself to the other's presence, the unasked asked, the answer given. Jerome turned away, unbelieving, his thoughts reaching out to Orith.

"We must tread carefully, for we are no longer in Skye, and everything is different here. Even what is above." Orith spoke to no one in particular.

The forest warrior remained where he was, looking down at the elder curiously as the warm breeze wended its way around them.

Orith leaned forward, holding his staff in front of him; it hummed with a new intensity. The small burls contained within its center were pulsating with a power that hadn't been there before.

The warrior of the forest pulled back, startled at what he saw. The staff, which Orith had been gifted with after the battle in the cavern when they had defeated Lord Nhon, had been new, untried. It had grown with its holder, its power limited, but now—

Jerome paused as the watcher pushed against his senses yet again. Words spoken, heard. Acknowledged, accepted. The others, the sentinels—

"Orith?" Jerome spun around, the words pricking along his spine as he searched the forest, his gaze seeking out the hidden places and the shadows that wished to remain as they were, undisturbed. Beside him, Orith remained calm, his staff held out before him, pulsating with a blue-white light that was nearly translucent.

The warrior leaned into the wind that blew from the four corners, the question unasked as he opened himself to the power within the power, gifted to those who allowed themselves to see.

§ § § § §

Leah felt the ebb and flow of the wind as it flowed over her, beside her, the warrior, the one known as The Hunter moved closer, his eyes scanning the fringes of the forest for anyone, anything, that would threaten the woman who stood next to him.

As the shadows had lengthened and deepened into late afternoon, they had journeyed deep into the forest's depths; not speaking, their silence their protection against what they could not see, the warrior and the woman walking close together, the wolves in front, the Old One lumbering behind. It would be much later, when the night deepened about them, causing them to stop, that they would speak of things that would change their world as they knew it, yet again.

"The warrior protects her."

Chera spared a quick glance at her mate, her look of distain caught as Gabriel looked at her in surprise.

"She is a young woman, Chera, it is good that she has found such a warrior to protect her." Gabriel paused long enough to nuzzle his mate gently. "We will not always be there—"

Chera lowered her head, quietly acknowledging her mate's words. He was right, and she knew it. She let her breath out slowly, knowing that the words that were left unsaid were hers to think on.

Gabriel knew her better than anyone. She had to let go and trust the two-legged one's intent; he had after all, protected Leah this far and kept her safe.

Without realizing he was doing it, his thoughts drifted back to that long ago moonlit night in the clearing. The battle for Skye was in its beginnings, and he and Chera had been called from the forest to protect two small ones thrown from another time.

Leah had been little, a young girl then, trying to protect her brother, Nickolous, with a fierceness that had nearly rivaled Chera's need to see her safe. Nickolous was younger, but his wisdom had belied his age, for he held within himself the memories of his forebears.

Gabriel closed his eyes, remembering. Like Chera, who had imprinted on Leah, he too had made a choice. The boy, so quickly turned to man beneath the watch of Skye, had been the catalyst who had helped to change their world. Chosen at the beginning by the elders. The seven. He had earned the right to be named *warrior.*

Yes, the big wolf thought to himself, the girl *had* become a woman and just as Chera would have had to allow her own cub passage into the world, so then must she allow Leah to do the same.

"Do we chance a fire?" Leah stood, looking up at the warrior, trying to keep her teeth from chattering. They were in the middle of a clearing, surrounded by red cedar trees. The warrior didn't hesitate as he nodded assent, for the night carried an unusual chill, and they were safe here, for it was a sacred place. He breathed in deeply of the air, the tension easing from his body. He knew this place. He had spent most of his youth here, the elders teaching him to listen... The warrior frowned, his finely arched brows drawing together as he wondered at the sudden emotions that pressed against his senses.

Where had that come from? The warrior remained where he was, his mind racing as he glanced surreptitiously down at the mere slip of a girl who stood beside him—she was more than that, and he knew it. She was awakening memories within him, along with other emotions he was trying to ignore.

Suddenly uncomfortable, he turned away. Away from the one called Leah. Away from the curious gaze of the others, the four-legged ones. Kneeling, he removed two pieces of flint from a small leather bag tied at his waist and began the task of making the fire.

Leah watched as the first sparks caught in the dry punk, the small plume of smoke quickly becoming a flame that licked its way eagerly upward, easily jumping unto the dry sticks that had been gathered and placed over the rotted wood that was tinder dry.

It wasn't long before the fire was arching upward into the starry night and she was kneeling beside it, grateful for the warmth it offered.

"This one you call the *Other,* we must guard ourselves against his deceit." The warrior's voice, so close, startled her, and she turned so quickly that she lost her balance. Strong arms caught her and held her as she looked into the warrior's face. He had, she thought almost absently, beautiful eyes.

She tried to pull back, out of his arms, away from the unease that his near proximity brought to her already muddled senses. From somewhere deep within the dark that encircled the small flames of the fire she heard Chera's softly growled warning.

The warrior ignored it. He was growing used to Chera's protective-ness toward Leah, and his instincts told him she would not attack. Still, he released Leah, but slowly, his hands running down the length of her arms to grasp her hands. Still holding them, he studied her face in the flickering light. Even by his clan's standards, she was beautiful.

He remained where he was, staring down at her thoughtfully, his black eyes betraying nothing of what he felt, his thoughts guarded as Leah pulled gently away. Her attention now on the fire, she knelt down, her hair spreading over one shoulder so that her face was partially concealed.

The warrior watched as she placed another dry stick within the fire's center, the flames flaring against the cedar. While the wolves moved closer, the Old One remained where he was, partially concealed within the nights shadow.

The warrior straightened, his hands running the length of his long bow, his thoughts centered elsewhere. He knew the dangers the night brought to those unused to it. Alert for anything untoward, he settled back to watch and wait.

Leah sat close, gathering the warmth to her as she stared into the flames, absently brushing at the little night stingers who welcomed the darkness with its cooling mists and dampness. Well aware that the warrior still watched, she kept her head down, her attention caught and held by the glowing embers nestled deep within the center of the fire.

Chera was there immediately as thoughts, memories fused. She, better than anyone understood the emotions that Leah was feeling for, she had lived through many of them with her.

§ § § § § §

"The night deepens little one—"

"I know. I know." Leah raised her head, pulling her gaze away from the fire's mesmerizing depths. Standing, she turned to face the warrior who remained where he was, his expression guarded. Behind her, she knew the others watched curiously, and she knew she was on her own now.

Chera and Gabriel would guard her with their lives, as would the Old One. The warrior, too. She shook her head to clear it.

"I just did not hear that—"

"—Yes, you did." Leah looked into black eyes that glinted in the shadows cast by the flickering light. The warrior was staring at her. Was it his words that had made their way into her deepest thoughts? She straightened her shoulders, at the same time she pulled the fur-lined cape more tightly about her, fastening it at her neck. She felt chilled even though she was standing close to the fire.

"It's not the night, with its unseen watchers, that makes you cold with the fear of the unknown. It's him." The voice whispered from somewhere deep within her subconscious as the fire, fanned by the night wind sparked, the tiny embers biting as they brushed against her exposed skin.

She pulled away toward the shadows as the warrior watched from beneath shuttered lids, his expression unreadable. Folding her legs beneath her, Leah curled up in the crook of an ancient red cedar, its gnarled roots exposed over time by the elements, forming a perfect place to rest. Wrapping the cape more tightly about her, she tucked it beneath her. The warrior did not move, and she shifted restlessly.

Might as well get it over with, Leah thought as she looked up into the starlit night. The wind had shifted, and with it the direction of the fire. The Hunter was watchful, his black eyes revealing nothing of what he was thinking.

Leah reached out, her thoughts probing his, the silence between them deepening as the warrior stayed where he was, not moving, saying nothing, but deep listening, then, "What of the *Other?*" The Hunter spoke softly. So softly that Leah barely heard him. She pulled the fur-lined cape more tightly about her shoulders, trying to bury herself within its warmth—the chill she felt had nothing to do with the night or the breeze wending its way softly around her.

"He is, I think, more dangerous than A-Sharoon. Her? She was as cold as winter's breath. Deadly. But him? He is different; more so because he deceives. His appearance is misleading." Leah stared straight ahead as she spoke, the words low and measured.

"*That One?* I know very little of except that he exudes an unnatural warmth. When I was pulled through the *gate* with him, I had no control. As hard as I tried to remain hidden to allow him passage, away from me, away from the others, I could not." Her eyes, luminous even in the half-light, glistened with unshed tears at the remembering of those she had left behind. Painful memories. Still, Leah pushed the rising emotions down, her voice carrying to the others who listened a short distance away.

"What I can tell you is that his sister holds the darkness to her like a shroud. She immerses herself in it. Revels in it." Leah paused long enough in the telling to laugh bitterly, her voice carrying upward, swept by the night's warm breeze to the silent watcher, who hovered unseen above them.

"The light? The light was her enemy, her machinations changing from one moment to the next so that we could barely keep ahead of her—but him? His warmth draws others to him, unwillingly they come, like a moth drawn to a light…" Leah's voice trailed off into the silence, then there were only the two of them. The warrior, who remained where he was, staring thoughtfully down at her, his steady gaze betraying nothing of what he felt, and the young woman. Both of whom were lost within their own thoughts. Seeing this, the others, Chera, Gabriel, and the Mukwa, withdrew further into the night's shadows, giving those of the two-legged clan their privacy.

§ § § § §

Jerome tensed, his grip firm on his war club. The sudden onset of night had brought things with it that had made him wary, his warrior's instinct warning him that all was not as it should be, and so he waited, watchful.

Orith bent low over the runes inscribed within the rock. His ability to decipher what had been written there turnings before his own existence had come into being, a gift he was grateful for. His thoughts on the task before him, he was startled by the forest warrior's sudden movement as something brushed past him, the warrior's heavy club finding its mark as the thing, crushed, gurgled, its last breath expelled in a soft sigh.

"What is it?" Orith asked as he stood looking down at the thing at his feet. It had no shape. Not even a face. Where there should have been legs there were only stubs of a sort, the mid section thin, the neck even more so. The only prominent feature was the fangs, which protruded from a lipless mouth. Shuddering despite himself, Orith turned to look at the forest warrior, his gaze sweeping their surroundings as he did so, his instincts warning him to be more diligent.

"It reeks of dark magic." Jerome used his war club to push the thing away from him, at the same time deep listening, but the forest remained quiet. Too quiet. Jerome remained where he was for a few moments more, his senses reaching out, probing the night and what was in it. Still nothing. He used a big hand to wipe the sweat from his brow, then, frowning, knelt down, his fingers splayed across the hardened earth, his mind focused on what lay beneath his feet. The earth diggers. The little ones. The watchers of the hidden places.

They were warning him.

The warrior stood, pushing Orith behind him as he did so, the hair on the back of his neck prickling as he stared into the darkness. They were not alone. The silence that wrapped itself about them warned of danger.

The war club struck with deadly accuracy. Behind him, Orith struggled with yet another of the formless things, his staff flaring, the shrill shriek of the thing dying to a shuddering sigh as the wind carried the scent of something unclean to them. Jerome sensed the next one to his left, his weapon unerringly finding its mark as Orith held the staff high, its glow against the backdrop of the night reflecting eerily off the rocks behind them as the night quickened and the unseen enemy was revealed.

Orith saw the thing as it approached; head low, the body twisted unnaturally, its foam flecked mouth working soundlessly as red eyes peered up through a darkness that threatened to overtake his senses. The staff was resonating beneath his touch, the burls pulsing along its length, the wood stretching, growing, as the creature crouched, ready to pounce.

Orith drew himself up, his ability to see through the shadows that were more than what they seemed coming to the fore as his instincts heightened. And his instincts were telling him that the thing that crouched before him was not what it seemed, that it hadn't always been like this. The elder drew in his breath sharply as the thing lunged, its misshapen forearm with its sharp claws sweeping upward as it aimed for its quarry's stomach. At the same time that the staff flared blue-white, Jerome's war club found its mark.

"There. In the shadows, there are more of them." Orith was peering into the night, his ability to *see* more acute than that of the warrior who stood beside him, his frustration evident.

"They're waiting. Gauging..." Jerome's voice trailed off as he squinted, trying to bring the shadowy forms into focus, but they remained where they were. Neither moving forward nor retreating, their dark forms barely discernible, the dull gleam of their eyes giving away their place of concealment.

"They're waiting for something—someone," Jerome muttered beneath his breath as the soft light that trailed across the forest's floor faded, the moon obscured by dark clouds that had not been there but moments before.

Orith clutched his staff tightly, the soft sound of it resonating, changing.

The burls glowed brighter, their centers swirling as the staff warmed beneath the elder's touch. Aware that the night had eyes, he waited for the staff to change yet again. Quietly acknowledging the power within the wood that had lived before them all, he held it in front of him, the heat resonating from it, traveling through him so that, for a time, the two became one.

16

Jerome tensed, readying himself as first one, then another, of the shadowy creatures crept out from the shadows, bellies low to the ground, their soft growls resonating as they focused on the light from the staff and the one who held it. Jerome hefted his war club, bouncing it off the hard earth, the sound carrying to those in front. The shapeless form paused; its eyes glowed eerily as it peered up at the forest warrior. Almost too late, the warrior realized that it was not him the thing was looking at, but something behind him.

The prickling sensation that curved up his spine as he spun slowly around warned him that something dark and deadly stood there, just out of his reach.

He was right.

§ § § § § §

Gabriel moved cautiously through the dense undergrowth, the sticky brambles embedding themselves deeply into his fur. Something—someone was out there, watching, waiting. He raised his head, scenting the night wind, the faint odor that wafted toward him indefinable, beside him Chera paused, the fur along her back rising as she caught the far off sounds of battle. The battle cry that wafted through the inky blackness of the night familiar.

Jerome.

The wind had shifted. Bits of debris, leaves, moldy and smelling of decay and earth, danced across the moonlit path, to fall aimlessly into the ditches that lined either side. The large emerald ferns that rose

145

majestically out of the black soil catching them, holding them. The wind shifted again. The dead leaves, swept upward by the sudden gusts dropped to earth, tumbling over and over to blanket one another at the bottom of the gully.

Leah stopped so abruptly that the warrior walking behind her barely had enough time to stop. He stood staring down at her, his dark brows drawn together, his forehead creased in a frown as he slowly unsheathed his knife, careful to remain silent, his skin prickling as the breeze swept around him. He knew instinctively that whatever the wolves had sensed, the woman had also, while he was unsure—and it irritated him.

He leaned forward, his dark eyes peering into the night, his sharp hearing picking up the faint sounds of battle. Beside him the woman had gone still, her face white, a sharp contrast against the blackness that now swelled around them.

"Jerome." The words were breathed out so softly that they were barely heard.

Then Chera was there, her presence lending strength as Gabriel, his head high, searched the night, his eyes missing little, his silhouette against the backdrop of the forest a silent challenge to any watchers who thought to catch them unaware. The Mukwa moved closer as Leah centered her thoughts, calming herself so that the others could hear. She turned to the warrior, her face upturned in the shadowy light cast by the moon and spoke, her voice carrying to the others.

"Help them."

§ § § § § §

Gabriel ran, his instincts guiding him as the sounds of battle grew louder. He knew Chera was not far behind, the sounds of her passage through the forest carrying to him even as the night echoed with the sounds of battle.

As he burst through the mass of tangled shrubbery into the small clearing, his roar of challenge was met by something unimaginable. He shook his head to clear it as he rolled, his hind legs kicking upward as his jaws locked on his advisory's throat, the low moaning the thing made cut off as he flung its body to one side, while at the same time seeking out another. Beside him Chera's roar of outrage filled the night as she met one of the creatures mid-air, the thing dying before it hit the ground.

And still they came.

"There are too many. Help *them.*" Leah watched in horror as the night filled with the shrieks of the dying and the living. The warrior grabbed her, his arm encircling her waist as he pushed her behind him, pressing her down so that she was partially concealed behind the dense bushes that grew so abundantly about them.

"Down. Stay. There." His black eyes glittered dangerously. In one fluid movement, he brought his bow up, aiming, the shaft of the arrow already released as it found its mark as just as quickly another was put into place, the quiver quickly emptied. Unsheathing his knife he stood, legs apart, his warrior's stance challenging as he beckoned, his challenge clear, the sharp two sided obsidian stone cutting a deadly swath as he stood in front of the woman, his need to protect her something that even he could not understand.

Leah stayed where she was, her breathing shallow, her heart beating painfully in her chest as the shadowy forms leapt from their hidden places, the shrill shrieks they emitted from formless mouths hurting her ears.

Aware that the warrior stood between her and the attackers, using his body as a shield, protecting her, gave little comfort as the night closed about her, holding her tightly within its dark embrace. She put her hands over her ears, rocking her body forward as she flattened herself against the cold earth trying to block out the sounds. The need to center herself overwhelming as she went inside herself, to her woman's place of knowing, her soft keening cry rising up, to be grasped by the unseen and carried to the elders who watched from their hidden places.

§ § § § §

Jerome stood with his back to the gateway; beside him, Orith, exhausted and coughing from overexertion, drew on an inner strength that amazed the forest warrior. Together they were holding the creatures at bay—barely. The big warrior knew the elder was nearly at the end of his strength and that more help was needed. Peering into the darkness, his warrior's vision seeking, he pulled back, shocked.

Beside him, Orith stiffened as he glimpsed what the forest warrior saw, hidden within the shadows—they were legion—Jerome drew in deeply of the night air, his grip on his war club tightening as his body tensed, readying for another battle; this one uncertain. Feeling a soft brush of warmth against his arm, he glanced down. The elder was looking straight ahead, his focus on what approached, but there was no tension in his body, nothing to indicate that this battle might be their last.

Like most of the clans of the forest, he accepted his fate and whatever it brought.

Orith looked up, meeting the forest warrior's gaze evenly, his staff flaring blue-white as the night gave up the hidden places, the skulking forms creeping slowly forward, their intent to destroy those who guarded the gate.

§ § § § §

Jerome. Orith—

Leah reached out, grasping nothing but cold empty air. She could see them and they were in danger. She tried to rise, failed. Strong arms pulled her up, the warrior's breath warm against her cheek as he held her tightly against him.

Around him, around them, there was chaos. Bodies littered the ground, while the wounded moaned, most staying where they were, their wounds so great it would be only a matter of time before they ceased to be. The more fortunate ones who could, were crawling or moving as quickly as their wounds would allow, back to the darkened places that once again concealed them.

"Where are they, the ones you seek?" The warrior's brows drew together, dark eyes glittered dangerously as he tried to piece everything together—to put everything where it was supposed to be. He knew there were others here. Strange ones like the two wolves who had forged on ahead, their voices rising, carried upon the restless wind as they sought their quarry.

The warrior's eyes widened slightly as the Old One moved closer, his hot breath rising in the night air as he opened his mouth, his fangs bared as he suddenly rose up, his massive paws swiping at something the warrior had missed. The dull thud a reaffirmation to the warrior that he had been careless.

The Mukwa went down on all fours, the vibration as he hit the earth with his forepaws an unspoken acknowledgment of his strength.

The Hunter nodded, grateful that he had remained nearby, for he knew it was not for his benefit, but the woman's who stood next to him, her wide eyes looking up into his, her small hands pressing against his chest, her whispered words reaching him as he lowered his head, aware that he wasn't the only one there to hear.

He raised his head just as quickly. The distant howling telling him what he already knew. Whatever—whoever—it mattered not. The wolves were in full cry, and that could mean just one thing...

"*Go.*" Leah pushed him away from her, her eyes luminous as she wiped at the moisture that threatened. She blinked, rubbing her eyes as she pushed down the rising emotions. "Go. I'll follow. The Old One will protect my path from the others." Leah nodded at the bodies, her meaning clear, for even as she spoke, the warrior had begun moving silently among the still forms, gathering his arrows, placing them in the quiver at his back. Reaching the forest's edge, he paused, sparing a look back, his gaze locking with that of the Old One who stood beside Leah, his expression guarded.

The warrior reached out, his thoughts probing gently as he eased his knife out from its sheath. He had to make sure—had to know that what he saw—what he felt—was true.

"Go. She will be as safe as if she were my own cub."

The warrior nodded. It was enough.

Leah watched as the warrior took off at a steady trot through the forest, her mind reeling with the knowledge that Jerome and Orith were here, somewhere close. She held her hand to her nose as she searched through her pockets for a handkerchief; the stench was nearly unbearable. Beside her, the Old One shifted his weight so that he was standing closer to her, his scent strong in her nostrils.

Leah didn't even hesitate as she leaned into him, her hands caressing the length of his back. She knew what he was doing. He was putting his scent on her so that any who followed would think that they followed the Mukwa. The bear. Most certainly not a young woman with the Old One as a protector.

§ § § § §

"Chera—" The warning was cut off as something flew past Gabriel's head, the rush of air carrying the putrid smell of death to him as the big wolf swerved sharply to his left. The night filled with sound as he zigzagged through the bushes, hoping to elude the predator that rode upon the edge of the night wind above him.

As it was, he nearly missed the skulking form who watched him from its hiding place, off to the side. The thing's dull, lifeless eyes glinting strangely, even in the wavering light that seeped through the tangled underbrush. The stifled sounds it made as he crushed it of little consequence to him as he tossed it aside, never once faltering as he continued to run, his instincts guiding him toward the blue-white light that beckoned.

Behind him, Chera followed, her footfalls on the earth echoing on the hard ground as she paced herself. Her strange silver eyes with their golden depths searching the darkened places for unseen things.

§ § § § §

The staff was tiring, the power it contained nearly depleted.

Orith was weary; the incantations he had cast were having little effect on the things that just kept coming at them. Inwardly he prayed for a miracle, even as he struck down yet another of the dark creatures that he knew belonged to the *Other.*

The knowing did little to help him as he used the staff as a weapon, the howl of pain the creature emitted somehow satisfying. *If,* he thought wryly to himself as his own strength began to ebb—*If* this was to be his last moments of knowing, he would go down fighting with whatever he had left.

Orith swung the staff again; it no longer glowed. The burls had shrunk back to their center and were no more than dark circles embedded with the lighter hues of the wood. Whatever power it had once contained was spent.

Orith swung it once more, the sound of the wood as it cracked hurting his ears as he realized what had happened. He threw the staff from him. It had broken in two; the pieces, jagged and weak, clattered against the hard ground at his feet. Pushing them aside, he let his cloak fall as he accepted his fate, knowing that he could not change things.

Shrugging indifferently, he turned to face the beast as it slunk toward him, its feral face upturned in the slivers of moonlight that danced through the trees, its yellow eyes with their small iridescent centers gloating as it crouched, preparing to jump.

Orith hesitated, but only for a moment, his vision going into the thing's center. The darkness that dwelled within its heart telling him that it was lost even to itself, for the master it served was Darkness. Beside him, the warrior of the forest tensed, readying himself. They were penned in against the rocks, and their only way out was a gateway that to unknowing eyes did not exist.

Jerome stared out into the darkness that was not the night, his mind seeking, while above him the unseen watched. As the wind brushed against his face he leaned into it, his warrior's sight probing, reaching out so that he saw what was behind it. Things with no identity floated in front of his blurred vision as he blinked, rubbing his eyes as he did so. Something—someone—was interfering with his warrior's sight. He looked down at Orith.

The snowy owl was tiring.

The journey *between* had taken its toll on his already scarred body, and he marveled that his friend still stood. A little beyond them, the remnants of the staff lay; the warmth and power had ebbed out of it so that it had grown cold. Idly, the big warrior wondered what Orith would do now, for it had never occurred to him that this would be their last journey together.

He looked down once more; Orith was turning toward him, looking up, his amber eyes speaking what his heart could not as the wind carried the sound through the night...

§ § § § § §

Gabriel saw the beast as it reared up, readying itself for the attack, its prey unwavering in front of it, his howled challenge thrown out, accepted. The thing turned, its attention momentarily diverted. It was enough. Chera leapt past, her fangs embedding themselves deeply in a body that was putrid and just as quickly flipped the body away from her, the sound of death so familiar that she didn't even flinch, but met the next one with anticipation.

Strengthened by the wolves sudden and unexpected appearance, Jerome moved forward, his massive frame in front of Orith as he protected him, his club meting out its own punishment for those foolish enough to get within range. And still they came. Pouring forth from their hidden places into the clearing, more than before, their numbers swelling as the wolves tore at the very heart of them.

"Stay—here—behind—the—rocks." Jerome grated out from between clenched teeth as he swung Orith unceremoniously around before placing him behind a large granite boulder. Orith nodded mutely. He was exhausted, and he knew his strength was ebbing. He would remain where he was, his silence his promise as the forest warrior turned away, his club already striking out.

His chest heaving with exertion, Jerome turned to face the otherworld hoard, his heart racing. He had thrown the prayer out and, even though he could hardly believe what he was seeing, the proof was there, in front of him. Gabriel and Chera, warriors of heart. Their courage and strength renewed him.

Pushing aside his exhaustion and weariness he stood, his massive trunk-like legs wide apart, his war club drawing a line in the earth in front of him. As his gaze caught that of Gabriel, he smiled, and the big wolf acknowledged what he saw there, buried deep within the forest green eyes that had seen endless turnings of change—

Let them come, it mattered not, they were part of the forest, and their cry had been heard. Gabriel nodded assent. He understood.

§ § § § §

The Hunter followed the path the wolves had taken, his instincts guiding him as the sounds of battle drew him steadily onward. His mind on what was in front of him, he didn't feel the brush of the wind as it soared past him, the unseen ones presence something that he had not yet learned to recognize. Somewhere behind him he knew that the Old One and Leah followed. His focus now on what lay ahead of him, he burst into the clearing, his arrow swiftly finding its mark as the creature howled its outrage.

Momentarily diverted, the attackers swung their attention toward the newcomer while Jerome used the opportunity to move forward. Placing his feet firmly apart, he bowed his head, centering himself, his thoughts reaching out as he went to the sacred place of the warriors, asking them to give aid—hoping that his prayers were heard.

They were.

The Hunter twisted sideways, turning at the same time, his arm coming up, the swift downward slash of his double-edged obsidian knife cutting a deadly swath through nearly formless shapes. Memories burst forth as a thousand images assailed him, and he saw what had been at the beginning, his inner vision seeing what lay behind him and before him.

"Quickly, to your left." Chera's voice, the words clearly spoken, gave warning as the warrior ducked. The creature snarled its outrage as it landed in a tangled heap at The Hunter's feet. He turned instinctively, twisting as he did so, his knife swinging up and out as leathery wings brushed against his face. The sudden wetness temporarily blinding him as he brushed it away, before reaching out, his hands seeking, his grip tightening on his knife that he held in front of him, his eyes glittering dangerously as he sought out another.

The challenge thrown out, met, the wolf's voice, low and throaty, giving her approval as she slipped away into the shadows.

Moments later, the cries of those hidden within were stifled as Chera moved swiftly in and out, her voice rising to match that of her mates as he joined her in the hunt.

Jerome flung the unclean beast away from him, the thing's stench nearly unbearable as he wiped the sweat from his eyes. Focusing on the myriad shadows that danced in the moonlight, just out of his club's reach, he did not see The Hunter until he was next to him, his knife arcing in the moonlight, the glint of the stone as it descended singing its own song as it found its mark.

Jerome shook himself, his limbs trembling with fatigue as he wiped his war club against one massive trunk-like leg. Behind him, sheltered by the rocks and shrubbery, Orith watched, feeling helpless. His emotions reaching out to the forest warrior.

Jerome knew the elder felt powerless without his staff—knew that they were still outnumbered. His gaze shifted once again as the warrior beside him met one of the beasts head on, his knife falling from nerveless fingers to fall at his feet, then just as quickly picked up, the adrenalin that raced through him pushing him, giving him strength. The dull thud of the thing as it hit the ground reminding the forest warrior of who and what he was.

Drawing on the visions of the elders from the sacred place of knowing Jerome centered himself, his warrior's vision seeing the unseen even in their hidden places.

Carried upon the night wind, the sentinel watched from his high place as knowledge, layered deep within primordial memories was offered. As the guardian of the once sacred places watched, the warrior of the forest looked up, his moss-green eyes searching the night, the wind that caressed his senses probing. The warrior of the forest nodded, understanding.

It was enough.

§ § § § § §

Leah felt the passage of something dark and dangerous even as she ducked. The echoes of rage bouncing off the rocks as the Mukwa used his massive girth to shield her, his roared challenge thrown out as he towered above her, his curved claws cutting a deadly swath as the few who dared to, challenged his strength.

The beast reared up before him, its eyes mere pinpricks of red. It was massive, long curved claws reached out to slash, to tear as the Old One pulled back, wary, his knowledge of the darkness that spawned things such as this warning him to be careful—to guard himself against even the slightest injury.

As the Old One blocked the blow aimed for his midsection, he threw himself at the creature. His massive weight catching the other off guard so that they both went down, their cries filling the night as two warriors, one of light, the other, brought forth from the machinations of the Lord of darkness himself, fought for what each believed was right.

17

Leah turned her head, listening. The battle cries had fallen off to mere whispers before finally trailing away into the silence. She wrapped her arms around the wolves neck as Chera nuzzled her, the unasked answered as Leah stood up. Her hand resting on the great silver-white wolf's back, she peered into the darkness, her senses probing the shadows while a little ahead of her the Old One moved back into shadow, his soft huff-huff telling her what she needed to know.

§ § § § §

The Hunter found himself looking up into forest green eyes as the early dawning washed away the night—he who had once thought certain things were lost within the mysticism of the circle elder's tellings now knew different. As the once mythical warrior of the forest changed back to flesh and bone, the vision of the great Oak, the most sacred of the forest guardians, faded before the warrior's eyes.

What was once myth, then legend, had become truth.

The warrior lowered his head, his gaze sweeping the clearing, seeking out the others. He sighed, visibly relieved, as he caught sight of the wolves, his eyes darkening with unconcealed relief as the woman, followed by the Mukwa, came into view. His glance of appraisal telling him she had come to no harm. The Hunter looked past her, to the Old One, the words, unspoken, heard.

"*Thank you.*" The words floated upon the wind that carried them to the Old One.

The Unseen watched from his high place as the companions, old and new, gathered together. Thrown together in a time of war, their purpose was the same. Each of them had been touched by the darkness. Each of them shared something in common, and whether or not they knew it yet each had something to give to the other. A learning, a sharing that would enable them to see the whole of what it was they faced.

It mattered little that they were from different realms, for they fought the same cause, and so there were no differences between them.

The unseen entity that had lived before them all sighed. Carried upon the winds that blew endlessly, it wrapped itself about the others who waited below. Wrapped within the unspoken words were the memories of the Ancients. The Old Ones. The Unseen paused as another sound, clear, distinct came to him.

The *Other!* Once more the *Unseen* wrapped his thoughts, his memories, about the one called Jerome, hoping that upon his return the giant warrior would have remembered—would know what it was that was needed.

Jerome shook his head to clear it, the red haze that shadowed his vision during battle was nearly gone. He looked down at the warrior, the familiarity that tugged at his senses telling him that they had met before. A vision of a seeker in the not too distant past flashed before him. He closed emerald green eyes briefly.

Yes. It was him—the vision seeker who had come to him but a few nights past, seeking answers that he already knew. Sensing the worst was past for now, the forest warrior looked more closely at the man, his gaze scrutinizing. He turned from his quick study as a familiar voice rang through the clearing while behind him Orith spoke softly, the elder's voice glad that they had all come together once again.

"Leah—" Orith was enveloped in a hug that took his breath away. Then it was Jerome's turn. The forest warrior had to lean down, but he managed it as Leah held on to him, her eyes watering as she blinked the tears away.

"Oh, Jerome, how I have missed you." She stifled a sob as she drew in a calming breath. Now was not the time to lose it. She pulled back, one hand on Jerome's massive forearm. "Nickolous? The others?"

"They are safe in Skye, little one." Jerome's tone was gentle for he sensed the turmoil within the young woman—for young woman she was. Gone was the child he had known in that other place. Like her brother before her, the journey *between* had somehow accelerated her maturity. He stood slowly as she released her tight grip upon his arm, her expression telling him that she had a new awareness of what was. He looked past her, to the warrior. Black eyes gazed back unblinking. Jerome suppressed a smile, his thoughts his own as he turned to greet the others.

The battle over, the danger temporarily past, there was much to do. Jerome bent to the task of doing what was necessary, disposing of the bodies that littered the ground. In death they were nearly unbearable, the smell rising up to clog his nostrils as he focused, his thoughts elsewhere, at the same time sorting through the memories—images left by the unseen one that had briefly touched the core of his remembering. His gaze momentarily shifted to where the warrior stood, next to Leah, his gaze sweeping over her guardedly and he laughed softly.

Beside him, the Old One snorted, the sound carrying to the wolves. The sharing that passed between them, for them alone. Jerome nodded. He understood. Later, as they all gathered together to share what they knew, so that the sharing would give them a better understanding, the forest warrior would once again appraise the warrior, the one the others also knew as The Hunter, and wonder...

The Hunter gazed down at the woman, grateful that she was here. Glad that they were side by side. It rankled a bit that he hadn't been the one to see her safe, his warrior's pride soothed by her nearness he reached out and drew her close, relieved when she didn't pull away. Realizing that she was cold, he wrapped her in his fur cloak, his touch lingering as he released her hands, tucking them carefully within the heavy folds of the warm wrap. He wanted to tell her how important she had become, but the words remained unspoken.

He was, after all, the one known to the people as The Hunter. His male pride such that it would be unthinkable to consider his words might be rejected.

Orith watched the warrior go. Watched through hooded lids as he picked the unclean bodies up as effortlessly as if their weight were nothing. But *he* knew better. The things were heavy by even Jerome's standards and without meaning to he had discerned what this one of the two-legged felt for Leah.

He sighed. Such pride.

The snowy owl shrugged. Some things remained the same. He remembered a time when he had been prideful. He pushed the remembering away. There were more important things to think about than reminiscing about a past that you could not change. He cast a surreptitious look in Leah's direction; dark circles rimmed her eyes, and she was thinner than he remembered, but beyond that, she carried something within her that hadn't been there before. Orith blinked, startled—she had the knowing.

"Orith?" The voice was questioning, Leah turned, her gaze seeking that of the elders. She squared her shoulders and, rising, she went to him, her hand on his shoulder, the sharing of thoughts between them for them alone.

§ § § § §

"Bring him in." The words were spoken in an ancient dialect known only to a few. The creature bowed low, backing out slowly, careful to maintain silence lest it displeased its Dark Lord.

The *Other* remained seated, the slow shuffling of feet irritating him as the visitor moved further into the room.

"Yes, what is it? What do you wish to tell me?" The dark head remained where it was, not bothering to look up as the candles flickered wildly, the wax splattering on the hand that held the parchment. "Speak." The hand never moved. Never flinched beneath the scalding pain as the wax hardened. Slender fingers peeled it off slowly, the redness beneath fading quickly as he muttered something beneath his breath. The visitor remained silent as the shadows splayed across the roof of the cavern. He hadn't come this far to be treated like one of the *Other's* minions. And so he waited for the dark head to rise.

To see.

"State your business or leave." The dark head raised slowly, the sharp intake of breath audible to the watchers who remained where they were, their silence warning the *Other* of possible danger as he rose cautiously to his feet, his hands clutching the silver amulet tightly as he drew himself up to his full height. Even then, he was not as tall as the visitor.

"What are *you* doing here?" The words had a hollow ring to them as he threw his woolen cloak to the earthen floor in front of him, the muscles in his neck tensing as he leaned forward; his gaze raking the others face. *"Leave. Now."* The words were slow, measured, broking no argument.

"I have come to warn you. Whether or not you listen is entirely up to you." The figure moved forward, his gaze penetrating. Eyes that had seen the world since its beginning burned into the *Other's* as the silence deepened, became poignant in the empty cavern.

"Leave. I have work to do." The dark one turned away in dismissal, the moment of indecision past. He had better things to do than listen to this *one*. Dark brows furrowed in remembering.

Once, they had been friends.

He squared his shoulders as the fire sparked, the dry wood beneath the green embracing the sap that dripped unto it. The unwanted visitor glanced at the *Other*, then at the fire that flamed against the moisture that tried to smother it. He looked around the room, then back to his reluctant host, who it seemed, had forgotten his manners.

"While you were seeking out your sister in her realm, your own was in dissent." The words carried through the pungent air to the listeners who watched from their hidden places. The *Other* leaned forward, his gaze locked with that of the visitor's.

Yes, they had once been friends, he thought wryly, tamping down his anger. But not now, not ever again. Something—a distant sound, caused him to turn, his gift of discernment allowing him to see the little watcher in the farthest reaches of the cavern.

"Ahhh, the little ones, those closest to the earth. They watch..." The voice trailed off as the *Other* uttered something unintelligible beneath his breath. The sound of falling rocks echoed in the cavern, but the little watcher was gone, its own sense of self-preservation saving it from being crushed. The visitor leaned forward, out of the shadows, his expression unyielding as he looked down at the one who he had once called brother.

Once, in the beginning when the one known as the *Other* had passed through the watcher's gate, they had been friends. The teacher and the student—but the student had surpassed the teacher, and they had gone their separate ways The one who stood before the *Other* now was older, wiser. He leaned closer, scrunching down slightly so that he was level with the *Other*, his gaze holding that of one who had once held such promise. After a few moments, he sighed deeply, knowing it would be useless to argue further.

The die was cast, and had he known the dark heart that beat within the little being he had found frightened and alone those many turnings past, he would never have allowed him entrance to a world that was just beginning. Dark eyes glared from beneath half-closed lids up at him as he straightened slowly, a quick glance around the cavern only confirmed what he already knew. He had come too late.

"You have no power here. That was taken from you long ago... Things are as they must be. The natural order of things cannot be changed." The rustling of rolled parchment as the *Other* turned away brought the visitor back to the present.

He should have known there would be no welcome for one such as he. Not now. Eyes the color of sapphires narrowed in a face aged with sorrow, the words spoken for all within hearing to hear.

"The little ones, the earth diggers, have returned to what they *were*. For too long has the forest slept, your spells and imagery darkening the world so that nearly all who dwelled within served you. My friend..." The voice softened as the speaker leaned forward, his face mere inches from the *Other's*. "Borne into the beginning of a darkness lost to remembering, you have grown into what you are. Remember, like A-Sharoon, there are choices to be made without losing your inherent nature."

"I am what I am. It was you who tried to change it."

"There is a seed born of light in all that come into being. You have blinded the forest and its inhabitants with your dark imaginings for too long—"

"—Go. Now. There is nothing you can say or do. You should have destroyed me when you had the chance." His voice harsh, the *Other* turned away, dismissing the visitor for what he was. Unwanted.

He didn't bother to look back, for he had no need to. He crossed his arms, his focus on what was in front of him, not behind him. It had been turnings since they had parted, too late now for his former mentor to talk of change. He smiled in the half-light of the dimly lit cavern. He had fooled them all and had played the helpless child well— he turned around, slowly, deliberately. His gaze resting on the empty space before him, the soft sighing that echoed around him the only reminder of what had passed between them.

The eldest of the forest clans was gone. The sudden draft of air that hit him, cooling him as the fire went out, the sparks hissing angrily upward toward the ceiling as the lesser of the creatures who hid in crevice and darkened places scurried hurriedly away—away from the unexpected—away from the *Other.*

As the shadows crept forward into the darkened places that the fire no longer protected; the man turned abruptly away, his thoughts now hidden from those who discerned. Still silent, he bent to the task of gathering his parchments to him, then, after securing them tightly and rolling them carefully in soft leather, he left the cavern to the darker things that would watch and wait for his return.

§§§§§§

Gabriel sat down, his pleased look not lost to the others who stood close by. The clearing was once again as it should be; the gate secured against the unwanted. Jerome, visibly relaxed, leaned idly against an outcropping of rock, one large callused hand stroking his chin thoughtfully.

Now that the danger was past, he could see for himself that Leah had come through the shifting *in-between* unscathed. Green eyes that were unfathomable narrowed thoughtfully as he studied her from beneath half closed lids, the slight unease that pricked the edge of his consciousness a telling thing. Leah looked up, her gaze questioning.

Jerome remained where he was, his eyes shuttered against the light—and from her. He was beginning to see why the Old One had sent Chera through so readily.

"She sees what others of her kind do not." The Mukwa had returned from the wooded places.

Jerome nodded, acknowledging the Old One's presence. Once, long ago, he had communed with ones such as he. The Old One tilted his head slightly to one side, studying this ancient elder of the forest; for, like him, he carried the remembering of his world within his weary body, and so they both bore the knowledge that had been offered in the beginning to all the knowing clans.

"Like yet not alike." The words drifted in the wind that caressed them both. Jerome quietly acknowledged the others words as his brows furrowed, his green eyes crinkling at the edges as he shifted his attention to the warrior who stood facing them.

And pulled back.

"That *one* has much to learn." The Old One's voice broke through Jerome's thoughts as he centered himself, his inner vision reaching out so that it flowed around the warrior. A dark brow rose questioningly when the warrior unexpectedly pushed back.

"Jerome?" Leah was standing next to them, her dark eyes looking up into his own, her expression puzzled.

"What is it little one. What troubles you?" Jerome asked, glad for the diversion, time enough later to decipher what he had seen, layered behind the warrior's dark gaze.

Kneeling down, he balanced himself against the trunk of a tree that, like him, had seen the world from its beginning. The slight vibration that he felt surprised him as a flicker of recognition sparked deep within, then just as quickly pushed back as Leah spoke, the words for him alone to hear.

"That which has been forgotten awakens; The Hunter needs to learn, he has the memories—like you." Leah was gazing at him intently, waiting for an answer. When none was forthcoming, she rushed on, the words tumbling out as she looked at him beseechingly.

"I cannot do this on my own. If I am ever to return to Skye..." Her voice trailed off as Jerome gazed thoughtfully into the distance, for once, at a loss for words. Even had he wanted to, he could not change what was inside someone. The Hunter alone held the key to his own awareness

"Things will be as they must, little one," Jerome replied, at a loss for words. Hiding his relief that the warrior was approaching, he moved away under the pretense of busying himself with other things.

From his place of watching, the *unseen* moved closer, the need to hear the words spoken between the woman and the warrior that would signal the awakening binding him temporarily to those who stood below.

Around them the silence deepened as the air changed, charged with a sudden poignancy that startled the wolves into watchfulness, Gabriel's growled warning reaching out to the others.

"The clan of the two-legged must choose." The Mukwa had risen up, his keen sense of smell overriding his poor eyesight as he glared at the warrior. They were in peril, all of them, waiting for the one, born to man, to see what was needed to make the whole. The Mukwa snorted in disgust while The Hunter remained where he was, unflinching, his gaze sweeping the clearing and those within its boundaries before returning once again to rest on the woman.

Chera moved closer, unsure as to the Old One's intent, her instinct to protect those she now considered part of her pack. Beside her, Gabriel growled softly, the sound carrying to the others who remained where they were, watchful.

"Observe and learn. This is not our realm, whatever force pulled Leah here is not for us to question. *They* must understand one another." The big wolf nuzzled his mate softly, for it had not been his intent to chastise. Chera nodded; she did not like it but she understood.

Leah felt herself pushed forward by something that would not allow her to turn back. She could feel Jerome's concern for her as he reached out, his warrior's vision seeking—knew that Orith watched and felt his frustration at the loss of his staff, the power it had contained within its burls now given back to the earth. She sighed, resigned to her fate.

Throwing her shoulders back, head up, she met the warrior's gaze with that of her own, the silent learning between the two binding them to one another as the wind whirled above them, the unseen watcher drifting closer so that the words spoken would be heard.

§ § § § §

The *Other* stepped carefully across the mossy bog, taking care not to get mired in the muddy clay, his journey was hurried, the rune spell he had cast earlier had cloaked his presence amongst most the forest clans, but not all.

Dark eyes glittered dangerously as he sought out the one who would guide him to the woman. As he threaded his way carefully along the narrow path, he looked neither to the right nor to the left. Aware that the little ones watched from the safety of their burrows, he cast a binding spell that would hold them immobile. Not a killing spell, it was, nonetheless, a powerful one.

It would be much later that they would awaken, their minds blurred, the uncertainty of what they saw keeping them from beating a tattoo against the earth to warn the others that death was moving unseen amongst them.

§ § § § §

There was something moving at the edge of his vision. Broad fingers brushed at the side of his face, the wetness that ran and pooled on the tunic at his neck not helping as the itch caused from the coarse fabric spread across his chest. The forest warrior knelt down, his broad hands flat against the earth, waiting for the familiar thrumming that would tell him what he needed to know. After a time, he turned to the Mukwa, his gaze questioning, the unasked asked. Receiving no answer, the warrior tried once more, his mind reaching out to seek the unseen.

There was nothing.

Straightening to his full height, he looked up into a cloudless sky; the azure blue was breathtaking, but something was wrong—his unvoiced thought reached out to Orith, the snowy owl nodded. He understood. He would guard the hidden places until the warrior returned.

Chera watched Jerome go, her instincts inexplicably heightened; she scented the wind, her silver eyes flecked with gold scanning the forest in front of her. Whatever was out there was not a threat—yet.

The silver-white wolf closed her mind, blocking out the sounds that whirled about her as if begging entrance.

"Listen." Leah was standing on tiptoe, her face upturned in the bright light, one hand resting on the warrior's arm. The silence deepened as she tried to convey what she could not speak in words, shivering as the wind wrapped itself about her, the slight trembling of the poplar leaves as they danced haphazardly above her head nearly unnerving her.

Nothing had prepared her for this. Nothing. Leah let her breath out slowly as she went to her woman's place of knowing.

"Remember who and what you are…" The warrior frowned as the words drifted to him. He looked down into wide eyes that were filled with concern. She was trying to tell him something. He reached out, one arm encircling her shoulders, drawing her to him and was pleased when she did not try to pull away.

For some reason that he could not explain, even to himself, he needed her close, her nearness a catalyst that pushed away the uncertainty. Lowering his head, his breath warm against her cheek, he spoke softly, the words barely discernible. "Woman from another realm, show me. Take me to the place of knowing. The forgotten place of my forebears."

"See me." The lone sentinel drifted downward from his high place. Waiting.

Chera felt the rush of air as the warrior and the woman looked at each other. The power of the circle elders surrounding them as they shared knowledge, the joining of their minds a gift they offered each other.

So different, yet the same. Worlds within worlds where time changes and nothing remains as it once was.

The Unseen drifted closer. There was not much time left. He who once had been forced to walk the darkened places felt the change—the echo of approaching danger.

The wind sighed about those waiting below him as he drew the sacred winds to him. He looked deep into the forest, seeking, his power flowing back to him from the center where the woman and the warrior stood, their faces upturned, their eyes now seeing the one who had been there from the beginning.

18

Leah stayed where she was, unmoving, her dark eyes wide with amazement as she focused on what was slowly taking on form in front of her. Thoughts, emotions, memories…

All there. Dormant since the beginning of her existing, they now surfaced, begging recognition as she acknowledged the ethereal vision that most, seeing, would think nothing more than the mist rising from the wet bogs within the forest on a morning when the air was cooler than what lie beneath. The emotions that swept through her an awakening that had always been there as she accepted the vision for what it was, the knowing within blossoming, spreading out to the others. The extension of all the knowledge of those gathered, shared. Understood.

§§§§§§

The *Other* remained where he was as the wind embraced him, pricking his senses, the forest around him resonating as the cooling breeze found him even in his darkened place of refuge. His face dark with rage he silenced the footfalls of the one who walked behind him—waited for the change in the wind before beckoning him forward. The whispered incantation once again binding the entity to him.

Eyes that had once seen everything focused briefly, the flicker of knowing rising as memories formed, and then just as quickly went blank, their swirling centers returning to the nothingness that bade them serve the one before them.

"Go to the sacred place and separate the woman from the other of her kind. Go. Now." The words were spoken in an ancient dialect, too old for anyone to understand except those who had been there from the beginning.

The sentinel nodded and left, knowing that his master would follow, but more slowly. The light streaming through the trees hurt his eyes, and so he moved off the path, gathering the shadows to him as he went, those hidden within the darkened places following at a distance as the smell of death and decay wafted through the morning's air. The clinging, cloying essence permeating the hidden burrows of the little ones who lived below so that the eldest of them ventured forth to see...

The *Other* watched until the sentinel was out of sight and the forest returned to what it was, the sounds of small scurrying things as he passed by something that had always been.

Throwing his woolen cape carelessly over his shoulder, he moved quickly forward, along the path that would take him to where he needed to go. Let the other—he who was once more than what he was now—thread his way toward the others. Whether or not he would be able to wrest the woman from the warrior mattered not, for he was merely a diversion.

The gnarled branches of the oak tree reached nearly to the ground. The *Other* ducked as he moved beneath them, his cloak catching on the protruding roots that rose upward from the hard earth. Cursing softly, he moved forward, one arm shielding his face as he used the other to push the low-hanging branch out of the way, the soft sighing as it fell back into place giving him pause as he arched a dark brow inquiringly, his gaze momentarily focused on the width and height of it.

He stroked his chin thoughtfully thinking it odd that he had never noticed it before, and then just as quickly dismissed the thought. It did not matter.

Moving quickly, he skirted the outer edge of the forest, the sun's light welcoming as he moved into the open; toward the top of the grassy knoll, his gaze locked on the valley that stretched out below him. The hot wind fanned him as he inhaled deeply of the scents carried upon it, his expression that of an animal seeking its prey. She was down there, somewhere beneath the thick canopy of trees. He started forward, down the steep incline that would lead him to the woman. Hopefully, there would be no need to battle them all. He only wanted the woman.

Dark eyes narrowed as he stared into the distance, his thoughts centered on what he would do when he found her, for there was no room for *"if."*

Jerome waited in the stillness, the shuddering sigh that ran through him shaking him to the core of his being. To suffer even the slightest touch from that *One* left him drained. He bent down to examine the footprints more carefully. Pinching the earth, he held some of it gingerly between thumb and forefinger, then released it, the scent heavy within the particles that fell back to the earth.

Rising to his full height, he stood for a moment longer, peering in the direction the *Other* had taken, his green eyes reflecting the color of the forest within their ever-changing depths as he came fully back to himself—his features and form once again that of the warrior.

He drew in a deep breath before releasing it in a shuddering sigh.

He had not used his ancient form for turnings, leaving the change to the younger warriors; their bones were more malleable, the return to themselves easier. The warrior flexed his muscles and then stretched. There. That was better. He picked up his war club; it too had changed back to what it was. He hefted it. Tested it. One brow arched quizzically as he decided what to do.

§ § § § §

Caught *"Between,"* Leah felt herself falling, her knees buckling beneath her as strong arms caught her. Aware that Chera was nearby, she tried to stay awake, her last lucid thought that of the others as the darkness took her.

"No!" The warrior shouted as he held her limp form to him, as if the holding would awaken her. He looked at Chera, his gaze pleading.

The big wolf remained where she was, her mate beside her, her silvery eyes with their ever-changing depths betraying nothing of what she felt.

"Awaken..." The words carried within the wind embraced The Hunter as he laid his burden gently down. Guided by something he could not see, he stood, legs apart, head back, arms spread wide, his voice rising—the supplication heard. As the wolves and the Old One watched, the frothing, roiling mist descended once more, fragile tendrils reaching out to draw the warrior and woman to it as those of the four-legged clans stood guard.

§ § § § §

Jerome moved quietly through the forest, pausing now and then to listen, his warrior's hearing so attuned that even the slightest sound caught his attention. While beneath him, the little ones, the earth diggers, the heartbeat of the earth, sought out those hidden in the darkened places, the muffled sounds of battle reaching upward to the warrior as he watched the path ahead of him.

Thoughts spiraled downward to the elders as he sought the one he needed for the task—they were too few. The *Other,* the dark one, was more powerful than what any of them had ever supposed, and the warrior misdoubted that even A-Sharoon would be a match for the power her brother now possessed.

Each time he had crossed between worlds, he had brought something back with him.

The warrior of the forest knelt, his large hands with their thick calluses digging deep into soil and rock, the black earth running between his fingers. It was moist and cool, rich in nutrients that nourished.

Jerome rose slowly, his hand shading his eyes against the light. Something or someone was following him, had been for some time. He reached out casually, his hand caressing the club at his side, the prickling that ran along the length of his spine telling him that he was not alone. Pivoting slowly, green eyes that had seen the world from the beginning looked deep within the center of the world—

—not surprisingly, the gaze was returned in kind.

§§§§§§

Peering into the mists swirling depths, the Mukwa saw what had always *Been,* the fine hairs that ran along the length of his spine rising as the entity, long lost to memory, embraced the warrior, while beside him the woman struggled to her feet, her voice heard as the wind found them in their hidden place. The essence of all they were—had ever been—reaching out to embrace the unseen.

The Old One turned his gaze upward, his heart seeing what his eyes could not. His memories reaching out to embrace the forgotten teachings within himself, his own voice rising, carrying to the wind that rode above him, to be joined by that of the wolves.

The choice theirs to freely give, they now offered a little of themselves to the one that had lived before them all.

§§§§§§

Jerome drew back so quickly that he nearly tripped, his sharp intake of breath loud in the sudden silence that pressed heavily upon him, eyes the color of emeralds blinked up at him as emotions surfaced.

The stripling that stood before him was a younger version of himself.

The warrior of the forest took a tentative step forward, his surprise at finding another like him slowly ebbing away as he went to his center, emotions reaching out as he gently probed. He rubbed his chin thoughtfully as he studied the young forest warrior through half-closed lids. The stripling was still a youth, barely past a thousand turnings—his gaze slid past him, seeking out the hidden places behind the youngling. There were more behind the first, the trilling of the young ones as they came forth a telling thing.

They were alone.

The warrior stood a moment longer, deciding, before looking deep within that well where all thought exists—the teachings of his ancestors—the young ones seeing what he saw—their minds opening to this new way of communicating.

Jerome rubbed his forehead thoughtfully. He needed to leave this place; the unexpected delay was something he had not counted on. The soft sigh of the wind interrupted his thoughts, his attention drawn to the stripling who had followed him, out from beneath the protection of the trees into the open, the others following, but more slowly. The curiosity that had driven him to reveal himself to someone unknown, obviously contagious.

Jerome smiled inwardly. They were young, true, but he had seen what was within them.

Their hearts, their thirst for knowledge—the warrior shrugged his massive shoulders in resignation. Placing his war club on the ground in front of him, he knelt, indicating to the watchers to do the same. He did not have much time but then again if he was right, neither did they.

It was not often that the student found the teacher. At least, that is what the warrior told himself as he began to speak of things long forgotten.

§ § § § § §

The Hunter released the woman slowly, almost reluctantly. The mist had receded, taking the *Unseen* with it. The warrior shook his head to clear it, but the images remained. His world, as he knew it, was no more.

In all of his imaginings, he would have never thought, never known—but for this woman who stood before him, her large brown eyes looking up at him, waiting for him to speak. To acknowledge the truth of what he had seen with his own eyes…

"They have always been there. It is you have who never listened. Never seen. You and your kind have forgotten those who have guarded you from the beginning. Help them…"

The warrior stepped back, glanced warily about. If the others had heard, they gave no indication.

"Warrior from the clan of man, I am all around you. I have always 'Been.' Accept the gifts you have been given. Use them."

The warrior brought his hand up to shade his eyes against the bright light, the words drifting into the sunshine, the remnants echoing, fading as he became aware of other things. Chera had moved closer, her concern for the woman evident.

He needed time to think. To center himself. So preoccupied with his own thoughts he narrowly missed knocking the elder down, sidestepping at the last moment he as he brushed against him. The snowy white owl was blocking his way, his large golden eyes unblinking.

"So you see with your heart what your ears cannot hear." Orith was studying the warrior—gauging his reaction.

The one known as The Hunter nodded.

"That is good." Orith stood a little taller; his cloak with its tattered hood fell back, revealing his scarred face to the warrior, something he rarely did because of the reaction he got.

The warrior remained where he was, holding the other's gaze evenly as Orith drew the hood forward, over his face, once again concealing his features from view. "Come," he said, motioning the warrior toward a place near the concealed gateway. "Come," he said again as he walked away, his gait slow and clearly painful, the words he threw over his shoulder nonetheless heard.

"It is time."

"Are you all right?" The voice, so close, startled her. Leah glanced down at Chera, then, the big silver-white wolf did the unexpected—she leaned against Leah, her warmth comforting, her nearness oddly soothing to Leah's frayed senses. Kneeling, Leah hugged her tightly, pushing back her emotions as she centered herself, not realizing until now that what she had seen earlier, carried within the mists that had ridden above them, had always been there.

She sniffled, burying her face in Chera's fur so that the others would not hear—would not know—

Chera nuzzled her gently as she waited for the storm to pass, for she knew that Leah carried a responsibility that most would have shirked. Sparing a glance in Gabriel's direction, she nodded, the action barely discernible, but the big wolf understood.

Moving quickly, he reached the edge of the forest, pausing just long enough to gaze over his shoulder before disappearing into the forest's depths.

After a few moments, the Old One followed, his soft huff-huff telling any who watched that he would not go far.

"Well?" Gabriel turned to face the Old One. They had traveled deep into the forest, stopping at a place that would conceal them from the unwanted, yet at the same time allow them to see any who would think to come upon them unaware. The Mukwa's silence was irritating.

The elder ignored him, staring into a distant place. What he lacked in sight he more than made up for with his sense of smell.

After a time, he turned to the wolf, the knowing between them leaving little room for spoken words. "An ill wind blows from the east—there are too few of us against the many..." The words trailed off into the strained silence.

The *'something'* was coming now.

§ § § § §

The sentinel moved cautiously forward, his silver eyes with their smouldering depths seeking out the hidden places. He pushed at the shadows that surfaced occasionally, the familiarity of the memories that pressed down upon him irritating him as he tried to remember.

"Once you were more—" The words drifted on the air that cooled him as he paused long enough to look around, leaning into the wind as he did so, his ability to seek out and find the reason failing him this once.

From his place among the forest's depths, the *Unseen* waited. It had been turnings beyond thought since he had come this way. Unbeknownst to the one who was once *more,* it was the way back to those like, yet unlike, his kind.

As he watched the lone sentinel with eyes that saw the whole of the nothingness that the other felt, the rain began to fall. At first little more than a fine white mist, it grew steadily, gradually, until it was spattering the leaves of the trees, rolling off the foliage to drop heavily to the earth.

The *Unseen* moved lower, embracing the rain, becoming part of it, at the same time releasing a part of who he was into it, in hopes that the one who walked below would remember. That he would come back to himself so that he could be once more a guardian of the forest. One of those ancient ones who protected.

The sentinel looked up into a smoky grey sky, the rain that hit him was warm and the sensation triggered more memories. More confusion. He reached upward to touch a leaf; heavy with rain, it trickled easily into the palm of his hand. He frowned, trying to remember. It was there, at the edge of his conscious thought. Just a little more...

The *Unseen* drew closer. Watching. Waiting.

He was almost there.

§ § § § §

Orith watched as the warrior prepared the fire, his silence his approval. Above them, the afternoon had turned overcast; the unusual chill the wind brought caused him to shiver violently beneath his robe.

From somewhere deep within his leather bundle of personal belongings, the warrior had drawn forth a heavy fur-lined cape. Taking his knife, he had sheared off a large portion of it, adjusting it so that it fit the elder, and Orith had sank into its warmth gratefully, accepting the unexpected gift with gratitude.

They had talked as the afternoon's shadows had deepened, the warrior listening, his voice tinged with a grudging respect as he had asked questions, and the elder had answered. Then, later, Orith began to speak of his own beginnings, letting the warrior see a little of himself, the dawning of awareness something that both of them shared as the day had worn on.

No longer questioning his abilities, the warrior had become an apt pupil, eager to learn, but at the same time, Orith knew much of it had to do with Leah.

The warrior knelt down, fanning the flames that crept slowly upward, the dry wood catching quickly. Now and then he glanced sideways, looking surreptitiously in Leah's direction. The big wolf remained close, and so the warrior remained where he was, the soft burr of Orith's voice drawing him back, his attention once again on the telling of the before time.

"Where is he? He should have returned by now." The words were spoken quietly, but Chera knew Leah was worried. They had taken refuge beneath an ancient oak tree. Its limbs grey and gnarled, it had seen many turnings of its world, yet despite that, it offered sanctuary from the elements to those in need. Gazing up at the dark clouds that scudded across the distant horizon, she turned to the big wolf, one dark brow arched. The dampness curled about them as the sense of foreboding heightened her already frayed senses while Chera peered into the distance, her thoughts her own.

Leah was right. Jerome should have returned by now. That he had not meant something or someone had delayed him. Chera sighed, the sound carrying to the warrior who stood a little apart from them, his dark gaze resting on the woman.

One brow arched quizzically as he shifted his gaze to Chera. The big wolf nodded.

Finally, they understood one another.

§ § § § § §

Cursing softly, the *Other* moved with a stealth that few, if any, of his underlings possessed, while the dark clouds roiled above him, the air heavy with a clinging, cloying, wetness that was suffocating.

Most, given warning, would have fled; but those who walked beneath, the little ones, the earth diggers, never had the chance as he spoke the words that would draw the others to him. Those who dwelled in the *"Between."* The bending of the trees from the unseen wind the only indication he had been heard.

§ § § § § §

It was his fault he had awakened them, so there was nothing left to do but to take them with him.

The words echoed in the stillness, unspoken but there. Jerome moved ahead, leading the way, the others following. As hard as he had tried to talk himself out of it, he could not. The big warrior sighed, the sound carrying to the young ones who walked behind him, their faces reflecting their eagerness.

The decision to bring them back had not been an easy one, but they had wanted to help. The warrior walked faster as he pushed the indecision aside, arguing with himself as he did so.

It *was* their world. They had been born into it, and yes, they were untried. However, they had courage and determination. He rubbed his chin thoughtfully, sparing a backward glance as he did so at those following; his forest green eyes crinkling at the corners as he smiled.

They would do.

He leaned down to move a heavy branch that had fallen onto the path out of his way, the sudden rush of pain that shot through him bringing him to his knees as he tried to focus, his senses reaching out as he sought to touch the hidden places with his thoughts. The echoing sighs had fallen silent. The warrior looked down at the earth beneath his feet in disbelief.

The others felt it too, their newly awakened abilities causing confusion as they pressed forward, their faces questioning. Jerome refused the offered hand as he stood, brushing the earth and leaves off him as he did so, his mind reaching out to the wolves, warning them.

Shading his eyes, Jerome looked up, the position of the sun telling him it was now late afternoon. He knew the others would be getting anxious, waiting for him, and it bothered him that he was still a distance from them. Yet he knew that he could not leave the younglings behind, for they were bound to him, and he to them. As he plunged into the forest, he could not help but wonder what Orith would say when he returned.

Not bothering to cover their tracks, knowing it was useless because there were too many of them, Jerome had thrown caution to the wind, his concern for the others growing as the sky above him darkened, the distant thunder warning him.

19

"Storms coming." Orith was looking up into a sky that had turned a sickly grey. He pulled the thick woolen cloak tightly about him to ward of the sudden chill that crept through him despite the fire.

The Hunter had built a crude lean-to, the thick cedar branches that crisscrossed across the top securely fastened with thick vines. It would protect him against the rain. Orith leaned back, satisfied, his eyes shuttered against the light cast by the fire's bright glow and dozed off.

The Hunter waited until he was sure the elder slept, his gaze focused on the fire's ever-changing depths. His world as he knew it was changing. He was changed. Knowledge, layered deep within his memories, poured forth as he accepted who he was, his handsome face turned upward as he welcomed the warm breeze that blew overhead, while at the same time he deep listened for the woman.

Without understanding how or why, he accepted the fact that she was important to him, the faint threads of thought echoing as he looked deep into the forest, certain that he heard the Mukwa's voiced approval.

Leah stopped a short distance from the warrior, watching him. She had felt the pull as he reached out from that inner place within himself, and she knew that he was readying himself for what was to come. She turned inward, her vision seeing what he could not; beside her, Chera growled and from the depths of the forest, Gabriel answered.

The warrior of the forest was returning and, he was not alone.

§§§§§

The *Other* moved cautiously forward. Concealed as he was beneath the thick canopy of trees, he knew the Mukwa sensed him and was not prepared just yet to battle one so formidable. Besides, he knew the others followed behind him, their numbers growing as they massed together. Vaguely, he wondered where the sentinel was and then pushed the thought aside. It did not matter.

He leaned forward, catching the scent of the woman—the one called Leah, and then drew back as the warrior, the one known as The Hunter, moved forward as if to protect her. Black eyes the color of polished obsidian swept the hidden places as if sensing the unwanted.

The *Other* rubbed his chin thoughtfully. So, the warrior of the clan of the two-legged had the *remembering,* did he? The man stepped back farther into shadow as the warrior's gaze found him in his hidden place, the musky scent of something unnatural reaching the wolves at the same time as the Mukwa, sensing the enemy within reach, roared a challenge.

"Get down!" The shouted words were lost to the winds wailing as Leah found herself unceremoniously being shoved face first against the hardened earth. Struggling against the hands that held her, she twisted around, half rising to her knees before being shoved back down again.

"Let. Me. Up." The words were grated out against the grass as Leah struggled to rise; the low growl to her left telling her Chera was close. The Hunter released her and stepped back, his hands falling defensively to his side, at the same time unsheathing his knife. Dark eyes glittered dangerously as his lips formed the unspoken words.

Run.

Leah felt, rather than saw, the vaporous form as it hurtled toward them, the sudden rush of wind as it came out of the west warning her, its slow downward spiral toward them giving her enough time to dive into the thick underbrush. As she hit the earth, rolling, the small rocks digging into her sides and shins, she heard Chera's roar of outrage, the Mukwa's own challenge rising above it.

The creature's hesitation was momentary; the translucent coils spiraling down did so with purpose.

It knew what it wanted.

It wanted *her.*

The Mukwa took the brunt of the blow to his chest, the low moan as he slowly collapsed echoing throughout the darkened wood.

Gabriel plunged after the thing, going deep into the dense wood, his roar deafening as Chera stood protectively over the still form. Her silvery-grey eyes ever-changing, she nosed the Mukwa gently, her voice rising upward into the night as Leah stumbled toward them, dodging the wraithlike tentacles that reached for her, her concern for the Old One so overpowering that she was careless.

The Hunter knew what he faced—knew who stood before him, barring the way. Long ago, he had seen this *One,* partially concealed within the shadows of his memories. Memories he had buried as a young boy who had been frightened and alone unable to face his darkest fear.

He was no longer that little boy.

He drew in his breath as he stepped forward, the knife he held in his hand glinting with a blue-white light as he swung it, the upward thrust carrying him forward as he lunged at the *Other.*

And missed.

The warrior stumbled back, his dark eyes wide with disbelief. The sound of the knife as it slashed through the air was still reverberating through his numbed senses as he stood looking for what was not there. He turned around, his gaze sweeping the clearing for the others—the woman.

"She's gone." Orith spoke softly. The low moans from the Mukwa as he stirred, groggy from the blow he had taken to his chest, the only other sound that the warrior heard as he looked helplessly at Orith. At the others. Beside him, Chera growled softly. Shaking herself as she looked around, bewildered by the unexpected turn of events, she sought out her mate, her sigh of relief audible to the others when he appeared at the edge of the forest, unharmed.

The warrior's gaze swept the clearing once more. His finely arched brows drawing together in a frown as he stared thoughtfully at the spot where Leah had been standing, his thoughts turning outward as he probed gently. Nothing. There was nothing except…the low moaning of the Mukwa drew him back from his thoughts as he went to aid him, Chera and Gabriel were there ahead of him, their concern evident even as they accepted what could not be changed.

She was gone.

§ § § § §

The wind reached out from its hidden place as the *Unseen* moved closer to the sentinel. Thoughts spiraling out as the one that had once been *more* paused, his hand reaching out to touch the tree that barred his way. The ancient fir tree, one of the Standing People, vibrated beneath the touch of the one who once had been a guardian while the *Unseen* watched from his place above.

He would wait. Beneath him the forest awakened, groggy from its long sleep as the sentinel leaned wearily against the tree, absorbing the memories, accepting what was offered.

Beyond the edge of his vision, the *Unseen* knew the *Other* was on the move, leaving chaos in his wake. He was powerless to intercede. At least not yet.

§ § § § §

Jerome silenced the young forest warriors with a wave of his hand. Something was wrong. He knelt down, his eyes missing little as he searched the trail in front of him, his senses tingling as he reached out to touch the broken branches. He closed his eyes—and saw—the seeing painful, for he was too late. As he burst into the clearing, the cry of the hunter seeking its prey trailed off into the eerie silence that surrounded them.

"*She's gone.*" The echoed words carried to the warrior of the forest as he stood, helpless in the face of what had happened.

"*Too late…*" The words trailed off into the silence leaving Jerome to wonder if they had ever even been spoken as he looked around. At Orith. At the wolves. His gaze swinging toward The Hunter, who returned the gaze in kind, unflinching, as one sleek brow rose questioningly.

She is gone. Taken by one who seeks to destroy that which was at the time of the beginning of the world. The disembodied entity was in their thoughts. Nowhere. Everywhere.

Jerome stopped mid-stride, his war club falling to his side. Behind him, the younglings paused, unsure of their place, the eldest of them inching forward, his forest green eyes taking in his surroundings, watching the others who stood in the clearing, his gaze wary. Gauging.

Jerome motioned him back as memories surged through him. A new awareness where before there had been caution—it was then that the realization of what was happening struck him.

He was a part of who they were. Born into the beginning, they had slept, but even in the dreaming time when the earth that enfolded them safely within its depths had changed—forged by the elements they could not control—they had garnered knowledge of the ever-changing cycles of life that had unknowingly surrounded them, drawing it unto themselves. The low moan drew him back to the present. A closer look confirmed his fears.

The warrior moved swiftly, kneeling, his hands running the length of the body, testing. Probing for broken bones. He sighed, relieved, as the Mukwa rose, unsteady at first, then growing stronger. Small brown eyes blinked as he shook his head to clear it, still dazed from the blow to his chest, he blew his breath out slowly, the huff-huff sounding loud in the unnatural silence.

The Mukwa moved gingerly forward, aware of the others, their concern for his well being something he was unused to. The last thing he remembered was Leah standing over him. He groaned inwardly, remembering.

She was gone. Taken by the *Other.*

He shook his head; just beyond his vision, something moved— shadows of a lost memory? He moved closer, aware that Jerome had paused. Everyone had.

Orith's voice echoed through the silence, his low melodious voice breaking through their thoughts.

"Well, just don't stand there." Orith stepped forward. His gait slow but steady; he looked from the forest warrior, back to where the young ones stood, unable to mask the emotions that ebbed and flowed through him as he beckoned the younglings closer.

He knew they had to find Leah, but he also knew that what he was seeing was an awakening of the forest and those who lived within it. He turned to The Hunter, his amber eyes speaking what his heart could not.

§ § § § §

"Put. Me. Down." Leah was furious, her anger toward her captor palpable even in the silence that surrounded her. She let her breath out in a whoosh as she landed unceremoniously in a corner, away from the fire that struggled to stay lit in the center of the cavernous room.

"Stay where you are." The man's voice was harsh, the dark plains of his face made even more so by the shadows that surrounded him.

Leah frowned, her eyes narrowing as she focused on the minutely whirling forms caught within the shadowed places. It took her a few moments more to realize that what she was seeing were spectres from another plain. She glanced uneasily around. They were all over. Were they his protectors?

She flinched as one of them began to take on substance, the elongated face that peered out at her, wraithlike, leered viciously as she tore her gaze away. She had to focus. Keep calm. The others would find her. She reached out, her mind seeking. The warrior pushed back.

Caution. The words formed in her mind—and were just as quickly pushed back, lest the *Other* see. Carefully extricating herself from the pile of musty robes, she rose gracefully, her gaze defiant as the figure stopped mid-stride, his back straight, the anger he emitted something that hung heavy in the poignant silence as he turned to face her. She lowered her head, averting her eyes so that he would not see—would not feel what she was feeling.

She stood there like that, the moments stretching out as the man's intense gaze probed her. Finally, satisfied that she would remain where she was, he turned away, to return to whatever task he had begun earlier.

Leah watched through narrowed lids as he went to the fire and, leaning down, threw more wood into the deep pit, watched as the flames caught, licking greedily at the dry wood until the red-gold streaks of flame rushed upward toward the ceiling. The breeze that blew restlessly through the cavern fanned the warmth, the brush of it against her face welcoming after the cold dampness of earlier. Lowering herself, her back against the rock wall, she ran her hands gingerly over her body, checking for bruises, as she did so, her every instinct warning her she was in terrible danger.

She instinctively shrank back as something reached out from the darkened place above her head. The brush of something prickling against her skin warning her there were unwanted watchers here. She rested her head on her knees wearily.

There was nothing to do but wait.

The *Other* watched the woman through hooded lids; dark eyes glittered dangerously as he pulled back, partially concealed with the shadows. His senses warning him caution.

He should have destroyed her before she made it past the gateway; instead, he had left it to others, thinking them capable of handling such a small task. The dark head raised, one hand stroking his chin thoughtfully as he leaned into the light, his dark eyes openly appraising his captive. The sigh of exasperation carrying through the silence.

He leaned back, giving it over.

They had not.

And now she was here.

And he had not.

His thoughts drifted to his sister. A-Sharoon had given much of herself to aid the sacred flame—and he had been complacent. Assuming the worlds had returned to their center, he had not looked back as he had entered the circle of ruins that would return him to his world. The resistance to his passage to and from the worlds between had waned over time as he had used his dark arts to open and close them, and none had ever entered or exited with him before. Except this time—this time another had been drawn through with him.

He rubbed his chin thoughtfully. The female was…interesting. A dark brow arched thoughtfully as he bent back to his work, aware that the woman watched from her place amongst the rotting robes. He shrugged his shoulders. It did not matter. What was—was. Of one thing, he was certain, whatever gifts this strange young woman had, they certainly posed no threat to him. He wanted to find out more about her unusual gifts, he could sense them, one in particular standing out from the rest.

And if that meant dissecting her piece by piece to get it…

Rising, he crossed the cavern in long strides, closing the distance quickly between himself and the woman, he reached down, jerking her roughly to her feet. Black eyes peered into dark brown ones as he tilted her head back.

He needed to see. Needed to know if what he sensed was coming from her.

§ § § § § §

"—and that, is all there is to tell." Jerome shifted uncomfortably as four pairs of eyes looked at him.

"It has begun."

"What has begun, Old One?" Chera asked; the asking something that was needed to understand.

"What was done to our world when the *Other* worked his machinations in the darkened places is slowly being undone. Those brought into existence at the beginning have slept too long." The Mukwa lowered his voice, well aware of the tension in the air.

Somewhere, in the far distance, the shriek of something unearthly carried to them on the distant breeze. The younglings shifted uncomfortably as the Old One approached them. New to their surroundings, they did not yet have all the remembering of their long forgotten past, and so they looked to Jerome for guidance.

The warrior of the forest nodded, the meaning clear, and so the eldest amongst them gathered his courage and stepped forward; his forest green eyes meeting that of the Mukwa's. The understanding passing between them.

"The day deepens, and with it the scent grows weaker." Chera growled, impatient. She needed to move. To return to the forest, even though it was not her own. Something—she was not sure what—beckoned, and Leah was a part of it.

She turned toward Gabriel, nuzzling him gently, her thoughts reaching out to him in her way of communicating when she wanted to him to hear her thoughts alone. Something was pulling at her, something primordial.

The Hunter watched as Chera shifted impatiently, her stance telling him she was ready to seek out the unseen. He drew a deeply callused thumb across the obsidian blade he held in his hand, drawing a thin line of blood as he did so. Impatient, he wiped it away, his black eyes searching the forest depths for signs of unwanted things as he moved closer to Chera.

Whatever her feelings toward him, and his for her, their purpose was now the same.

"Go. Look for her in the hidden places. The forest awakens, and the Ancient Ones who dwell in the high places will guide you. *Go.*" Orith watched as the warrior took off at a steady trot, his bow slung over his shoulder, his knife unsheathed.

A few moments later, Chera followed.

The forest warrior watched from his warrior's place of knowing, for he knew that the silver-white wolf was bound by something ancient and deep—her need to protect Leah something that had always been. Jerome put the thought aside. He had his own growing suspicions as to why the wolf was bound to Leah.

Sighing deeply, he turned aside, his focus now on the younglings that waited patiently behind him.

Chera would take care of what was necessary, and Gabriel would protect them both. The forest warrior sighed again. Weary, and temporarily at a loss for words, his concern now for the younglings that gathered about him, their faces anxious as they reached out, their voices heard.

§ § § § §

The Mukwa moved slowly, cautiously, along the path strewn with fallen limbs and jagged rocks, the decision made. Orith would stay behind to guard the hidden gate while Jerome and the younglings searched the forest floor, their senses more attuned to the nuances that carried through the concealed places, he would follow the path the others had taken.

The Old One snorted disdainfully as he caught the scent. The Hunter and the wolves were being followed.

The Hunter moved silently, his breathing even as he centered himself; beside him, Chera matched his pace with her own, so intent on the trail in front of them that neither saw the sentinel until they were nearly upon him.

Above them, the *Unseen* watched as he who was once *more* pulled slowly away from the sacred tree. Eyes the color of pewter opened to look upon the ones who had come under cover of darkness to this sacred place of knowing. There were no irises within their center. Their otherworld glow caused the warrior to stop, startled, unable to move or even to have a coherent thought so mesmerising was the figure before him. Beside him, Chera stiffened, amazed at what she was seeing as the figure stared at them, through them—before the night embraced them.

The voices that were not their own hushed as the sentinel began to change, his gaze locked on the warriors as he became vaporous. The soft keening of the wind hurting their ears as he who was once more became what he had been at the beginning. Chera stared at what was left of the empty shell before the wind took it, lifting it, carrying it to a place where it would never be found.

The *Unseen* reached out, the caress so subtle that most would not have noticed it. Nevertheless, Chera did. She leaned into it, inhaling the essence of something so ancient—long forgotten by even most of her kind that could she have wept, she would have.

She turned to look at the warrior, trying to impart a little of what she felt to him. The cry of the whippoorwill as it passed overhead reminding her of where she was. Who she was. The night once again filled with the rush of sound and the beating of wings as the forest centered itself, becoming naught but a darkened wood, where only the four-legged and now two, walked.

"Come, Hunter. We must leave this place." Chera had turned to face the warrior, the fur on her neck rising. *"Now."* Without waiting to see if he followed, she dove into the thick underbrush, her keen hearing telling her the warrior was not far behind. Unsure of how far ahead Gabriel was, a part of her grieved that he had not been with them, to see what they had—but she knew that if he was needed, he would know and return.

A few moments later, a dark form paused at the base of the oak tree, its long curved claws digging deeply into the earth as it struggled to hold itself upright. Yellow eyes narrowed in an elongated face as it searched the hard ground in front of it for signs of those it tracked. There was nothing. Frustrated, it began to change; to grow into something more. The Mukwa heard the rustle of leathery wings opening and closing and knew he was close. The changeling had almost completed its metamorphoses into something darker as the companions burst through the clearing, the change from four-footed beast to winged nearly complete, but not quite.

"Hurry, Hunter." The words were thrown into the wind as Chera moved forward, belly to the ground, avoiding the jagged branches that barred her way.

The warrior ducked, the low-hanging limb was barely visible in the dark, the sting of the branch against his cheek reminding him that he had to be more cautious, for he knew that he and the wolf had an uneasy alliance at best. He reached out, probed gently and relaxed. Leah was out there. He could feel her. She was waiting for him. Them. Ahead of him, Chera growled softly. A warning? His bow already strung, the hiss of the arrow as it was released the only sound that filled the night as they hurried past the still form. The Hunter stopping long enough to retrieve his arrow before moving on.

Behind them, the Mukwa followed, but more slowly, his pace steady. The changeling had died where it stood, returning to the nothingness it had been as he cuffed it, sending the body into the deep ravine where the shadows had concealed it.

20

Jerome stayed where he was, watching as the younglings quickly fanned throughout the forest, their shrill trilling telling him they were learning fast, drawing the essence of what *was—had always been—* into themselves. They were growing. The warrior scanned the trees overhead, watchful, as he waited for the change. It was not long in coming.

The Watchers, guardians of the ancient places, moved purposefully amongst the warriors of the forest unseen—memories, born into the beginning now theirs to take into themselves and keep. Jerome watched as the eldest of the forest warriors returned, his green eyes reflecting the forest secrets deep within their depths.

Jerome nodded, understanding as he looked around him, for this was a sacred place of knowing. This was where the young ones had been brought into the beginning, their very essence the forest floor they now walked upon. As they drew from it, learned from it, they began to grow, the forest growing with them as they grew with each other, the shared knowledge—the connection so strong that the warrior from Skye bowed to its power.

"There was another, once, in our beginning. We are not so far apart, I think."

Jerome looked at the speaker in surprise, for the young one spoke of a memory of his own distant past. As he stood there, watching from beneath half-closed lids, he slipped into another time of remembering. His own. And he saw.

From his high place, the *Unseen* watched as events unfolded the way he had hoped. He turned to the other—the one so recently returned to himself as the invisible became visible in the high place where none who were mortal could see. Below them, the clans of the four-legged and two struggled against the dark. The *Unseen* sighed. Such sorrow. There was too much.

The young ones, those born to the forest, were growing quickly, absorbing what the forest offered. Awakened from their long sleep, they had shaken the darkness from themselves and had embraced who they were. The *Unseen* rode the wind, spiraling downward, the leaves on the trees resonating with their own voice as the younglings paused, looking upward into the night, their faces illuminated by the moon's subtle glow, the caress of the wind upon their bodies a telling thing.

"The trail disappears into the '*beneath.*'" One of the young warriors had hurried ahead of the others and was standing in front of Jerome, breathless. Pleased beyond measure that he had found something—a clue perhaps to what the forest warrior was looking for.

Jerome nodded his thanks, for had not he himself thought as much? Of course, the dark one would conceal his path, for his footsteps were not bound to the mortal realm, as others knew it. The big warrior shrugged broad shoulders indifferently. It did not matter; he himself was of an ancient race of warriors and could traverse the in-between places in safety. He looked around, his gaze searching the expectant faces of the forest warriors and the unasked was answered...

So could they.

§ § § § §

The *Other* leaned forward, his concentration on the parchment set out in front of him broken as the tremors beneath his feet ran the length of the cavern and back again. Cursing softly, he pushed away from the roughly hewn table, the wax from the overturned candle burning his hands as he swept the yellowed parchment aside to save it from further damage. The soft hiss as he blew his breath out angrily not lost in the dampness that pressed relentlessly upon him as he looked about, his dark gaze seeking out the huddled form of the woman in the farthest corner.

"So, the warriors born to the forest at the beginning seek to find you." A midnight brow arched in Leah's direction, his dark brooding gaze settling on her as she stayed where she was, her every instinct warning her to be cautious, to betray nothing of what she felt as the man slowly approached.

She, too, had felt the little ones, the earth diggers, their presence comforting. Cringing inwardly, she instinctively pushed back, her shoulders scraping against the jagged rocks behind her—and found herself being jerked upright, off the moldering pile of robes, toward the cavern's center.

He had moved so quickly she did not have time to guard herself, and he saw... Leah twisted out and away, her instincts guiding her as she spun around, her elbow catching him in his midsection. The sound of male laughter, dark and deep, drifted upward as he grabbed her again. This time around the neck as he drew her back toward him, choking her as he held her up off the earthen floor so that they were eye to eye.

Leah felt herself being swept upward, the movement so swift that, even if there had been time to guard her thoughts, it would have been useless against what she now faced. Fighting for breath, she tried to shift her weight, but the grip on her neck only tightened as the *Other* drew her closer, forcing her head up and back as he looked into her eyes, seeking answers to the unasked.

And was furious when there were none.

§ § § § §

"There, in the center, there is a doorway to the '*beneath.*'" Jerome knelt down, peering into the darkness. Around him the young warriors gathered, their thoughts centered as they too looked into that place of shadows. Jerome reached out, cautious as he shielded the young ones lest they be detected. He sighed. They had slept so long, their awakening bringing them into a different world from what they had known before the darkness—before the *Other.* He looked up, startled at the touch on his shoulder. It was the eldest of the young ones. His face was close to Jerome's, his expression troubled.

"Something blocks our vision, something dark and shadowed."

Jerome nodded. He knew what lie in front of them. Knew that the dark ones guarded the path their master had taken. He shook his head, his thoughts reaching out as he listened to what the others could not yet hear. Beneath their feet, long caverns stretched endlessly, guarded at each turn by something dark and dangerous.

He rose slowly, his gaze sweeping the forest in front of him. He knew the others, Chera and Gabriel, would find them. He also knew that the warrior who traveled with them would come. His thoughts reached out to the Old One, the Mukwa. He now walked beside the warrior, the one known as The Hunter, sharing what was his to share at his choosing.

Jerome stroked his chin thoughtfully, remembering something more, closing his eyes as he went to his warrior's place of knowing. When next he looked, it was to see the others standing about him, their expressions puzzled.

"We wait." Jerome moved back, settling himself against the nearest tree; his arms crossed, he peered into the night. Wordlessly, and without argument, the others followed his example, silently moving into the shadows, becoming one with the trees that surrounded them. Jerome, noting this, breathed a sigh of relief, grateful that the young ones had not argued, had not questioned his decision.

As the dawn swept away the night, Gabriel found them, his low growl of inquiry not necessary as the warrior of the forest stepped out from beneath the trees that shielded him to greet his old friend.

"Chera follows close behind. She brings the warrior."

"And the Old One?" Jerome was looking past the wolf, deep listening as he tried to pick up anything untoward.

"Do not worry, old friend." Gabriel nudged Jerome gently; unsure of what the others could see, he was cautious, for some things could not be shared. The warrior of the forest understood. He stood up, words unspoken, heard, as the others gathered anxiously about, wondering at this new thing that had passed between them, for with the passing of the night, they had grown yet again, the very earth they stood upon offering the learning.

Jerome looked around, pleased that they had accepted what was theirs by birthright. Beneath his feet the little ones, those closest to the center of all that was—had ever been—stirred sleepily, the darkness that had sought to silence them dispersed by the presence of something more.

He looked up, his gaze questioning, the lines at the corners of his eyes crinkling against the bright light as he shielded them with his hand. Turning toward the big wolf that stood beside him, he nodded, the tension he had felt momentarily easing as he reached out, his mind seeking, and drew back, his question answered.

Beside him Gabriel relaxed, the apprehension draining away as he opened himself to see what the forest warrior saw, the knowing almost too much to bear, for, like Chera, he knew—had always known—there was more to the wind that blew about them, wending its way through the hidden places. Not seen—never seen—but heard as the leaves trembled beneath its rush as it passed by.

Gabriel shivered as the wind rippled the fur along his back. *From the four corners to the center...* Gabriel turned to Jerome. He understood. Loping to the top of the small rise, he looked back the way that he had come. Chera and the others were close.

The fine mist that heralds the night still lay damp upon the forest floor when the others appeared.

The Hunter had his bow already strung as he topped the rise. He knew they were close even though he could not sense the woman. *He should have protected her. It was his fault she had been taken. He should have known!* He berated himself silently as he gave Chera the lead, gradually falling back so that he could observe from a distance the strangers who had come from an unknown place to offer aid.

I could have done more... the unspoken thought nonetheless rankled, more so than if someone else had spoken the words aloud.

"You are not to blame for the woman." The voice, so close, startled him. The Old One had come up behind the warrior; his stealth for one so large was impressive. "Patience, warrior. The learning is not yet complete." Saying nothing more, the Old One moved ahead of him, leaving the warrior to wonder at the words spoken.

So deep in thought was he that he barely noticed it—the passage of the wind, brushing against him. It was Jerome who interrupted his thoughts, drawing him back, reminding him of who and what he was. He straightened his shoulders as the answer came to him, carried by the thoughts of the others.

The Hunter quickly closed the distance between the wolves and the warriors of the forest, his instincts guiding him as he sought out the hidden entrance to the *"between."*

§ § § § §

His breathing ragged, the *Other* moved back—away from the woman—away from her barely discernible form that crouched in the corner where he had thrown her, nearly knocking her senseless as he had hurriedly spoken the words of the rune spell that would bind her. Still in disbelief of what had just happened, he withdrew to the farthest corner of the cavern.

His movements calculated, he carefully piled the wood on the burning embers, layering it until the heat was nearly unbearable, the flames reaching upward to touch the ceiling. Then and only then did he return his gaze to the woman, uttering the words once more, binding her even more tightly as he wondered once again at the wisdom of his allowing her to live. Yet, even as he wondered, deep within his dark heart he knew why.

He turned his attention back to the pieces of yellowed parchment, but the words of the Old Ones remained silent, their meaning unclear—

Even then, the dark one did not falter in his resolve for he would show them all. Laughter, dark and deep, drifted upward to seep outward to those who waited above, seeking entrance. He knew they were there, and he welcomed the chance to destroy them. Eyes that were full black blinked against the grey smoke that wafted toward him. Stifling a ragged cough, he bent over his work, his senses attuned to any nuance. He knew now why the woman was so important, knew that her coming had been no mistake.

He stared into the darkness rimmed at the outer edge of his vision, past the light splayed haphazardly across the cavern's floor. Things had changed. The woman, the one known as Leah, was growing, changing into something more, and she did not even know it. He closed his eyes, inhaling deeply, for he needed to focus; he needed to choose the right moment. He blinked in the half-light cast by the fires shadows. Good. She was still in the exact same position he had left her.

He leaned back, his expression thoughtful as he rubbed his jaw gingerly where she had hit him. It still hurt. His dark head lowered as he made up his mind. He would wait.

Leah stayed where she was, her senses reeling. Unsure of what had just happened, she tried to focus, her every sense warning her to be still. Chilled from the dampness, she resisted the urge to shiver as she went to her place of knowing, seeking answers—and closed her eyes against the disappointment. There was none.

She curled up, her head on her knees, shifting slightly so that she could observe the man without him knowing it, his dark head bent over what appeared to be some kind of parchment. She remained silent, watching. Finally, sleep came, and with it something else.

As Leah struggled against the visions within herself, halfway across the cavern a dark head raised, the *Other* watching as he deep listened, his senses reaching out to see what the woman saw. He pulled back, disappointed, and returned to his work, temporarily dismissing the woman from his thoughts. Confident that the rune spell would hold her fast, he shut out all thought save one—the symbols and strange markings inked in black that lie in sharp contrast on the yellowed paper in front of him.

§ § § § § §

"There has to be another way." The Hunter was standing a little apart from the others, frustrated. Despite their combined efforts, the stone remained impenetrable, barring the way in. It was one of the younglings who broke the strained silence, his voice carrying to the others as he spoke, Jerome and the others moving closer so that words were heard.

"There is another way."

"How? Show me and I will do it." The Hunter moved toward the well-concealed doorway that would allow him passage to the beneath.

"A world within a world—have a care warrior lest you find more than you bargained for..." The Hunter whirled about to find the Old One standing behind him, so close that he could feel his breath upon his face. He stepped back, his instincts warning him as the Mukwa moved past him, toward the path that led upward, into the high place, the youngling leading the way, the warrior not far behind. It was there, at the top of the rise, that the young forest warrior stopped, his downward gaze pointing the way.

The warrior knelt, brushing at the yellowed grass, pushing it aside. Hidden by trailing vines and grey moss flicked with golden hues on the end, he brushed at the rock beneath, tearing away the lichen that covered the opening, revealing a thin line that at first glance appeared to be a fissure.

"Look closer, warrior." The Hunter resisted the urge to shiver, unsure of where the disembodied voice came from, but knowing the words were meant for him. The Old One drew back, giving the warrior room to move forward, his expression that of a teacher watching the pupil as The Hunter reached out, his touch upon the grey stone tentative, his mind going to that place he had so recently discovered within himself.

The *Unseen* drifted closer. Watching. Waiting. Knowing that the warrior had to see—to acknowledge his own power before he could accept what his world offered. Had always offered.

"No!" The Hunter reeled back, his heart racing, his mind numbed by what he had just seen.

"What is it, Hunter, what did you see?" Chera pressed close, her instincts warning her of a danger that she could not identify. Frustrated, she looked to Jerome, her glance sliding back to the warrior while the wind whipped about them, warning them they were not alone.

He had gone to his warrior's place of knowing; even farther, as that part of him that could *"see"* left the physical self and entered the darkness through a fissure in the rock. Once inside, he had drifted down the darkened corridors, drawn inexplicably forward until...

The Hunter recoiled against the vision in front of him, withdrawing quickly as Leah looked up, her eyes widening, sensing his presence. Stumbling backward, the essence of what he was retreated; in his current state of awareness, he was powerless to help. As he had turned, he had sensed, rather than seen, a dark head rise in the distant corner and knew who it was as he had returned to himself. Aware of the others as they surrounded him, their concern evident, he shook himself, his hand going out to touch the wolf—to share the seeing—to ask the unasked. The long, drawn out howl that echoed through the forest going out to the others as they opened themselves and saw what the warrior had seen.

The warrior moved quickly, his bow and arrows placed at his back where they could be easily reached, his knife, never far from his hand, placed securely within its leather sheath as he felt carefully along the jagged rocks.

He knew there was a hidden mechanism that would allow him entrance, and he meant to find it. His teeth grated together as his jaw tightened, the muscles in his neck tensing as his eyes narrowed dangerously.

She lay bruised and in pain, and he was going to destroy the one who was responsible! The warrior turned at the sound of approaching footsteps. It was Chera, her strange silver eyes with their golden flecks speaking what words could not. Behind her, the others waited. With a start, the warrior realized what they were waiting for.

Him.

"Lead us warrior, for this is your time. This is what you were born for." The voice was everywhere. Nowhere. The speaker not one of them, but all. The Mukwa reaching out to the one known as The Hunter, offering an understanding between them.

"No. I cannot do this thing alone." The Hunter stood where he was, unmoving. Were those his words?

"Yes, you can. The power of the elders—the old ones—courses through you. Listen, warrior. Listen to the wind that blows. Listen to the water as it trickles over the rocks, rubbing them gently 'til they are smooth. Kneel down and feel the earth, for it speaks of the eternal. That which was at the beginning; you, the clan of the two-legged. Man. The caretakers, who once protected. Into the beginning was your kind brought, a gift given so that the earth and those it nourished would be cared for.

It is not too late warrior. Take all that you are and become more..."

"We will follow you, Hunter, for this is not our world, but yours. You must make the decision." Chera had stepped back, away from the warrior as he looked around, a little dazed and awed by what had just happened. He shook his head, pushing his long black hair away from his face as he thronged it loosely at the back of his neck. Inhaling deeply, he stood there a few moments more, undecided, unsure. Like a child taking its first steps, he wavered. But only for a moment. Chera was right. This was his world, and his people had forgotten— he frowned, his dark brows coming together as he tried to remember.

It was a distant memory at best, but it was there, recessed within the darkness where all unexplained memories dwelled. The warrior opened himself to what had been his to accept from the beginning, exhaling sharply, the sound loud in the stillness that surrounded him. *Them.*

The final coming together, something the *Unseen* had waited for, hope rising within the smallest of the watchers, those little ones who dwelled beneath as the warrior glanced around, seeing a little more, the understanding coming slowly.

But it was there.

Beneath his feet the little ones sighed in relief.

"Here, where the rock is weakest." The Hunter pressed himself against the gray slate; running his hands along the nearly invisible seam, he followed it downward, along the sides to the earth. It was solid, nearly impenetrable. He pulled back, away from the rock, his gaze traveling upward to the top of the knoll. Saying nothing but moving swiftly, he topped the rise, his strides taking him away from the others—but not for long.

In moments, the others had followed. Chera, her body tingling as it responded to a primeval instinct, ran beside the warrior, her heart racing, for she also had seen Leah in her hidden place, had seen what the warrior had not.

Leah. Lying upon a bed of moldering robes. Dark circles rimmed her eyes as she struggled with her disbelief of what was happening to her—

The big wolf swayed beneath the realization of why she had been drawn to this young daughter of Skye so many turnings past, her primordial instincts warring with her common sense even as she had heeded the call. She closed her eyes, remembering.

She and her mate had been summoned by the elders of Skye, those Ancients who watched from their sacred places—called forth from the hunt, urged to leave their forest and protect—and they had. Never once had they questioned the elders, and now she knew why.

Guarded by the clans of the four-legged, the young girl had swiftly become a woman, her gifts concealed within her deepest memories as she grew into them. The pull of the moon and earth, the tides, the ebb and flow of all she was—

The silver-white wolf spared a glance toward the warrior who was moving steadily ahead of her. He cared for Leah, she knew that now, and as she cleared the dead fall that blocked the path, she accepted what was.

The Mukwa paced himself behind the others while the younglings followed Jerome eagerly. Each step they took provoked memories that they absorbed readily, and they were growing quickly. Nourished by the very earth they trod upon, they would soon realize their potential, although, the Old One thought wryly to himself, they would still need guidance.

He watched as Chera paced herself with The Hunter, her concern for the female something he could now understand, for had he not himself begun to realize the warrior's worth. Too many turnings since his own youth when their world was young had passed; the time of the sacred fires when his kind had sat with theirs, the smoke rising to touch the velvety darkness that shaded the night as each had taken what they needed from the other. The learnings shared.

He sighed wearily as he moved to catch up, his instincts telling him that before this day deepened into night, all their strengths combined would perhaps not be enough…

21

"I said, get up. Now." The voice was tinged with barely controlled rage as Leah felt herself being yanked unceremoniously to her feet. The long rope that tethered her to her tormentor burning into her skin where it chafed at her neck.

"What—" Whatever she was trying to say was cut off, the words dying in a sigh as she instinctively put her fingers up to the rope that threatened to strangle her, desperately trying to wedge them beneath the knotted cord to protect herself from further damage as she fell to her knees gasping for breath.

She could feel herself losing the battle, pulled forward so that she was closer to the darkness that threatened to smother her. Struggling to rise she tried to swallow the panic that rose in her throat, as she tried to focus. It hurt. As the darkness swirled about her, she thought she heard Chera calling her, the silver-white wolf with her silver eyes that matched the moon's pale light receding into the black void that cradled her, as she fell limply to the cold earthen floor where she lay unmoving.

"You think to control the woman with runes cast from the before time and fear?" The voice was incredulous as the speaker remained guarded, concealed within the shadows. He did not intend to reveal himself, at least not yet, for he knew he was not welcome, especially not now. His gaze slid over the woman, coming to rest on her face briefly before sliding away. He tried to hide his shock but was too late.

"Surely you cannot think…?" The words trailed off into the silence as the *Other* glared balefully in his direction.

"Leave. Now." The voice resonated with feral undertones that threatened. The *Other* yanked on the rope to get his point across as he whirled about, his dark gaze furious as he spoke the words once more that would bind the woman and hold her fast, helpless, should she become fully aware of what she was capable of. It was the only way—at least for now.

"What are you doing here?" The words were grated out through clenched teeth as he turned to face the one who, long ago, had allowed him entrance to a world just beginning. Something, he knew the other now regretted.

The elder stepped out from the shadows cast by the fire's rising flames, the cold draft of air coming out of nowhere. Chilled, he pulled the heavy feather cape more tightly about his thin shoulders, his gaze locking with that of the one he had once called son. A part of him sorrowed for he knew now that his journey had been in vain.

He had been too late; he turned away, his expression masked as he hid his pain.

The Old Ones had been right. He could not change what *was*. Had always *been*. He had been blinded those many turnings past by a young one who had begged entrance to a world just beginning and as the eldest of his kind he had allowed it. Now, the others were gone, destroyed by the *Other* and the darkness that he served.

The elder moved slowly toward the entrance that would take him away, back to his place of watching. He regretted that he was unable to aid the young woman, for he had grown too old, his abilities weakened by the presence of the one who drew the strength from his world by his very existence within it, the distant sounds from the above to the below reaching him even here, in this desolate place of emptiness.

Sparing one last glance back at the woman, he reached out to her, his mind probing. And pulled back. A weathered brow singed with the frost that comes with turnings beyond count, arched thoughtfully. Then again...

The *Other* snorted derisively. Did the elder really think to thwart him? Impossible! He blinked. Where the elder had been there was nothing—he was gone. As he turned back to the inert form of the woman, he made a mental note to close all the gateways. All.

It did not matter how hard she struggled, the darkness held her fast. Caught in between two places, neither here—nor there—she was powerless, the bonds that held her not the only reason she could not move. He had cast a rune spell on her to hold her and until it weakened; she was helpless against what was not familiar. Unless—Leah went limp. She waited, barely breathing, her heart pounding as she resisted the urge to shiver, for the earth she lay upon was cold, and the dampness chilled her so that part of her was numb.

She couldn't feel her feet or her hands; still dazed and confused by the events of the past day, she remained where she was, unmoving. Finally, after what seemed like an eternity of waiting, the soft echo of footsteps on the hardened earth moved slowly away, although she did not need to open her eyes to know he paused now and then to look back, as if to assure himself that she was secure.

Unfortunately, she was. She let her breath out softly, unaware she had been holding it, before giving in to the darkness that wrapped itself about her, the temporary release from thinking—feeling—a relief.

The *Other* moved closer to the fire, his black eyes watching the woman through narrowed lids. The more he thought about it, the more he decided she *was* the one.

Glancing at the yellowed parchment that lay spread out in front of him with its undecipherable letters, a dark brow furrowed thoughtfully as realization dawned. He, better than anyone, should have known. Now, he knew why the woman's coming had wrought such changes to his world. Sweeping the parchment aside, he brought his fist down on the roughly hewn table, sending the candles flying from their crude holders as he stood up; his face mottled with barely controlled rage, he strode across the dimly lit room, his ability to *see* seeking out what was needed.

It was as he knelt down to retrieve an object that he had placed beneath the stone for safe keeping turnings past, that he felt it—a faint stirring—the brush of something against his skin and he tensed. His sanctuary had been breached. Breathing shallowly, he rose cautiously from his kneeled position, the muscles at the side of his neck tensing as he turned, pivoting slowly around.

Ahh. There it was. A slight movement off to his left. So, the elder thought to return unseen, to wrest the power that was rightfully his away from him did he? As the figure stepped out from the shadows embrace, the *Other* started forward, his lips curled upward in a feral smile, confident it would be a short battle.

§ § § § §

Leah opened her eyes slowly, carefully, stifling a groan as she tried to move and found that she could not. One last final tug and she laid back, her head flat against the hard earth. She was weak. She groaned inwardly, angry with herself for letting her guard down. Angry at herself that she had not listened to The Hunter when he had tried to protect her.

She had been foolish to think that she could defend herself—just look where it had gotten her.

Here. In a cave. With a man who was darkness itself. She knew it. Felt it with such a burning intensity that it made her feel sick. Something terrible was happening to her, and she did not like it. Not. One. Bit. She stilled, willing her heart to slow down, her breathing to even out as the footsteps faltered, hesitated. The musky smell that permeated her senses recognized as the man knelt down, his face inches from hers.

She kept her eyes closed. It was almost as if—Leah pretended she was still unconscious as the man's breath fanned her face. The scent was earthy and sweet.

Darkness within the light. Careful. Do not let him see inside you. Your memories. Your thoughts. He will take them from you, and he will destroy you. He wants what you have.

Leah went still. So still that she heard the *Other's* sharp intake of breath as he moved abruptly away from her, her senses telling her he was still close. Too close. As she sank back into oblivion, she wondered exactly what it was that she *had.*

The *Other* backed slowly away from the woman, his instincts alert as he returned to the fire and the warmth it offered. Unlike his sister, A-Sharoon, who reveled in things cold and dark, he preferred the warmth. He spared a guarded glance toward the woman. Soon her defenses would be stripped from her—and then?

Fire and frost. Yes—the darkly handsome head snapped around at the sound of someone approaching. Eyes that were blacker than the darkest night set in a bronzed face that was ageless blinked, as full lips drew back in a feral smile. The first intruder had been dealt with; the inert form lay lifeless where it had been tossed against the rock wall. Black brows arched in anticipation of this next adversary.

§ § § § §

The sound of rock crumbling against his continued onslaught gave little satisfaction as the Old One reared up, his massive paws coming down once more upon the rock as he moved back, then forward, again and again until he was weary. Then it was Jerome's turn.

As the others moved back, giving him space, the warrior of the forest centered himself, partially becoming a part of the earth he stood upon, his gaze focusing on what lay in front of him. There. His war club came down with a thwack that echoed as The Hunter pressed close, the warrior impatient for his turn. Behind him the others, Chera and Gabriel waited, readying themselves for what was to come. They did not have long to wait.

Jerome brought his war club down yet again, the sound of stone cracking echoed hollowly as the dust rose, curling upward as it dissipated, swept away by the cooling breeze that sighed around them. Silently the *Unseen* entered the underground cavern ahead of them.

The Hunter paused, his skin prickling as he caught the faint scent of wood and earth. He knew that smell. It pricked the edges of a distant memory, jabbing at his subconscious as he quickly moved toward the opening, his knife unsheathed as the obsidian blade warmed to its owner's touch.

Of one thing, the warrior was sure: he would see the woman freed before this day ended.

"There. In the corner. Get it."

"I see it. There is another. Over there." The voices echoed in the darkened cavern as Chera and Gabriel swiftly dispatched those that thought to stop them. Their limp forms thrown carelessly aside as the wolves moved steadily forward, The Hunter and the forest warrior keeping pace side by side, Jerome looking into the hidden places with eyes that missed little while the warrior sought out Leah, his instincts carrying him forward, into one long darkened corridor after another.

"Careful," the words were whispered into the darkness as The Hunter rounded a narrowed corner, the rocks that jutted outward catching his fur cloak. The ripping sound it made caused him to pause, the dim light ahead telling him that he was nearly there.

Nearly there but not quite, his inner voice cautioned.

Aware of the furtive movement off to his right, he kept going, moving past the watcher, not bothering to look back as the shriek of rage was cut off, Chera's low growl carrying to him as she moved swiftly to intercept another of the *Other's 'best.'* This one bigger, more deadly.

It was borne of rock and earth, part of all that was—had ever been—there since the *knowing,* brought forth from the darkness by one who knew how to control the very essence within the creature's center. The growls it emitted tinged with pain and regret as it faced Chera, its long curved claws ripping at the earth in front of it as it surged ahead, then back, its indecision evident. Chera centered herself, her primordial instinct warning her to be cautious as she moved forward, wary.

This one was not like any of the others that had crossed her path. Driven by pain and hunger, its need to be set free poured forth from within the very center of its essence—she took another step forward as the creature lunged toward her, its intent clear as it rose up, standing on two legs, readying itself to attack.

Chera leapt upward, her jaws closing on the thing's throat, and was flung against the earth where she lay for a few moments, winded but unhurt. Quickly rising, she tried to circle around it but could not, for it moved with surprising agility, its dark form nearly indistinct as it became more than what it was.

Then the Mukwa was there, pushing the big wolf aside, his bulky form moving ahead of her, shielding her as he embraced the thing head on, his low growls mingling with that of the creatures as they struggled.

As Chera watched, helpless to intercede, strength met strength, the one melding with the other, the choice to choose offered.

The Mukwa pulled back in disbelief. The two combatants stood slightly apart from one another, each breathing heavily, the sound carrying through the air that smelled of dampness and musk.

Shaking his head from side to side, he who had once sat at the fires of the two-legged in that long ago time of the dreaming sorrowed. He knew this one! Once, he and others like him had sat in counsel with the Elders in the high place, those Ancients who saw the world as it had been in the beginning.

Now twisted and corrupted by one who knew the ancient arts of change, a part of the Old One sorrowed, for the being that faced him had once been *more*. Much more.

The Old One blew his breath out slowly. Small brown eyes narrowed as he reached out to the other. Thoughts, unspoken, passing between them like quicksilver, bridging worlds that most would never think to cross.

"Never. Too. Much. Pain." The words were choked off, smothered, as someone—something—reached out across a chasm where few dared enter. The Mukwa reeled back, stunned as the beast hesitated. It was enough.

The forward lunge was swift, unexpected; long, curved claws cut a deadly swath through flesh and bone as the beast fell forward, the only sound to be heard the soft sighing, as the dark form stilled forever.

§ § § § §

Jerome shifted his weight; at the same time, not knowing why, he drew his war club slowly, carefully, from where it was thronged at his side, his warrior's sense warning him.

They had passed through a maze of connecting tunnels, leaving the sounds of the wolves and the younglings behind them as the passageway widened, went deeper into the earth. The forest warrior spared a glance down at The Hunter, who returned his gaze in kind; black eyes looked into emerald green, as a thought, a question, passed between them.

Something, someone, was shuffling toward them, his gait unsteady. Jerome reached out, his warrior's sense seeking. His hand on his war club as he steadied himself, disbelief mirrored within as he reached out to grasp the elder, his grip firm as gently laid him down.

"How bad is it?" The Hunter was kneeling beside him, his voice barely above a whisper as he searched the shadowed places for things unwanted. Jerome did not answer; he was too busy moving his big hands gently over the inert form. Hope waning as he searched for life where there was barely a flicker, his anger rising at the one who had dared to harm one of the Old Ones.

§ § § § §

Consciousness, when it came, brought with it a heaviness that made Leah wish she could sink back into the darkness of oblivion. But she couldn't. She opened her eyes slowly; even then, the dim light set her head to aching as she tugged at her bonds.

Which. Were. Not. There.

Suddenly she was sitting bolt upright, her head spinning, her eyes aching as she rubbed one wrist, then the other. She sighed, relieved, the sound carrying in the silence as her gaze swept the room, and then back to her wrists, which carried the proof of her nightmare, imprinted on the fragile skin.

The red welts had begun to sting, the burning sensation spreading from her touching the raw welts. She shook her head as uncontrolled laughter bubbled up in a throat that hurt from too much screaming. As the memories washed over her, she edged back, cautious as she tried to focus, to look past the flames that flared, their reds streaked with gold reaching up and out as if to test the air that flowed around her. She could sense the *Other,* and as she centered herself, knew he was watching her, gauging her, to see if she would run.

No, she would not run. At least not yet.

Leah squared her shoulders, guarding her thoughts as she edged forward.

So, he thought to play games did he? she thought to herself, as she reached the outer edge of the fire. She could not see him but knew he was on the other side of it, his black eyes watching her. She also knew that he was tensing, his muscles bunching, ready to spring if he felt threatened and for the life of her, she could not imagine why.

The *Other* knew he could not hold the woman forever. Had known even before the elder had suggested it, then tried to wrest her from him. *Him.* He who had looked into the flames, and saw her for what she was—could be—if she only knew her true self.

He leaned forward, watching her, black eyes that had seen what lay just beneath the surface of her seemingly fragile form blinked, their even darker centers glowing with anticipation as he returned to himself.

He crossed his arms over his chest, his breathing even. It would not do for her to see what *he* could be should he chose to reveal himself to mortal eyes. He was more powerful than even his sister, A-Sharoon. And once he got what he needed, well, he would see what would be done with the woman. For now, he would not harm her.

Perhaps, he thought to himself—perhaps he could persuade her. Coerce her to willing aid him. Give him what he wanted. She *was* different. Therefore, it was decided: he would not reveal himself. Not yet. And that was why, after his battle with the elder that had once nurtured him, protected him—he had then returned to the woman and removed her bonds.

Sitting back, he had waited for her to awaken; he hadn't gotten where he was from being stupid, and having caught a glimpse of what she could become, he had no desires to build a wall between them when cunning could get him what was needed. She was, after all, a woman.

A naive one at that.

He laughed to himself in the darkness, the sound abruptly cut off as he saw her coming through the shadows, her movements slow, graceful.

Her regenerative abilities were remarkable, considering what she had been through; even though her small frame shook from the dampness, he knew what a toll it had taken on her just to remain as she was.

He glanced at her from beneath half-closed lids, her dark hair trailed down her back to fall in soft waves about her slender waist. The man pulled back, the darkness shadowing him so that he was partially hidden, protected from her piercing gaze. He knew if she looked into his eyes, she would see what was layered behind their depths. And that wouldn't do. Not yet.

He had freed her from her bonds, but the rune spell was still upon her; layered beneath her skin, it would remain dormant until the time of his choosing.

His dark head nodded curtly as she seated herself carefully across from him, her body soaking up the warmth it had been denied earlier as she leaned into the fire's warmth, her hands reaching out, palms down to test the flame's heat as she drew it into herself. Saying nothing, the *Other* remained where he was. Watching. Waiting. Gauging.

The warmth returned to her, but slowly, and it was some time before she quit shaking. The fire had been replenished several times, and still *he* watched her, his voiceless silence unnerving her even though she did not show it.

§ § § § § §

The Hunter moved back, away from Jerome, his instincts warning him of unseen danger. So far, they had been lucky. Somewhere behind him, he knew, the wolves followed, the Old One and the younglings doing what was necessary to protect.

He stood in the darkness, his breathing even, his hearing attuned to each small nuance, each small noise that carried through earth and rock to warn him and the others that the path they walked a dangerous one. He knew she was close; he could feel her.

Something—a sound—caught his attention. He knelt down, cursing softly; he had nearly missed it, the imprint of a small foot in the soft earth. Rising, he centered himself, deep listening as he focused. Beneath his feet, the little ones, the earth diggers, moved; they were trying to tell him something.

He looked into the darkness, the thrumming beneath his feet moving upward through rock and soil so that was all he felt. This time, when he looked into the darkened places, he saw with eyes of knowing.

"Hold, warrior." Jerome's deep voice resonated through the darkness so that The Hunter stopped mid-stride, his bow already strung, the shaft of the arrow ready to be released as he swung around.

"Patience, young one of the two-legged clans."

The cavern's echo made it hard to tell where the voice was coming from as the warrior of the forest laid his burden gently down.

Closest to the center of knowing, he was not surprised when the heavily cloaked figures detached themselves from the shadows, taking on form as they released the robes that concealed them from the others—those dark ones who hid within the darkened places, waiting for their unsuspecting quarry.

The warrior of the forest inclined his head slightly, waiting.

"Come." The words, softly spoken, carried through the darkness as the *Unseen* hovered slightly above them.

Powerful guardian though he was, his existence drawn from a thousand beginnings and endings—he needed Jerome and The Hunter. He who was born of earth and air needed the strength of those who walked *between.*

He had seen into their hearts. Together they would make the whole.

22

Jerome watched as one of the Ancient Ones approached. Under cover of darkness, it was hard to see the other's features, if there were any to be seen. The soft tread of footsteps trailing behind him the only sound as they moved deeper into the cavern's depths, finally stopping in a secluded chamber.

Jerome looked around, stunned by what he saw.

"Our kind has many faces."

They were sitting with their backs to the wall, the warmth seeping into their weary bodies, strengthening them as they gratefully accepted the food offered. Their hosts had removed their robes, and The Hunter was flooded with memories of his childhood—of sacred places. He leaned back into the shadows, ashamed he had forgotten such things.

"Who are you, and why do you remain hidden from those who walk above?" Jerome asked, his senses tingling as he looked up, his gaze taking in his surroundings—the weapons that were so much like those that had been in the underground caverns of Skye.

"We have many names. We are those who walk within the worlds of creation. We cannot intercede, we can only watch. Sometimes, like now, when the gates have turned in upon themselves, we can *become* more. We can gather substance so that we can help—a little."

"Can you heal the one who lies dying, there in the shadows?" Jerome inclined his head toward the inert form, not surprised to see others bending over him, their hands hovering above his body.

Jerome thought he caught the faint sigh of the elder's breath, uneven but there, as he turned his attention back to the speaker who stood facing him. The light glinting off a face that was familiar—but not, as his mind drifted back to Skye and the others they had left behind, those who would guard the gate so that when the time was right, he and the others could return home.

"We do not have a lot of time. Things are different here. The worlds within worlds are ever-changing, their life cycle numbered by the caretakers who have been placed within the center of all."

Jerome's sharp intake of breath rang through the poignant silence as the elder's words struck him, their meaning taking his breath away as he centered himself, his warrior's heart weeping at the words spoken by someone who had seen the beginning and ending of many such worlds as this.

The big warrior rubbed his chin thoughtfully, casting a sideways glance at the warrior beside him as he did so, his gaze thoughtful, wondering if he knew where he was—if he knew what it was that they were seeing.

The warrior, the one known as The Hunter nodded, the movement abrupt, an acknowledgment that he understood.

"The worlds within worlds sometimes align with others. It is during this time that those, like us, can enter and for a time, we can offer knowledge. Each listener takes away something different. It is how they use it…"

The voice trailed off, the unspoken meaning clear as Jerome leaned forward, his mind reaching out to the other so that which passed between them would not be imprinted into their surroundings—to be heard later by those shaded forms who were part of the living rock that surrounded them.

The Hunter leaned forward, his conscience pricking him. He wanted to confront these beings with their ageless faces and rune-covered bodies that were constantly changing form. He stood up, not caring that those gathered about looked at him from beneath half-closed eyes that were dark with hidden knowledge they kept mostly to themselves, giving it out in small bits, here and there, as they chose to. The warrior drew in a deep breath. It was time.

He centered himself. He knew these Old Ones. They had come to him when he was a child. And again when he was a young man. They had whispered to him in the dark of things he did not understand. Each time they had left, he had felt more confused and, at the end, empty. The elders in his village had tried to help, their wisdom guiding him to understand a little of who he was—what it was that he sought, but it had never been enough.

In the end, they had left him there, alone in the forest where he had drawn his first breath. One by one withdrawing to the safety of their hidden places, away from him. Away from the *Other.*

To watch.

To wait.

To see.

It had been the watchers themselves who had waited at the edge of the clearing the night the warrior had found the woman, and later had watched as the Old One had entered the circle.

Watched as the woman reached out to one of the four-legged.

It had been decided. The warrior had to recognize what was within himself. And so he been left with the woman. To learn. To grow. Some things, he now knew, could not be taught. As he faced the elder, he knew Jerome watched, helpless to intercede, for this was his journey—it had seemed an endless journey—'til now.

"Ahhh, the warrior, the one known as The Hunter, finally understands."

The fire flickered wildly as Jerome watched from his place by the fire, eyes that had looked out at the beginning now seeing something else. Seeing bits and pieces of what the warrior was seeing, but knowing it was not his place to intercede, he remained where he was, his own thoughts guarded. Like the others, he watched, the watching at a distance. There was power here, in this sacred place. But it wasn't meant for him.

No. It was the warrior's.

Jerome leaned back, the unspoken becoming the spoken as The Hunter and the ancient faced one another across the fire, each choosing their own side. Each wary. Each taking a little from the other as thoughts bridged an endless void that had once seemed impassable.

The shadows in the cavern deepened, but no one looked up. Moments later, The Hunter moved back, away from the searing flames that threatened to scorch through his fur cape. Black eyes narrowed as the warrior sought out Jerome; the big warrior leaned forward, grasping his war club before slowly turning around, his intent to reach a larger corridor where he could stand and stretch.

The elder they had found so grievously injured was gone, taken by the ones with the strange runes that ran through their bodies, everchanging as they went from gate to gate. Realm to realm. It was,

Jerome supposed, how they entered unscathed, the guardians that remained at the entrance allowing them passage *"Between."*

§ § § § §

He was watching her. Leah bent forward, brushing her hair to one side, her face partially concealed from the man's intense stare. She flicked a spark off her arm, pulling back, away from the intense heat, her mind blocking his.

She needed to escape. Wait for the right time—she stiffened, the chill that ran up her spine warning her. *Beware.* She turned her face toward the light cast by the flames, the soft caress of the heat, as it brushed against her cheek strangely comforting despite the fact that he was there. Across from her. Staring at her. His eyes boring into hers as if...

Never! She jerked back, closing her mind, putting the barriers up so that she once again returned to herself. Pushing back the anger, she swallowed the words she was tempted to throw at him. When she did speak, her words were tempered with a tinge of distaste that left her with the feeling she had swallowed something vile.

"I don't know what it is that you want, but whatever it is, you will never get it. Not from me. Never." She spat the words out from between clenched teeth while her captor remained where he was, staring with those black eyes that were blacker than black. Eyes that were soulless.

He was darkness and light combined—

Warmth to her light—

She turned her head away so that he could not see, and silently wept.

The *Other* pulled back, away from the fire's flickering light, at the same time the woman did. She was strong, this one was. Already she was adapting, changing, and soon—soon he would get what he needed from her and then, he shrugged broad shoulders as he brushed long black hair back off a face the color of burnished copper.

He was changing. And it felt good. He stood up, his dark gaze sweeping the shadows. He had placed the rune spells carefully. She would not escape him. She was bound to him. She just did not know it, and even if she did, she was powerless to do anything about it. He laughed softly, the sound carrying in the tense silence as it echoed off the rock walls that surrounded them.

§ § § § §

The Hunter unsheathed his knife, slowly, so that the obsidian blade barely brushed against the leather, the sound as it scraped the soft underside muffled by his palm sliding over the sheath as he carefully pulled it out. He could hear Jerome as he moved ahead of him, the warrior moving cautiously down the damp corridor.

The Hunter grimaced, remembering the spoken words of the elder. Words for him alone to think upon. He glanced up, the brush of something across his face in the dark startling him.

It was one of the little winged ones. Its soft squeak of protest faded into the distance as the warrior turned down yet another seemingly endless corridor, Jerome following behind. The light they had followed earlier had been nothing more than the florescent moss that clung with unending tenacity to the wet rock that fed it from an underground stream.

The warrior ducked, the low overhang of rock nearly invisible in the semi-darkness that rose up to embrace their passage. The dampness that seeped from a hundred places was mind numbing. He thought of the flint he carried and wished they had dry wood, and then just as quickly dismissed the thought. It would only draw attention. Unwanted attention.

The Hunter probed the darkness, seeking the wolves and the Old One as the forest warrior muttered something unintelligible behind him.

Jerome straightened slowly, the whisper of the unknown running the length of his spine as he turned cautiously about, his mind seeing what his eyes could not. He had thought they traveled alone, but there was something—someone—there. He breathed deeply, centering himself, not moving, brushing at the side of his face as something passed him in the dark. Something indefinable.

§ § § § § §

Chera stepped back, her every instinct warring with the need to intercede. Gabriel stopped her, his intuition warning him this was not their battle. The Old One knew what he faced, for he had walked the forbidden places, watched from the shadows as his world had changed and he, with it.

As the sound of earth and rock—all that was—had ever been— met, Gabriel turned away, his heart heavy as he waited in the darkness with Chera.

A few moments later, the Old One joined them, his soft huff-huff caught within the air that moved around them. Saying nothing, for there was no need, Chera and Gabriel followed, neither bothering to look back, for each knew what the other felt.

The Old One moved steadily, his pace never faltering, for he did not wish to tarry in a place that held such sorrow. That such a one could be manipulated...

It was unthinkable. But it had happened. While he and others like him had stayed safe and protected in their hidden places, hoping that the *Other* would fade with time and their world would return to what it once was—he shivered as the brush of the unseen breeze rippled across his back—felt the center within himself responding to the unspoken.

"Hurry," they said.

§ § § § §

Leah moved slowly back. Aware that the shadows splayed across the rocks above her head moved with her, she closed her eyes, hoping to shut them out. When she opened them, they were still there. Indefinable. Formless. But there. Only her instincts kept her from running from something she could not see.

"Here." The voice, so close startled her; even though she knew he was still there, shrouded within the shadows that protected him, it was still unexpected. She took the bowl of broth he handed her, careful not to touch his hand lest he contaminate her. Look into her mind. She sniffed it suspiciously. The man—if man he was, threw back his head and laughed; the sound of it was dark and deep.

Leah brushed absently at the side of the wooden bowl, as if to wipe away the essence of where he had touched it.

"You need to eat, to keep up your strength." The voice was soft, cajoling. She held the bowl beneath her nose, wondering if he had put something into it—something that would make her more malleable.

She decided that he had not.

The *Other* watched in silent approval as Leah drank the broth he offered; rarely did he need sustenance, but when he did—he turned aside so that she would not see—would not read what was there in the darkness that swirled behind eyes that had seen the beginning.

Tread carefully, this one is different. If she realizes what she is...

The man moved away, just far enough that the fire's light could not cast his shadow where it could be seen. *No,* he thought to himself as he studied Leah intently from beneath shuttered lids.

No. It would not do at all. He turned aside; the fire's warmth was inviting, but he would leave it to the woman. Soon enough she would tire of the heat.

He watched as she set the now empty bowl down and then wrapped herself snugly in the old robe he had thrown to her earlier. Lying on her side, she closed her eyes, but he knew she did not sleep. He leaned back, his black eyes watchful as the shadows deepened.

If it were not for the fire and the searing heat—the *Other* silently motioned the unseen watchers back as they crept from their shadowed places. It would not do for them to see.

Not yet.

Leah lay with her back to the fire, her eyes closed against the shadows that danced against the walls where the fire's light could not reach. She knew that *He* watched from a distance. She shivered with the knowing; her every instinct urging her to get up and run. But where? She had no idea where she was or why and she felt different, somehow changed.

As she drifted into a dreamless sleep, she thought she heard Chera calling her. Then for a time she knew nothing.

The *Other* turned his head, the scent of impending danger in his nostrils as he stood, pivoting slowly before moving to the edge of the flickering shadows that shot out, then just as quickly retreated back to their place of concealment. The man turned toward the messenger, his gaze dark and forbidding.

"Stop." The words were hissed, the dark head whipped around as the entity drew back, wary, its soft sigh barely heard as the fire raced up the blackened logs. The red-gold tendrils reaching out as the wood cracked, crumbling into blackened coal.

The *Other* leaned forward, stirring the coals with a piece of iron-wood kept for just that purpose, placing more wood on them before stepping toward the creature that bade him come closer. Born in the darkened places, it could not bear the touch of even a spark of warmth or light cast by the fire.

Concealing all but his need to hear why one of those forbidden entrance here would dare enter uninvited, he inclined his head slightly to one side, listening, his senses attuned to the woman's breathing.

She slept.

"Why do you come here, you know it is forbidden." The voice was even but the unwanted visitor nonetheless withdrew, beckoning the *Other* to it, further into its shaded world where it felt more secure.

"They come through earth and rock. They come for *her. For you.*"
The voice hissed as the man leaned forward, his features changing.
Black eyes that were fathomless roiled unnaturally in a face that darkened with unvoiced rage. The blue-black runes etched beneath his
skin became visible, glowing with a pre-eternal light that faded as
quickly as it had appeared.

His faced the entity calmly, his feelings, thoughts, masked as he
accepted the images that poured forth from one who was older than
the rock that surrounded them.

It was the *Other* who broke the contact, pushing down the rage that
he had missed it. The unforeseen. His fists clenched as sweat beaded
his brow, and for the first time in his long remembrance, he felt the
faint stirring of the unknown as it reached out from its hidden place to
touch him.

He turned away, his expression guarded against the messenger, lest
he see what lay behind his eyes. He drew himself up proudly, exhaling sharply as he did so.

He was the master of his world and no one else. "Go." One word,
the meaning clear. The voice was edged with steel, and the messenger
left, not wanting to incur further wrath from one such as *He*...

Later, as the *Other* stood at the edge of the darkness, his back to the
fire's inviting warmth, he reached out, into the darkened places, his
mind seeking.

In as many days, he had lost two of his sentinels, now returned to
what they once were, and as far as he was concerned, they offered little threat to him. The others, those who followed him, offering of
themselves, their strengths, their very essence, to serve him, to do his
bidding—they were born of the darkness that nurtured them, and
already their numbers had dwindled because of *them.* They sought to
displace him and his world with their meddling...

A man who thought himself warrior; still growing, his knowledge
of his world sketchy at best, like the others of his kind, most of it had
been forgotten. This one, he could dismiss, but the other one? A forest
warrior, he was one of those Ancient ones who could shift, powerful
in his world—but this was not his world.

The dark head turned to look at the woman who lay so still beneath
the robes, her dark hair framing a face that was fragile in sleep. He
laughed softly, the sound smothered by his hand.

The woman was anything but fragile, and he had work to do. He
knew now why the wolves followed so doggedly, the Old One hoping
to use her presence as a catalyst, to create the storm that would see

him gone from their world. He blew out his breath, the sound loud in the stillness as he centered himself, the darkness rising, shrouding him as he made a decision.

They might get their world back, but it would not be what it had been.

§ § § § §

"Wait." Jerome stopped so suddenly that The Hunter nearly ran into him. The warrior inhaled sharply, his black eyes questioning, his hearing attuned to the smallest nuance as he waited. Waited for the forest warrior to speak as the silence about them deepened, the shadowed places taking on movement as those hidden within crevasse and darkness began their subtle movements forward. The glint of obsidian in the warrior's hands stopping them so they stayed their movements, remaining where they were, watchful.

"Listen, warrior. The others, they come."

The Hunter turned his head, listening, wondering how he could have missed it. The sound of footsteps approaching cautiously carried to him in the unnatural stillness that had settled about his shoulders. He cast a sideways glance at Jerome.

The big warrior was tense, his fingers caressing his war club as he prepared himself for anything untoward, his eyes peering beyond the boundaries of the darkness, watching to see if the others had been followed. Behind him, the unseen ones, those hidden in the darkened places, retreated, back into their world of nothingness. The Hunter understood.

Too much light to their dark.

Moments later, the others, Chera and Gabriel, followed by the Old One, came into view.

"This being, he was borne of the beginning? When the world was no more than molten rock?" Jerome had leaned forward, his green eyes glinting in the semi-darkness.

They had found a place where the rocks were covered in the strange silver moss, tinged with flecks of gold that gave off light from the tiny creatures that dwelled within, their life force feeding it, and it, them.

The companions appreciated the companionable existence as they gathered about one another, while the younglings stayed to the shadows. They had taken the task to themselves of watching, following at a distance; all the time learning, both from the earth that had borne them and the others—the forest warrior from another time and place—the same—but not.

The Old One, his kind had long walked the earthen places, their memories of a time, born into the beginning, something that could not be ignored. Jerome cast a questioning look toward the eldest of them. The stripling nodded. He understood. A few moments later, the entrance was closed.

"I'm sure." The Mukwa's voice was strained. For him, it was a painful telling, for he had looked into the face of one who had lived before them all. To think that one such as *He* could have been turned to the dark—and was no more—

It was unthinkable.

Jerome said nothing, his silence his voice as he turned to Chera; the big wolf was impatient to leave, her need to go to Leah understood. But they were tired, and being tired meant they needed to rest, at least long enough so that their senses would be attuned to the unknown, not weakened by fatigue. They needed their strength, all of it, before they went any farther. Chera grudgingly nodded assent. It was decided. Jerome knelt down, his war club placed across his massive trunk-like thighs.

He would take first watch.

23

Leah opened her eyes slowly. The fire still burned hot in the pit, but the flames had died down. The pile of red-hot embers in the center glowed with an intensity that was hard to ignore. She stretched carefully. Her muscles responded by cramping, and she drew in her breath sharply, seeing what before she had missed. Something *was* different.

She eased herself up on one elbow and looked around, careful to make no sound as she lifted herself up slowly, first to her knees, her kneeled position allowing her to pivot as she stood, her legs unsteady as she swayed uncertainly. After a few moments, it passed, and she was able to focus. To look around.

She was alone—the thought had barely registered before the prickling sensation ran the length of her spine, curling softly at the nape of her neck, warning her.

She looked up into the shadows. The scream that rose in her throat choked off as the translucent tendrils trailed slowly down, their touch electrifying, paralysing her as she writhed beneath their caress. A few moments later, another scream echoed through the stillness.

It was not hers.

Placing her hand on the angry red welt that ringed her throat, while telling herself that what just happened hadn't, really, Leah stood, swaying slightly beneath the realization that she had somehow destroyed one of *them* or at least sent it back to whatever dark abyss it had come from.

This time when the sensation of being watched crept up her spine, she knew without turning who it was.

The *Other. He* had been there all the time, embraced by the shadows, watching her. Waiting. Testing her strength—

As he stepped out of the roiling blackness, his mantle of dark invisibility gone, Leah looked up into black eyes that were not disappointed.

Well, then, she thought to herself as she tensed, readying herself, for she was no longer frightened. She had had enough, and if *He* wanted to play games, well, right now, she was more than willing. As the strength ebbed and flowed, coursing through her like wildfire, she turned, her shadow caught and held against the rock wall by the fire that had inexplicably surged upward to touch the ceiling of the cavern.

Leah stopped where she was, frozen in place, and for a fraction of a moment, *she* ceased to be. All that she had been—ever been—was gone. Confused, she shrank back against the wall, stifling the scream that rose in her throat, threatening to pour forth into the world of the living. As she turned away from the fire's bright light, the burning, stinging sensation ceased.

She opened her eyes once more, this time to the darkness. The shaded forms that shrank back from her stare scrambled to find other hidden places. She blinked uncomprehendingly as the *Other's* voice broke through her numbed senses. Somehow, he had managed to get behind her.

"Ahhhh," the voice whispered against her back. "You have become *More.*"

"More what?" She whirled about, her glare tearing through the darkness, peering into a hundred places that she had not noticed before. She shaded her eyes against the fire's glow, the heat searing her face as she stumbled back against the rock, her back to it, her other arm caught behind her. She winced at the pain. There was something different—she was different.

She looked down at her body and shuddered violently, the nausea rising up in her throat as she tried to swallow and found she could not. She shut her eyes, opened them. Looked at her hands and sighed in relief.

She must, she thought, have been seeing things. She shook her head to clear it as a vision of Chera, her silver eyes with their effervescent centers that were ever-changing, searched for her in the darkened places—and wished for the briefest of moments she could call to her.

The sound of male laughter, dark and deep, caused her to turn once more, her gaze traveling up the length of him to rest upon a face that was darkly handsome. Black eyes that had never seen anything less than the darkest recesses of humankind blinked then became shuttered against her blatant appraisal.

She drew in her breath, at the same time gathering her wits about her. She knew the others were close. She could sense it. She also sensed something else. *Her.* She was changing. Becoming stronger. It was almost as if…she turned to face the shadows that had begun to crowd about her.

The darkest of the dark—Leah bowed her head, thinking, her thoughts probing. When she looked up, they were gone. She turned at the feather soft touch on her shoulder. This time when she gazed into the dark fathomless eyes, she was able to return something in kind.

And he did not like it.

Leah edged cautiously, slowly, back.

No! She could not help but shudder as she felt the power rising from the center of her knowing.

The *Other* threw one last apprising look at her, his lips barely moving as he uttered unintelligible words that she could not hear, before turning. His woolen cloak thrown carelessly over his shoulder, he disappeared down the long, darkened corridor.

Leah watched him go, knowing that something—someone—was still in the cavern with her. She did not have to look around to know that it was there, behind her, guarding itself. Watching her. She ignored it, knowing it posed no threat. Not anymore. She remained where she was for a few moments longer, staring into the darkness. She could still sense where he was. Could almost smell it.

Resisting the urge to shiver and feeling suddenly very cold, she turned back to the welcoming warmth of the fire. Placing more dry wood upon the red-gold coals, she huddled close until the flames were licking at the uppermost edge of the pit. She bit back a bitter laugh as she remained there, enduring the singeing heat, drawing it into herself as she waited, watching as the flames slowly died back while the wood blackened, then slowly crumbled into ash.

Like her, they too wished to escape their prison. Sighing, she put more wood into the pit and leaned back, settling herself against the cold, grey rock to wait.

§ § § § §

He should have destroyed her himself, before the change, before she became more. The *Other* stood just behind the thin wall of rock, his fists clenched at his side, his eyes closed as he drew on his memories. He had missed something. With all his knowledge and power— he turned angrily away. He needed to regroup his thoughts before the others came for her.

He knew they were close, and even now, knew it was not too late. He could destroy her.

Should...

The darkness beckoned, and he allowed it to envelop him so that even *she* could not sense him.

Sliding soundlessly into the small room where none but he dared to enter, he waited until the stone slid silently back into place, before lighting the torches that were wedged tightly within the small crevasses that ran the length of the rock wall. The warrior, the one known as The Hunter, was coming for the woman.

Dark eyes glittered dangerously as the *Other* peered into the gloom. He did not have much time. He made up his mind even as he reached for the relic that had been his from the beginning, its original maker long lost to mortal memory. He held the staff aloft; made from the wood of the yew tree, the carvings, etched deep, glowed iridescent as it warmed to his touch.

The runes that ebbed and flowed beneath his skin drew closer to the surface of his coppery skin as he flinched, the movement so subtle, it went unnoticed by the little ones who waited breathlessly in their hidden places. Nearly too small to be seen, they waited patiently for him to be gone from them and leave them to their peace.

It was not to be.

Black eyes widened as nostrils flared in a face that had grown feral. Too long had he controlled himself. Too long had he waited for what was now within his grasp. He turned in the darkness, seeing them in their hidden places. The little ones. He turned away, not bothering to look back as the earth heaved upward and the rocks that sheltered the smallest of the clans shattered.

A smile curved the *Other's* lips as he strode away, the staff he held now silent, no longer resonating it had begun what was necessary, the warmth from the wood spreading upward, traveling through his body. He stopped once more, the spasm passing through him as the runes beneath his skin settled back to their center, once again sleeping.

§ § § § §

The Hunter did not bother to look back. He knew the others followed. He could hear Chera's low growl as she broke off to his left, Gabriel to his right. He centered himself, focusing on what lay ahead.

He could smell the smoke, knew he was close, and as he broke into a run, his bow was already coming up, the arrow released into the darkness, the shouted warning echoing off the cold rock as he ducked, the stinging sensation temporary as Jerome swung his war club, as the others, the younglings, joined him. Their instinct for survival giving them a slight advantage as they became a solid nearly impenetrable wall of solid oak, the memories surging upward through earth and rock as they changed yet again, their war shields where before there had been none, protecting as the unclean beasts leapt at them.

The sound of wood striking against flesh shattered the eerie silence. The wetness that pooled on the ground sinking into the earth, the soft sighing rising toward the sky to swirl about the companions as they battled the unseen things in the darkness while below them, the earth trembled as the blood from the younglings seeped deeply into the heart of what was—had always been—then there was nothing.

Nothing save the roaring of the wind as it swept through the tunnel, sweeping the attackers aside, crushing them against the cold grey rock, their limp forms falling lifeless to the earth before drawing back to itself.

"It would seem the Old Ones watch and give aid where they can." The Hunter turned his head, looking up. Jerome was beside him, the forest warrior's height allowing him to see what The Hunter could not.

"Hold." The words echoed loudly in the darkness. The cavern had widened, and they were looking down a long corridor lit by torches. Jerome drew himself up to his full height, his senses reaching out as he felt the earth heave beneath his feet. Behind him, the younglings had fallen silent. They had returned to themselves, their wounds already healing as they took what the earth offered, for their healing was a part of who they were. The eldest of them stepped forward, his height now almost matching that of Jerome's. He inclined his head slightly, the question unasked, heard.

Jerome nodded assent. It was time to let the young warriors do what they must. Although their journey was not yet complete, the younglings had embraced their new beginning with a enthusiasm that would serve them well.

Silently, the young warriors melded back into the shadows, their path to the outside world marked by the barest whisper of sound.

The Old One moved slowly forward, his abilities heightened as he drew closer to all that was the "beginning." To think that he had lived these many turnings and had not known it was this close.

A part of him sorrowed for the loss of self—*he should have known. Should have sensed what was beneath.* He drew himself up slowly to his full height. Beside him, The Hunter remained where he was, looking up at him, his gaze a little impatient, each of them sharing their thoughts as they took unto themselves what their world offered.

"It is time to see."

The Hunter turned, his expression questioning. Something moved off to his left, at the side of his peripheral vision. Then there were more. Dozens more. The little ones.

The warrior let his breath out slowly; unaware he had been holding it. He glanced at the Mukwa. The elder said nothing. He did not have to.

Once, long ago, when the world was new and just beginning, the Old Ones and the clans of the two-legged had walked together, their spirits touching. At night, when the mists had crept along the ground, damp tendrils softly seeking, the clan of the two-legged had built their fires—

In the time of the beginning, the two-legged had dwelled peacefully with the four-legged. Each of the clans taking only what they needed to survive. They had respected each other in that long ago time, and at night, when the dampness had crept along the ground, soft tendrils seeking, they, the two-legged had built their fires and had gathered about, some with drums to sing their songs honoring the earth and all those who walked within it.

As the moon had risen taking her place in the velvety night and the white mist had curled lazily about them, the Old Ones had come, their spirit-self listening and advising as the clans of the two-legged honored them and the ancestors who had walked before.

But that was a long time ago, and they had been forgotten—

The Old One shook his head sadly as he looked down at the warrior, the one who was called The Hunter. Deep-set brown eyes blinked thoughtfully as he decided. The Hunter met his gaze evenly.

It was time.

Chera paused as she looked from her mate, to Jerome, then back. Gabriel nudged her gently as he reached out to her in the old way of communicating. Chera bowed her head, her silver eyes with their swirling centers glowing iridescent in the shadows cast by the torch's flickering light. She sighed, the sound loud in the stillness. Without a backward glance to either Jerome or Gabriel, she left, the darkness swallowing her as the warrior of the forest and the wolf stared after her, then, they too, followed, the shadows closing in behind them, the secretive ferret like things following in their wake.

§ § § § §

He was close. She could feel it. The heat from the fire was so intense that she pulled back, but not before she saw into the heart of it. She pivoted around, her gaze raking the darkness for *Him.* She could hear him. There. Off to her left. A shadowy form detached itself from the darkness, an indistinguishable mass of nothingness. Leah shivered, for she knew who it was.

She spun sharply about, her hands held out in front of her protectively.

He laughed then, the sound dark and deep and it chilled her. Unsure of what it was that he wanted from her, of one thing, she was certain, he would destroy her after he had gotten it, whatever it was. Her back stiffened defensively.

Not if she could help it, he wouldn't.

She had watched the flames as they had crept closer, the heart of the fire burning blue-white as it reached out. She knew it reached for her and she had embraced it as the power curled through her body; understood a little of what she had seen within herself earlier. She turned dark brown eyes toward him, her fists curled into balls as she fought down the urge to throw herself at him.

"Not yet," the still small voice whispered.

He had her. His vice-like grip tightened about her throat as he tried to bring her chin up. He wanted her to look into his eyes as he ripped it from her and yet—she fought him with a strength that surprised him as she twisted out of his grasp, her eyes blazing as she went into herself.

The *Other* stepped back, his hands dropping to his sides, staring at her. Uncertain for the first time in his long remembering, he searched his memories, seeking the knowledge that would reaffirm what he had come to believe. It was not possible for one of the two-legged to own such a thing. It could not be hers by her birthright. A dark brow arched thoughtfully as he went over the events that had brought the woman into his realm.

He had been the one to cast the incantation, the spell that would see him safely returned to his own ever-changing world, but unknown to him he had brought her through with him. Something—he was not sure what—must have happened as they passed through the gates in the *between. Yes,* he mused thoughtfully to himself, that had to be it.

He stared down into her face, his black eyes apprising her openly, the runes layered beneath the surface of his skin stretching as they writhed restlessly, sensing what should have been theirs.

Leah glared up at him. How dare he! Leaning forward she struck out blindly. Missed. What happened next was a blur of motion, as she struggled, not with him—but herself. The last thing she remembered was the *Other,* leaning over her, whispering words in an ancient language she did not understand, her body arching as *she* began to change, to become the thing he needed to gain the absolute power he sought.

§ § § § §

The sentry died without making a sound. Then another and another as The Hunter moved methodically, in and out, moving so quickly that the last of the guards expired without even a sigh to mark their passing.

"Patience, Hunter," The Old One spoke softly. The warrior nodded. He understood.

They were nearly there. He peered down the dark passage that opened before him, the feral sounds muffled as things dark and terrible hid behind any barrier they could find. The warrior scented the air, his nostrils distended, the smell of death carried to him, choking him as he brushed absently at something on the side of his face.

Beside him, the Old One had gone down on all fours, one massive paw scraping the ground in front of him, the unspoken challenge thrown out as the shadows roiled and frothed above him. The Hunter edged forward, his hand on the long obsidian blade, the knife warming to his touch as he brought it up, knowing that what awaited them in the hidden places was nothing compared to what had begun to materialize in front of him.

Chera and Gabriel were there ahead of him. This one, they knew.

As the wolves battled the unnamed thing, the warrior moved swiftly along the dark passageway, the Mukwa clearing the way. The shrieks of protest dying as the shaded things moved back into the darkness, their deepest remembering of the Ancients and the power they possessed holding them at bay. Later, when they had shaken off the vision that had held them fast, it would be too late. They would come to themselves, staring blankly into the darkness, trying to remember what it was they were supposed to watch for.

§ § § § §

Impossible. It was his by his birthright—

—*Then again, perhaps not.* The *Other* reached down, furious, as he grasped nothing but empty air. Somehow, she had shifted away from him and was now behind him. Turning swiftly, he threw himself back, his body, reacting to the incantation he had cast, was still changing. He glared at Leah as he reached for her once more, his intent clear as his eyes glowed eerily in the half-light cast by the dying fire.

She would not own what was his. He should have killed her that day. Now, it was too late. He knew that, regretted it—he, who had thought never to regret! The Other looked up into the gloom that overshadowed them both. Drawing all that he was, had ever been, to him, he went to that dark place knowing that what he now summoned could destroy even him. Full black eyes looked up into utter darkness.

It was agreed.

He would give all to have what the woman held...

It was like looking through shaded glass, Leah thought wildly as she balanced herself on the balls of her feet. Gone was the fear and indecision. The need to be protected. All gone. She could protect herself. And would. Only thing was, she was not quite herself. She looked down, then up. Into eyes that had bartered with something no one could name, and in that moment she saw herself reflected in the *Other's* glare.

She did the only thing she could think of, she struck out at him, hoping to catch him off guard. Dropping to all fours, she tucked and rolled as he shouted something in a dark voice that reverberated in the dead air around her. The runes he had placed beneath her skin roiled just beneath the surface as they answered in kind, and for a moment Leah felt as if she were being ripped apart. The distant echoes reverberated off the rock walls as someone called out to her; powerless to answer she struggled with the thing that he had placed within her. Then she was falling into a dark abyss, and she was something else.

Silvery eyes looked down at her, and then there was only the darkness.

Leah sank into it gratefully, the ebb and flow comforting as she looked down at herself from a distant place of knowing.

Truly, she had become *more...*

24

"What is wrong with her?" The warrior was kneeling beside Leah, his brow furrowed as he shook her gently. Chera pushed him out of the way, her concern evident. Gabriel stood over her, his expression guarded, his senses reaching out, seeking the unknown. The cavern was empty, the fire dead, and the grey ash within its center cold. He glanced down at Leah's limp form. She was cold. Too cold. He spared a glance at Jerome; the forest warrior's fingers caressed his war club absently, something he did when he was at a loss for spoken words—when he needed to think, to seek answers.

Jerome turned away, his back to the companions as he stroked his chin thoughtfully with a craggy hand. A few moments later, the Old One joined him; thoughts, unspoken passing between them as Jerome tilted his head to one side, listening. They had searched the cavern more than once, finding nothing. Nothing except...

He looked down into ancient brown eyes that gazed back, unblinking. Jerome nodded. It was decided.

Moments later, the others flanking him, the warrior, the one known as The Hunter, carried a small bundle effortlessly back the way they had come. As they passed, the others, those ones who reveled in the deepest shadows, pulled back, farther into their shaded places.

Better to live to fight another day. The unspoken thought was heard and echoed by them all.

§ § § § § §

Leah wakened slowly to the sound of familiar voices. She opened her eyes, closed them. It was morning. The light that filtered through the lean-to brushed against her face as she buried herself deeper beneath the warm furs that had been thrown over her during the night. When she opened her eyes again, it was midmorning. The soft growl of inquiry next to her caused her to turn. "Chera." One word. She buried her face in the silver-white fur, wiping at the wetness that ran uncontrolled down her cheeks.

"Are you hungry?"

Leah looked up, her gaze sweeping lazily across the warrior's features. More time had passed since she had awakened and slept. She pulled herself up to a sitting position. The Hunter knelt next to her; he was holding out a gourd filled with hot broth. The smell was tantalizing, and she accepted it gratefully, drinking it greedily as she savored the warmth as it slid down her throat. She could not remember when something had tasted so good.

"Slowly. Drink it slowly." The warrior took the gourd from her and set it aside while Chera moved back, watchful. Although the silver-white wolf was still protective of her young charge, she had grudgingly acknowledged the young warrior's right to be there, and they had come to a truce of sorts over the last few days.

Strong hands cupped Leah's face gently as The Hunter drew her to him. His face inches from hers, one hand brushed her hair back over her shoulder as he looked at her, his black eyes apprising her as if searching for something, anything to reassure himself she was unhurt. Dark circles shadowed her eyes as she gazed, unblinking, back at him, but it was not weakness her saw within their depths. It was strength.

Strength of the women. Strength of the grandmothers...

The Hunter turned toward Jerome, his eyes speaking for him as the big warrior nodded. A few moments later, Leah was sitting in front of the fire, her friends gathered about her as the younglings kept watch. They too, had become *more*. Their journey from where they had begun to where they were now had made them complete.

Young warriors now, they held within themselves the ability to see into the darkest heart. They were part of the whole, the earth that they walked upon a part of them, and they, it.

Jerome, too, was a part of what they were—had become. It had been he who had inadvertently awakened them and had taught them to see through his eyes while they had quickly learned to see through their own. Wherever he journeyed from this day forth, they would be with him. Memories shared. Lessons learned.

The big warrior shook his head sadly. He wished it could always be like this for them, but knew it would not. Catching the Old One's attention, he moved to the edge of the clearing, where he stood staring up into the late afternoon sky. Dark clouds scudded across the distant horizon. A storm was coming. He could smell it. Beside him, the Old One stood tall, scenting the air, the fine hairs along the ridge of his back bristling as his spirit-self went to that other place that only his kind could go to. A few moments later, he returned to himself. Wordlessly he dropped down, his front legs making a soft thud as they hit the ground, at the same time pivoting around, his gaze settling on something just above Leah's head. Beside him, Jerome muttered something unintelligible.

The Hunter leaned forward, into the light breeze that blew around them. He could not see what the elder saw, but he sensed it. They were not alone. Turning slowly, he edged toward Leah, the fine particles of dust that swirled within the warm breeze irritating him as he rubbed at his eyes.

Something made him stop, look up. He squinted, shading his eyes against the bright light. Caught within the center of the prism of gently flowing light something moved. The fine particles caught and held, spinning, taking on form as the unseen moved closer. And stopped. Hovering just above Leah, as Chera, silver-white fur bristling, growled softly, questioningly, her gaze swinging back to meet that of her mates, Gabriel responding as he acknowledged what Chera saw. What he saw. And as he turned to look at the others, what they all saw.

It was there. Then it was not. An infinite being that moved like quicksilver, the prickling that ran the length of their spines telling them that it was there. Everywhere. Within the very essence of the air that swirled about them.

Leah shivered beneath the velvety touch of the breeze that curled about her head and shoulders, while the runes the *Other* had placed beneath her skin roiled uneasily as she flinched, the movement so subtle that it went unnoticed by the others.

The Hunter placed his arm about her protectively, but she shrugged it off gently as she reached out, one slim arm disengaging itself from the tangle of robes as she acknowledged the most ancient of the forest guardians. Her memories of moonlit nights long ago, the forest alive with sounds that soothed her shattered senses as she went to that still small place of her childhood when she saw with eyes of knowing and acceptance of what had lived before them all.

She sighed softly, the sound carrying to each one of the watchers as they remained where they were, unable to move, to react, the air swirling around them charged with power that ebbed and flowed through them like a river. Their abilities to see the unseen heightened as they shared the seeing as one.

Chera trembled with the understanding, the knowledge that this was the reason she had been thrown though a gateway into the unknown—to protect a young girl who had grown into a woman beneath her watch. This was why her primordial instincts had pushed her nearly to her limits. She was Leah's protector, and as she watched incredulously, she was allowed to see something else. Something the others could not see but a few suspected.

Leah was *more,* she was... Chera's gaze narrowed, her silver eyes shuttered against the ethereal vision as the unseen gently embraced Leah, the acceptance of her outstretched hand an acknowledgment that she saw what was really layered above the earth and beneath. She trembled beneath the feathery touch as her eyelids fluttered.

The *Unseen* once again became what it was—nothing more than the rise and fall of the breath of the wind, its gentle caress soothing.

Chera turned her head to look at her mate and caught the sound of his sharp intake of breath. He saw it, too.

Beneath the pallor of Leah's skin, something moved. Something dark and dangerous. Something they had missed. Something the *Unseen* had wanted them to see.

The *Other* had found a way to see them, even in their hidden places.

The wolves watched, helpless, as the runes moved, restless beneath the fragile skin, their shadows blue-black, growing, as they sought refuge from the winds painful caress while Leah moaned softly, her eyes closed against the discomfort the shadows within her caused as the *Unseen* showed her what to do.

This time, when Chera growled, they all heard it. It was a call to battle. The earth beneath their feet responding in kind as the little ones surged upward from their hidden places. The cry of the eagles as they flew from their aeries echoing as the forest awakened.

The *Unseen* reached out, tentatively, the caress feather soft as it brushed against the woman. The most ancient of the Ancients offering her what had never been offered to any other. Since time before time, their kind had wandered the forest, protecting without being seen, the breath of the night the cover that aided them.

But that had been in the long ago time, before the one known as the *Other* had entered their world.

The wind picked the leaves up, twirling them around and around, brushing lazily up against the woman. She remained where she was, poised, her face betraying nothing of what she felt. Not even what lie so restlessly beneath her skin.

The entity swept lower, knowledge layered deep, the seeing—the very essence of all that the woman was, something that she did not yet understand. Because he and those like him had been trapped within the shadows, kept from their world as it had darkened, and they, forced to serve a dark master, their senses numbed by spells, their true forms masked...

The decision had been made.

To defeat the *Other* and return the balance of their world to what it *was,* they had to all come together. It was the only way. The clans of the four-legged and winged needed to go back to their place of remembering. To the before time.

The Hunter was still struggling, the denial of who he was warring with what he had been taught, while the woman accepted what she could not change.

The *Unseen* sighed, the wind taking him as the warm breeze wrapped itself about the others.

Too late would the Dark One discover the truth about her. Who she really was. What she held within her. The dark runes he had placed so carefully would be rendered useless.

Dark brown eyes widened as Leah focused, the translucent mist, caught within the lights prism began to spin, faster and faster rising upward until nothing remained.

Nothing except the memories. And the shadows. Swirling above her. Within her.

Leah went into herself.

Into that still small place where she had walked those many turnings past, first as a young girl, then later, as she balanced precariously on the cusp of womanhood. The journey to that place within herself something that only she knew about. She had never shared it with anyone.

Until now.

Silver eyes watched from beneath the low-hanging branches of the red cedar, the delicate fronds brushing against the silky white fur as the big wolf edged back. Unsure of what to do, she remained where she was, watching from that distant place, her spirit-self protective of the young woman. She understood now.

In some distant place of the before time, she had been named guardian to this small one who belonged to the clan of the two-legged.

Chera centered herself, focused on what she saw taking place as her primordial instincts surfaced, the memories coming together, merging into a distinctive thread of thought. She growled softly, the slivers of silver pooling within the depths of her eyes as she looked out from beneath the heavy branches, the pungent scent of the cedar strong within her nostrils.

This was a place of medicine from the long ago time. It was the place where the women had gathered to learn their strengths, gain insight into who and what they were, and accept the wisdom of the elders.

Leah stood beneath the heavily branched copse of trees, her feet planted firmly upon the ground, arms raised, head thrown back. She did not speak the words aloud. She did not have to. She had been heard. Now, it was up to her to take the learning and make it more. Dark brown eyes opened to look upon a world that she knew as she spared a glance downward. She understood. She knew what she had to do even as the runes surged restlessly beneath her skin. No longer painful, the journey *between* had altered them, the dark intent that had writhed so restlessly earlier had been rendered useless.

Brought forth from the beginning, they knew no middle. No ending except what the user poured forth from their own emotions. The tingling sensation that ebbed through her body no longer confused her as she started forward, changing, her senses reaching out as she embraced all that she was.

"Chera." The voice was unexpectedly loud. Chera looked around dazed, as Gabriel nudged her. "Careful." The words were whispered as he pressed against her, his blue eyes warning her. She shook her head, scenting danger, the distant cries alerting her to her own peril as she closed her mind to what she had just seen in the sacred place.

The sudden rush of wind carried the putrid smell to her as she sprang out of the way, the creature screaming its outrage, the sound choked off as the Old One swept it carelessly aside, his small brown eyes flashing angrily as he delivered a death blow to yet another of the loathsome things.

"Go to Leah, she needs you. *Now.*" The words were snarled as the Mukwa shoved Chera roughly aside.

The foul-smelling creature bellowed its fury as yellow eyes glared balefully out from an elongated face. Long fangs snapped at them from a mouth that had rows of teeth that seemed to grow as the thing crouched a few feet away, its powerful hind legs readying themselves to spring.

Chera flipped sideways as it pounced, twisting with an agility that belonged to only those of her kind, her teeth sinking deeply into its neck as she shook it. Tossing it from her, not bothering to look as it rolled lifeless into the ravine, she shook herself. The taste of the thing in her mouth was revolting. A few feet away, The Hunter crouched, his warrior's stance challenging, his knife slashing upward, the black obsidian blade glowed eerily as the afternoon deepened into an unnatural darkness that was haunting.

Chera looked wildly around for Leah, her thoughts reaching out, probing. Amidst the cries of the dying and wounded she found her.

§ § § § §

"This cannot be…" the voice trailed off, shocked into silence as the *Other* paused, his stride temporarily broken while the shadows coiled about him in confusion. Eyes, full black, narrowed angrily as he brought his arm up, sweeping his robes aside as he brought forth the silver amulet. Ripping it from the leather that had held it bound, he uttered the words that would awaken it from its eternal sleep. The heart within the stone's center glowing with an ethereal light as it recognized its master.

He held it up, into the light that filtered through the trees, the shafts of sunlight glancing off it, bouncing back so that the effect was blinding. But only temporarily. He motioned the others back. Some things were needful, and right now, *they* were not. His palm burned with the sheer power that nestled within as he absorbed what the stone offered and after a time he turned around, his gaze finding the one he sought.

"Bring her to me, unharmed." The dark head nodded to the others curtly, the unvoiced command to follow acknowledged as the lesser of them followed in the shadow beings wake, the smell of something unclean lingering long after the wind had left him. The elders whispered pleas carried within its embrace lost to the one who now stared into a distant place, drawing his dark warriors to him as he prepared for war.

He should have destroyed her at the gate.

The *Other* knelt in the shadows, ignoring the whispers that swept over him, the stone slipping from nerveless fingers as the dark head bowed, the incantation uttered from bloodless lips summoning those from the lower realms, awakening them from their long sleep. Rising slowly, he picked up the stone, its surface now cold and dark; he placed it securely inside his robe before moving forward, his gait steady, black eyes narrowed, the decision made.

He would go into battle, placing himself at the center, and he would take back what was his before the woman drew her last breath. Ahead of him, the sounds of battle quickened while the skies above him changed. He looked up. Eyes that had seen the world from its beginning stared starkly out of a face gone suddenly pale, the incredulity etched within the shadows that splayed across his features quickly pushed back, concealed once more by what lie beneath.

He pushed himself forward, head up, his cloak flung carelessly across his shoulders as the runes beneath his skin coiled blue-black, restlessly moving as they strained against the thin covering that held them fast.

§ § § § §

The Hunter flung the creature from him, the putrid smell it emitted clinging to his nostrils as he wiped his hands on his leather leggings. It did not help. Rising from his kneeled position, he met the next one head on, its strangled cry choked off as the sharp obsidian blade found it mark.

"Careful, Hunter," Gabriel growled. The big wolf had come out of nowhere and was standing next to him, his muzzle stained red, the crimson splayed across his chest. Another of the things lay at his feet. The warning to be more cautious remained unspoken as blue eyes looked into black, before disappearing into the frothing white mist that was everywhere.

The Hunter squinted, trying to focus on the slithering forms that were moving rapidly in and out of the frothing roiling mass that snaked its way around them. He tried to shake the feeling that this was nothing compared to what was coming as he loosed an arrow into the swirling whiteness that had descended, listening in satisfaction as it found its mark, the soft thud a telling thing.

§ § § § §

Leah looked down at her hands. Brought them to her face. She was burning up, as she had back there in the cavern, when the Dark Lord had held her prisoner. She felt him, that *One*, before she saw him through shuttered lids as she centered her thoughts. Remembering where she had been. Remembering what she had seen—had accepted as part of who she was. Beside her Chera growled, the sound low and threatening as she warned the others back.

The big wolf's silver eyes glowed dangerously, her gaze sweeping the forest in front of her, her relief evident as the *Unseen* caressed her gently. The ancient guardian of the forest giving of itself so that the others, those who could *see,* would know they were not alone.

Jerome warned the others back, his war club whistling dangerously as it swept through the air. The trees in front of him sweeping from side to side, bending beneath the force of the unnatural wind that raged around them. The cracking of limbs and trunks amidst the shrieks of things unnatural and dark—he went into himself—to his warrior's place, drawing on the teachings of the elders and accepted what he saw.

His warrior's vision focused on the shrouded figure in the center of the unnatural storm that swept toward them, changing form and feature as he came. His power undeniably dark, his intent so focused on Leah that the warrior of the forest took advantage of own abilities.

The Hunter pushed himself forward, his warrior's instincts guiding him as he fought his way through the tangle of bodies. The odor was nearly overwhelming. The fear and despair that clung to him so strong that he wavered uncertainly, before pushing it back, seeing it for what it was—more dark magic.

He blew his breath out slowly, released it, the sound rising upward to be swallowed within the wind as something flew past, wing tips brushing softly against him so that he ducked. The shrieks of rage echoing hollowly as the golden eagle rose upward, the turning twisting unknown thing gripped tightly in its sharp talons. Behind The Hunter, the Old One snorted his approval as the air filled with the cries of the winged ones.

They had come from the high places. Called to battle by an ancient one who had once guarded the sacred places below, now returned to what it once was, it had reached out. The unspoken understanding of what was needed passing from clan to clan.

The Hunter sidestepped as the eagle released its prey, its triumphant cry echoing through the mist as the thing hit the ground, whatever essence of life it carried expelled in a sigh as it stilled forever. The warrior met the next one head on, his blade tearing through unnatural flesh and bone; he stood back, his breath rasping in his chest as he looked around.

There were more. Dozens more.

He moved ahead, the Old One guarding his back as Orith's voice called out to him. The elder was somewhere ahead of him, the white mist with its translucent tendrils was climbing upward, the chilly dampness seeping through clothing, numbing his senses.

"Have a care, Hunter." The voice, so close, startled him, Gabriel's growled warning nearly lost in the rush of sound that tore at him before he was flung backwards, where he landed unceremoniously on the ground. Momentarily stunned, winded, but not seriously hurt, he rose to his feet, his senses reaching out, seeking the one concealed within the hidden places. He could not see it, but knew it was there.

The warrior went to his place of knowing to 'see' the calm that washed over him a prelude to what was coming. This time when the obsidian blade swept upward, there was no mistaking that it had found its mark.

§ § § § §

From their high place, the Ancients, those old ones who rarely traversed the plains layered in the *Between,* watched, their silence their approval. The warrior had finally come into being. *He saw.*

The warrior had found his center—an instinct that was inherent to all of the clans, a gift from the Ancients instilled the moment they came into being. They watched as, unafraid, he threw himself into the mass of roiling things that had been called forth from their dark abyss where all despair dwelled.

25

Leah rose slowly to her feet, her back arched, the emotions flowing through her so great that she could barely contain the ebb and flow of them as she steadied herself, the wind rushing past her as she looked out upon the destruction the *Other's* entrance had wrought.

She saw *him,* his darkly handsome features changing as he strode toward her, flanked on either side by things that held no semblance of intellect within their misshapen forms while behind him, the lesser of them followed. Leah took a step forward, faltered, her head swung up, her gaze meeting that of Chera's.

The great silver-white wolf nudged her, giving a little of herself to this one, she now named sister…

§ § § § §

Leah looked down at herself, then up. The moment of indecision past, she flung herself at the *Other,* the air above her ringing with the cries of the winged as they went to earth, their talons cutting a deadly swath as they circled back, flying high, their intent not to retreat but to surge back. She sent the first of the guards flying, her voice heard above the baying of the dark things that surged hungrily forward, toward her, toward them, the others: Jerome, Orith, and the Old One.

She knew The Hunter ran beside her, but, like her, he too was changed. She voiced her silent approval as together they dove into the snapping snarling throng that closed rank about them, the *Other's* voice rising above the rest, calling her name as the red haze descended, primordial instincts taking over as the day swept swiftly into the night. Her vision changing as she looked into eyes that roiled dangerously, their centers blacker than black, the outer darkness rimmed at the edges that should have been white nothing compared to what moved restlessly within.

She went into herself once more...

The *Other* shifted position, tensing for the final attack. He would take back what should have been his—the ability to shift—to change.

Power surged between them, a palpable shifting of the wind that blew unfettered through the night as the runes expanded once more beneath his skin, reaching upward to strain against their prison, greedily accepting what their master offered even as he reached out, his cry of frustration heard as he grasped at nothing but empty air.

Jerome struck at the vaporous being, the high keening hurting his ears as it writhed angrily, its pain making it even more dangerous as it lashed out blindly, seeking what was not there, letting his breath out in satisfaction as the entity went into itself, dissipating into the darkness. It would not be returning. Green eyes narrowed as he went to his warrior's place, calling forth the memories that made his kind who they were.

The shrill trilling of the young forest warriors as they poured forth from the forest echoed against the night as the dark sentries revealed themselves.

It was what the *watchers* had waited for—the accumulation of events triggered by the dark one himself. Placed there at the beginning, they had lain dormant. Waiting.

'Til now.

The wind sighed over them as the *Unseen* released the whole of himself into it, riding upon the currents that spiraled earthward, to settle silently upon those who walked below.

The light, blue-white and cooling, pooled about him, its comforting mantle of power enveloping him within even deeper folds of remembrances as he went to that place where nothing remained but the memories... The Hunter rose up, his body reacting to the change as he centered himself, seeing what was before him before plunging blindly into the unknown. Leah was somewhere ahead of him, words, tossed into the wind carried back to him as he knelt, his bow already coming up, the soft hiss of the arrow as it found its mark satisfying.

He did not need to turn his head, the Old One's soft huff-huff telling him that they stood side by side. Brothers now, in battle they would guard each the other. The Old One went down on all fours as he reached out, his thoughts probing, the unspoken words carrying to the warrior.

With each turning of thought, with each setting of the sun and rising of the moon, that which we hold within our self—accepted. The Old One was watching him, gauging him. His soft brown eyes peering into the warriors dark ones as he blew out his breath softly.

"It will get easier, warrior…"

§ § § § § §

Leah circled around behind the *Other,* her body stretching, growing as she ran, her vision changing, becoming more acute as she saw with different eyes. Eyes that saw into the dark, layered places held in-between that were invisible to most, but not to her.

Not now. Not ever again.

She reached out, her mind seeking, and found the warrior. Saw the other *self* that he now owned, her voice rising into the night as she became a part of it. The warriors answering cry echoing as thoughts joined, visions shared.

Leah turned slowly, the muscles beneath her skin bunching, her body taut with the power that surged through her as she faced the one who had pulled her from all that she had ever known.

§ § § § § §

How could he have missed it? The *Other* had watched as Leah disappeared into the tangle of ancient oaks, the night enveloping her as the Standing People closed rank about her. Black eyes glittered dangerously as he started after her but stopped before he reached the forest's edge.

He turned his head, listening to the wind while the runes surged restlessly beneath his skin. He did not need to look at them, for he was all too aware of what was happening. To him. To *them.* He had been so eager to garner more power that he had failed to see it. The gift the woman carried was not just the ability to shape shift. It was more. Much more. Both the woman and wolf had been chosen, even before their existing for this moment.

Hands clenched. Tightened into fists. The rush of the night wind as it curled against his back warning him as he went to that place where all things dark existed. He knew she was there. In front of him, her other self rising.

The one known as the *Other* looked into eyes that were tinged at their center with silver—eyes that should have been brown.

His mouth curved slowly upward into a smile, the harsh plains of his face shadowed as he, too, became what he was. *More.*

Chera moved cautiously, her heart racing as she circled around the two combatants who now faced each other. Knowing she was literally powerless to help did nothing to assuage her concern for her young charge as she paused, alert for the hidden things that laid in wait for her to pass.

She need not have been concerned. While she had made the way clear for Leah, protected her while she had embraced the whole of who she was, Gabriel and Jerome had been there ahead of her.

She settled down to wait, focusing all of her remaining strength on what was needed.

Their silence their truce, the *Other's* dark army waited within the forest's fringe. As with all who moved within the circle of creation, they had reached within their memories and remembered. While the subtle shifting of the night wind had blown away most of the seemingly unending mist, they had watched as the woman and warrior changed—the bear and wolf waiting, committing themselves to the old ways that had been there from the beginning, the clan of the two-legged holding the power within themselves to shape-shift in order to protect.

They would not interfere in what was to come, for it was an unwritten law that was embedded within the very essence that bound them to it. Borne into the beginning, it would not be disputed.

And so those born to the realms that existed in the *"Between"* remained where they were, the dark places reaching out to shadow them.

26

In the time of the making, the Ancients had poured forth their memories so that the realms of the clans that existed below could gather knowledge to themselves. To learn. To grow. To become.

As with everything born within creation, some were gifted with special abilities—this advantage made them protectors. The clans of earth and sky coming together in times of need to aid each other—the clans of the four-legged and winged lending their power to the clan of man. An understanding that the gift was only lent and so would return to the one who had offered a little of himself to the one like, yet unlike, himself.

And so the keepers of the sky realms watched. Watched as the woman and the warrior accepted the gift their protectors offered. The acceptance binding them together, changing them so that their paths would always be connected.

An unending circle, they would always find their center. Within themselves. Within each other.

27

The moon hung low against the velvety backdrop of the night sky as The Hunter edged forward, cautious, nerves taut, the sensation of oneness with the Mukwa growing, becoming more as his mind accepted what was. He turned his head, acknowledging Jerome's formidable presence, and behind him, the younglings. If any of the scurrying things thought to break the laws of the Ancients...

The warrior smiled grimly in the dark as he positioned himself, his vision of how he saw the night and those within it changed—watched as the shafts of moonlight washed over the woman and the *Other,* bathing them in ethereal light as they faced each other across a seemingly endless void. Both poised to accept what their center offered, each making a different choice.

The darkness and light merging on different sides as the stillness deepened. The watchers in the hidden places cautioned once again not to interfere.

§ § § § §

The dark head bowed as the *Other* remained where he was. Powerful before the change, he was even more so now. Not bothering to raise his head even as the runes surfaced, rising above his skin, writhing with a power of their own as all that had been before and after the making now met in a crescendo of sound that was deafening.

Leah shifted, moving out of the way, the rush of power from the *Other* as it passed over her pricking along her spine. She shook it off, her body barely reacting to it as another image assailed her senses; the runes writhing above the one who faced her across a seemingly end-less void that seeped pure evil. She blinked, brushing at the moisture that gathered at the edges of her eyes, her heart racing. Such sorrow layered so deep within the entities bound within a darkness they could not escape!

The eyes she now saw through seeing more than what her mortal self would ever see as she went to that still-small place within, the image of her other self rising up. The final joining something that would always be remembered as the moment she truly came into being.

She started forward at the same time as the *Other.* The sudden silence in the wood absolute as the watchers remained where they were, the need to fight temporarily forgotten as their world changed yet again.

Jerome and Orith watched, helpless to intercede. The air above them charged with indescribable power as light and dark met. The whole of who they were joining as the ethereal began to take on form, the seeing something that none would ever forget.

"Come now, is that your best?" The taunting words rang through the night. The blow had jarred him, but not enough to let the woman see it. "Silence, beast." Words, tossed carelessly into the air as he turned to look briefly at the silver-white wolf that had approached from the side of his vision, her growled warning rippling against his senses as he focused.

The runes were rising above him, joining; their oneness infusing him with power, dark and ancient. More power than even he had ever thought possible. He paused to savor it—to draw the darkness back to himself. To become part of the whole that the dark masters offered. A feral smiled curved about bloodless lips as he threw back his head, the laughter that bubbled forth not entirely his, the hiss of something black and terrible coming from the runes as they settled back upon him.

Chera was close. Leah knew it without turning. Sisters now, both were bathed in the warmth of the light that pulsed around them, the *Unseen* embracing them with the knowledge given to a few, under-stood by even less.

The Dark Lord threw his arm up to protect himself from the surge of power, blue-white and blinding as the woman and the wolf shared the joining. The wolf rising above him, her gaze fierce and unforgiv-ing, while the son, born of darkness in a long forgotten place, went into himself.

Words flowed like quicksilver between the warrior of the forest, and the younglings as they watched, unable to interfere.

All this time the Old One and Chera had been the protectors. Each of them born into a different time, the events that had brought them together had been predetermined by an unseen force greater than them all.

Beneath his mantle of silence, the Mukwa was thankful that he had listened to the voices of the unseen ones. Those ones he knew as the Grandfathers. The Seven. His prejudice against the clans of the two-legged put aside, he too had learned, the learning giving him more, helping him to grow. He and the warrior now sharing a bond that would last for the rest of their lives—in times of need the sharing benefitting them both.

Jerome stood slightly in front of the younglings. A solid impenetrable wall of solid oak trees blocked the way to the gateway of the "*Between.*" His warrior's vision seeing into the hidden places as he centered himself, waiting for the moment when the warriors behind him would be needed.

The warrior of the forest knew the younglings stood ready to take their world back. To finish what had begun before the *Other*—before the shadows had darkened their world with forgetfulness.

§ § § § § §

Leah saw her chance and took it. Words, spoken in an ancient tongue not heard since the dawning of the beginning, drifted upon the night, swallowed by the nothingness that was. Neither seen nor heard but there, it dwelt within all living things, a part of themselves, the unknown. The fear of what could not be seen or explained, it built upon itself, growing until it became the unimaginable.

Jerome pushed Orith behind him as the light, brilliant white and blinding, washed over him. The younglings remained where they were, unwavering, their strength of heart their unity as the vision of the white wolf and Mukwa rose upward, the ethereal vision pressing upon their senses so that the reality of what was seen or not merged together into a oneness that all could accept and understand.

The *Other* felt the darkness wash over him, soothing him, calming him, the tendrils of power burrowing into that part of him that had always *been*. He leaned into it. Breathed it. Drawing it into his lungs as he savored the feeling of being absolute in a world where he was the master and the clans of earth and sky his to command.

Now, while he savors a victory that can never be his…

The watchers in the wood pulled back, some of the smaller of the clans in alarm, others because of the quickening within themselves. The air pressed down, heavy, electrified, the fine particles of mist rising up from the dampened places, white and thick, their cloud-like appearance taking on form, settling over the woman, nearly touching, but not quite.

Leah did not stop to wonder. Instead, she reached up, embracing all that was offered. The change had come naturally, the spirit-self of the wolf embracing her. Becoming her as she opened herself to become the whole. The vision of the white wolf standing out in sharp contrast against the darkness that was the *Other.* The unspoken thought thrown out. Caught.

She circled him once more, at the same time emptying her mind of everything, pushing the memories back as she went to her place of knowing and found what it was that she sought.

Chera was there. Within her. Together. The sharing as one. The soft growl of the wolf becoming her own as she accepted the challenge the *Other* offered. Her one thought to protect. Her acceptance of her fate what the Old Ones had waited for—the selfless gift of giving all that she had so that she could be all that she was. Their oneness empowering them as the wind swirled about them, the subtle shift as it pressed down not lost to the *Other's* senses as he stiffened, his mind seeking out allies in the hidden places, those who would challenge the forest warriors, the young ones who were still attaining their memories.

They were the weakest link.

Black eyes narrowed in a face that was livid with unsuppressed rage. There was none to answer his call to arms, none.

The thought had been passed from one dark lair to another and just as swiftly laid aside. None dared to challenge the unwritten laws that had been there from the beginning—or Jerome.

The forest warrior's stance carried a silent warning to any who thought to interfere this night.

If help came to the dark one, it would not be from any of these. Jerome turned to the youngling, his unvoiced thoughts acknowledged as the rest of the warriors returned to themselves, their shields placed to the front of them, their trunk-like bodies forming a partial circle as the vision of the white wolf rose above the *Other,* while the wind pressed lower.

It happened so fast Leah barely had time to move out of the way. The jolt of electricity as it grazed her shoulder stinging as she moved swiftly, averting the next one, steeling herself, throwing up her own barriers as she turned swiftly and met him head on.

The impact sent them both reeling back.

"You cannot defeat me." Black eyes that were soulless glared out from a face that was changing, shifting into something unimaginable as the runes settled once more against his skin, the becoming of both, yet neither, nearly complete.

Incantations whispered against the darkness in an ancient tongue rose upward to curl against the breeze that pushed them back as the *Other* lost himself to the power that coursed through him. Laughter, dark and deep, echoed through the stillness as he opened himself to the watchers thoughts. All of them.

It was too late to undo what should have never been.

The faint ripple of the unknown washed through the *Other* as he looked out into the night, his breathing stilled as he focused, the need to shut the others out so they would not know—would not see that his call for aid had been answered. Beneath his feet, the first faint tremor rippled through the earth. The *Other* opened his arms, the runes once more rising above him, reaching out.

This was what the *Unseen* had waited for. The *darkening.* The shifting of power between realms. The moment when the *Other* would be weakest as he accepted that which now poured forth, unhindered from the realms beneath

The *Other* closed his eyes, inhaling deeply of the darkness and what it offered. No longer caring the consequences of opening himself to something he could not see, he accepted the change without question. The unwritten laws of the before time put aside as the door from the beneath began to open.

The Lord of Darkness paused, the chant falling from bloodless lips into the quickening silence as he looked up, his lips parted in a feral snarl. Black eyes widened in disbelief, then outrage as the *Unseen,* one of the most ancient of the forest guardians, brushed against him, the caress imprinting countless turnings of thought—the memories coursing through the entities that drew back in terror, away from the dark one, away from the light, returning to their world. Closing the gates to the beneath as they fled back to their hidden places.

"Careful." The word rippled though the unnatural darkness as Gabriel tensed, his eyes warning his mate to be tread softly. She was weakening, her spirit-self taking from her to lend to the woman the very essence of that which was a part of her, rising higher, the Old Ones reaching out from their place of watching as the woman and wolf shifted once again—each one taking what was needed to make the whole.

Chera collapsed, exhausted, as Gabriel stood over her, his protection accepted. In this weakened state, she was vulnerable. She closed her eyes, the wait between something that was needed.

Bathed in light from countless stars, the spirit essence of the wolf settled over the shoulders of the woman, the gentle embrace as they became one no more than the sighing of the wind as the *Unseen* swirled around them.

Unable to physically use his own strength against the one who had held him captive these many turnings, he could still use what he had learned in his mortal form from the *Other* to tip the scales. The night was lit with a thousand lights from a thousand unseen beings. All of which had waited for this day, this place—to stand here and breath in the night that was the night, the stench of the Dark Lord weakening as the woman, gifted with the knowing, and the warrior, still learning, combined their knowledge and strength of heart to do what the Old Ones could not.

Leah wrapped herself about the *Other,* pressing herself against him, drawing from him what he had taken from countless others, releasing it into the air that blew around her, the soft sighing nearly shattering her senses as those who had been lost within the dark void now entered that place to which they needed to journey.

§ § § § §

Black eyes looked out from a body caught between the plains of making. The *Other* closed his eyes. Opened them. He was alone, returned to what he was. Neither immortal nor mortal, once more *in-between,* he had been stripped of all save what was his by birthright. Drawing his heavy woolen cloak about his shoulders, he spun around, the incantation rising into the shadows of the waning night.

The younglings surged forward to intercept him but were too late. The *Other* was gone. Returned to his dark caverns deep within the earth. Returned to the warmth of his fire where he would gaze broodingly into it, desiring things once again as he reached into himself.

That he would return one day Jerome did not doubt. The big warrior looked up into the cloudless night, at the distant mountains rimmed with the dawning that was not far off. The trilling of the younglings as they faded into the forest, seeking out the unwanted telling him that their journey was now their own to make, their world once more centered, the balance between darkness and light where it should be.

Jerome let his breath out slowly as he looked down at Orith, the elder's golden eyes speaking what words could not, the thought that passed silently between them the same: home. That other place where their friends waited, guarding the gateway so that they could return to what they knew, the returning bringing with it more tellings that would be remembered long after their time ceased to be.

Skye. The Old One. Their old one. With her leathery skin and wizened body, the memories of her kind giving those who were just in their beginning insight into a world that was ever-changing—where nothing was as it seemed, the unexpected around every corner, the possibilities endless.

Jerome smiled at the memories as he turned aside, busying himself, collecting more dry wood, the chill from the mist that curled about the companions damp and seeking as the night gave way to the morning's dawning.

Leah returned to herself slowly, the centering a bit more difficult. The warrior knelt beside her, watchful. His world no longer in peril, the gifts that had been lent had returned to the Old One, both he and Chera sinking wearily to the ground. The earth beneath them offering strength, the offering accepted as they took what was needed.

The little ones, the earth diggers, moved below them, returning to burrow and den, placing them once again at the center—the heartbeat of the earth, returned to their vigil of watching.

28

"It was never his to own," Jerome spoke succinctly, turning away from the fire to look at Leah. The big warrior was grateful that she had come to no real harm while in spirit form. Glancing to where Chera lie, Gabriel curled against her protectively. He was glad it was over. They all were.

Leah leaned back against the sturdy backrest made from the cedar boughs, the oil from the bruised fronds that wafted out soothing to her battered senses, her body still recovering from the spirit sharing as she wondered at the changes within her.

This time it was she who reached out to grasp The Hunter's hand, her small fingers twining about his as he looked at her, his gaze approving as he brought her hand to his heart as the others looked away, busying themselves with menial tasks, their thoughts their own. They would not intrude. Let The Hunter and Leah have their time alone.

They too were in a new beginning.

Epilogue

It would be later, much later, when the night deepened and the moon rose full and round, that the Old One and others like him would return from the forest, the mist carrying them to the places where they were welcome.

Once again, the spirit-self of the great one, the Mukwa, would sit at the fire of the two-legged between the dusk and the dawn, speaking of things lost to memory.

Jerome and Orith would remain with the wolves. Chera, reluctant to leave her young charge—the knowing that what they shared was something binding. Gabriel, understanding this, did not hesitate. He would not leave his mate to journey back to *Skye,* for deep down he knew they were still needed. The *Other* even now was working his dark magic somewhere within the hidden places deep below them.

About the Author

Thérèse Pilon was born in Kingston, Ontario, and attended Sharbot Lake High School. She grew up in a farming community surrounded by forests, rivers, and lakes. Her deep respect for nature and all things living were the catalyst for her early years of writing, and later, the teachings of The Native American People. Her main focus in those early years was raising her children. After winning the poetry competition for Southeastern Ontario in the early 1980s for best category for her poem "Moon," the adventures of Skye began.

What began as a bedtime story for her children, Naiomi-Leah and Nickolous, changed and grew until it became Son of Skye, and later, Daughter of Skye. It has been a journey influenced by the aboriginal teachings and Ms. Pilon's own teachings that is ever-changing, with the beginning yet to be written...

Her first book, *Son of Skye*, (sonofskye.authorsxpress.com) was published in 2011. An exhilarating young adult novel:

Born of two worlds—belonging to neither—Nickolous is thrust into a world where the clans of the four-legged and winged rule. Guided by an old she-rat and his own instincts, he learns who he is while fighting to protect a world that has awaited his coming since its own dawning. Those who walk within the sacred places give of themselves to protect him so that legend, once myth, can become reality.

253

Thérèse currently lives in Uxbridge, Ontario, working on a horse ranch with her husband and sons, and writing in her spare time. Her husband, Dan, is a member of the Mattawa/North Bay Algonquin First Nation, while her own roots are linked to the Haudenosaunee, the teachings of her grandmothers part of the way she writes, her understanding always changing as she continues to learn.

Thérèse's summer weekends are spent on the powwow trail. She is a woman's traditional dancer and never misses an opportunity to learn from the elders she meets; their wisdom and their teachings are a continuing cycle of knowledge to be passed on. She still finds time to prepare her own preserves and make medicine from the abundance of plants that surrounds her. With her children mostly grown, she now spends more time on her writing.

Her next book is a sequel to *Daughter of Skye*, in which Leah and The Hunter must find a way to return to Skye.

Something dark has awakened. Something that threatens the worlds of knowing...